Printed in Great Britain
by Amazon

WHEN BLOOD BURNS

A HOLT & FISKE CRIME THRILLER

REGAN BARRY

INFINITE BOOK

What is history? An echo of the past in the future; a reflex from the future on the past.

— Victor Hugo

PROLOGUE

The track leads into darkness. Rough, wild landscape spreads out on each side of it, thick with brambles and bracken. Patches of black, moist, peaty soil are exposed, and a cool, humid, autumn breeze blows.

She shivers, grips her dog's lead tighter, and casts a glance over her shoulder at the car park where a car is leaving, headlights piercing the night, beams wobbling as the driver navigates the potholed road. Her car is one of only two vehicles parked there now.

Damn. I've left it too late. I should have gone to the lake.

At the lake there would be other people about, even at dusk. Lamps illuminate the paths. Here, at the fen, no artificial beams shine to guide her steps.

Her dog strains against the lead and whines before giving a single, short bark: 'Hey, what are we waiting for?'

She's been here many times. She knows the route so well she could walk it blindfolded. In the distance a copse of silver birch stands, ghostly in the meagre light of the cloudy night. It'll take about ten minutes to reach it.

'Okay,' she relents. 'Just a little walk, then straight home.'

Her dog yips happily as they set off.

Less than five minutes later the dog moves off the track. She fishes

in her pocket for the plastic bag and, after sliding her hand into it, she waits. When the dog has finished doing his business, she bends down to clean up.

Something catches the dog's attention. He pads away from her into the vegetation until he reaches the extent of his lead then he strains against it. His ears prick up and his spine turns rigid as he stares into the dark.

'What is it, Toby?'

He must have heard a rabbit or a bird.

'Come on.'

She tries to tug him away from the distraction, attempting to return to the path, but the dog resists. His collar digs into his neck and he refuses to budge.

'Come *on!*'

Like a husky hauling a sled, the dog digs his paws into the soft soil and pulls against her, softly growling.

'No,' she says sternly. 'No investigating. Let's go.'

Abruptly, he complies and obediently walks towards her. The lead slackens. She steps onto the path, but then there's a rustle in the brush. The dog leaps away, jerking the lead from her grasp.

He's gone.

She curses loudly and stares into the night. 'Toby! Toby! Come back! Come back here right now!'

Why didn't I go to the lake?

Crashes, crackles and snapping noises signal his progress through the vegetation.

'TOBY!'

He'll come back eventually, once he's lost interest in his quarry, but maybe he won't. Then he'll be lost in the fen in the dark.

She drops the full plastic bag in an open spot where she'll see it when she returns that way and, sighing, she steps off the path. Forcing a path between tall fronds of bracken, avoiding arching clumps of bramble waiting to snare her clothes and skin, she repeatedly calls her dog's name. Every minute or so, she checks her bearings, using the car park with its lonely single light and the birches. Soon, she can no longer hear her dog.

Where has he gone?

Trying to reassure herself, she imagines how she will scold him when she finds him. She'll cut the walk short and take him straight back to the car.

Several more minutes pass as she searches and calls.

If I'd gone to the lake we would be on our way home by now.

At the edge of her vision, a shadow shifts. She turns. Darker than the surrounding darkness, the shape of the thing is indistinct, about fifty meters away. It is too large to be a dog.

She inhales sharply.

The figure is human. Someone else is out here. Is it a man or a woman? She can't tell. She can barely make them out at all.

Should she say something? Shout a greeting?

No.

There is something menacing about the stranger. He or she isn't going anywhere, only standing and watching her.

'Toby,' she calls querulously.

She turns and heads for the path. Or perhaps she should cut through the vegetation to reach the safety of her car. As she moves, she hears more sounds than the ones she's creating.

She looks back and her heart plummets into her stomach.

The person is following her.

If she can just reach her vehicle and lock herself in...

Maybe she should call the police, but she would have to stop, take out her phone and dial, giving the person time to reach her. It would take the police at least ten or fifteen minutes to arrive, by which time...

She changes direction, making a beeline for the car park. Instantly, thorns snag her coat. She rips it free. A thorn drags at her hand, tearing the skin. A stem catches on her trouser leg. She pushes forward, ignoring the snagging and scratches.

She doesn't dare look back again, but she can hear the stranger approaching.

A huge clump of brambles appears to rear up, barring her way. The curving stems reach higher than her head. Where did it come from? She pauses, panting, her heartbeat loud in her ears. She can't

see how far the barrier extends. Which way should she go? She has no time to think about it. She turns right. Hopefully the bramble patch will come to an end soon.

It doesn't end.

It extends.

She should have gone left.

She pushes on. It's too late to change her mind.

The wall of thorny stems seems to go on forever, but suddenly she realises she can only hear her own progress through the landscape. Straining her ears, she listens for sounds of movement behind her, but there's nothing.

She halts, gasping.

Where is the stranger? Did they stop? Or did they go a different way, planning on cutting her off?

Terror rises.

Feeling for her keys in her pocket, she manipulates them so each jagged edge protrudes from between her fisted fingers. She stands with her back to the brambles, her gaze searching the shadows.

Something leaps at her.

She screams.

Toby!

The dog bounds about, ecstatic at their reunion. Sobs catching in her throat, she scrabbles for his lead on the ground, painfully aware that if the stranger had lost sight of her she's just given away her location.

There's a rustle to her right, too loud for any nocturnal creature.

It's the stranger.

She drops the lead and bolts.

There's the sound of a scuffle and a dog's whimper.

Poor Toby! What's happened to him?

Running through the darkness, thorns grabbing at her, exposed roots catching her feet, she doesn't know where she's going, only that she must get away. Her pulse pounds in her ears. Her breathing is ragged in her throat. But worst of all, an iron band of fear tightens around her chest. She doesn't want to die. Not yet, not here on the bleak, desolate fen.

Something long and yellow flashes into view, stretching across her path. She can't avoid it. She runs right into it and it cuts into her middle. Her momentum carries her onwards and she somersaults spinning head over heels until she lands heavily on her back, knocking the air from her lungs.

She struggles to breathe, struggles to move. She must get away from her attacker, but she cannot.

With a groan of despair she manages to turn onto her front. Painful tingles of anticipation run through her as her mind moves a step ahead, imagining the stranger grabbing her, hurting her.

But nothing happens. No one seizes her.

The noise of pursuit has gone. Someone is moving away with quietening crashes through the bracken.

She gulps air and peers into the darkness but she can't make anything out. The noises soften until they entirely fade away. Still fearful, she watches and waits. Minutes pass but the stranger doesn't return. She sits up, becoming aware she is wet and muddy. She weeps.

Why?

Why chase her across the fen only to abandon the chase at the last moment? She was entirely helpless and at their mercy. Was the stranger just getting a kick out of frightening a woman out alone at night?

A sudden pattering sound makes her stiffen, but then she recognizes the jangle of a dangling lead. Toby has arrived. He licks her face and she holds him close. He seems okay.

'Not much of a guard dog, are you?'

He wrestles free and trots away behind her, apparently interested in something. She snatches at his lead and grabs it just before it moves out of reach. Then she swivels on her bottom to discover what it is he finds so interesting.

The dog is sniffing at a bundle of clothes. Beyond the clothes a wide, dark hole yawns.

That explains the tape. It was safety tape, to prevent people falling in. The middle of the fen is an odd place for a hole.

She gets to her feet and scans the landscape. There's no sign of

anyone, though it's so dark it's hard to tell for sure. Someone could easily be lurking in the shadows or hiding under a bush.

'Come on,' she murmurs, 'let's go.'

She's fairly sure she knows where the car park is. She contemplates calling the police, but what would she say? Someone chased her but then left her alone? Maybe she'll call them in the morning.

Toby is resisting her tugs, intensely sniffing the pile of clothes.

'Let's go!' she hisses.

Her new view of the pile of clothes enables her to see it more clearly.

A pale face sits among the textiles, glowing faintly in the gloom.

She gasps.

It isn't clothes.

It's a body.

She fumbles for her phone. Her hands trembling, she presses the nine key three times.

1

I'm coming for you, bitch.

Shauna read the text, deleted it and slipped her phone into her coat pocket before returning her attention to the body.

The dead woman was lying on her side a couple of metres beyond a strip of yellow safety tape at the edge of a wide hole. Brilliant floodlights lit up the scene, casting deep, dark shadows. The victim faced the glare washing out the blue of her lips and sightless eyes. She looked young, maybe early twenties, though it was hard to tell in the definition-erasing light. A rectangle of parcel tape covered her mouth.

Outside the floodlit perimeter, the night was pitch black and the threat of rain hung heavy in the air.

The Scene of Crime Officers were doing their work quietly and methodically. She hoped they found something useful. It would feel good to put this young woman's murderer behind bars.

'Not anything important?' asked Will.

'Huh?'

'Your text wasn't something about the case?'

He'd spotted the phone she'd checked had been her work mobile. His powers of observation certainly came in handy for his job but sometimes she wished he wasn't so nosey.

'Um, no.'

'Right. It's just it's odd to receive a message about work this time of night, isn't it?'

'If you could concentrate on the crime scene, DS Fiske, that would be great.'

'Sure. Sorry.'

Their little exchange had attracted the attention of a few of the SOCOs. Some looks were passed among them, then work continued.

Will squatted down and ran his gaze over the victim. 'Fully clothed. I can't see any blood.' He peered closely at the face. The victim's left cheek rested on the mud and her chin was angled downwards, her short brown curls hanging forlornly over her brow. 'No older than thirty, I'd say. I think I can see burst capillaries. Might have been strangled.'

'Let's see what Dr James says. He's on his way.'

'Any ID on her?'

'No, not a thing. All her pockets are empty. If she was carrying a handbag she was separated from it at some point. DC Payne has run her description through the mispers database but nothing's turned up, though it's probably a little early for her to be reported as a missing person. She can't have been here long, only a few hours.'

'Another burning question,' said Will, 'is why has the council dug a great big hole in the middle of a field?'

'It wasn't the council. This is an archaeological dig. That's how we know the victim was placed here within the last few hours. There were people working at the site all day.'

'Archaeology? That makes sense. There's a lot of that goes on around here.' He stepped away, as if to investigate further.

'Be careful where you tread,' said Shauna. 'The ground's soft. We don't want your size 12s contaminating the evidence.'

'Size 10s, actually.'

While Will examined the site, she took another close look at the victim. What had she been doing out here? Was she one of the archaeological team? But she wasn't dressed for digging. Her mid-length woollen coat, jeans and heeled boots were more suited to shopping or hanging out with friends.

If the victim hadn't been working on the dig, why had she been

out on the fen? A public footpath originating at the car park passed by about fifty meters away. Why had she crossed the difficult terrain to the dig site? How had she done it? Her coat didn't seem to bear any traces of passage through the vegetation like dead leaves, weed seeds, or embedded thorns.

There was something odd about the position of the body. Her legs were akimbo, one of her arms was flung out and the other lay loosely across her chest. She looked like a rag doll discarded by a bored child.

Shauna inspected the soles of her boots. They were only a little dirty.

Will returned.

'See anything interesting?' she asked.

'Very big hole in the ground. Whatever the archaeologists are digging up they've covered it in tarpaulin.'

'We can find out more tomorrow but I'm not sure it's relevant. I don't think the murder took place here. I think she was carried here and dumped.' She explained her observations. 'She's short. I would say she weighs about eight stone and a half, if that. A strong man could carry her quite a distance.'

'Or the murderer had a wheelbarrow.'

She lifted an eyebrow.

'What? I wasn't joking. We should check for tyre marks.'

'I suppose it's a possibility.'

'Someone pushing a wheelbarrow might not look out of place around an archaeological dig,' he reasoned. 'Less out of place than someone carrying a body.'

'A wheelbarrow with a body in it?'

'If it was after dark, who would notice?'

'Well, if there are tyre marks the SOCOs will pick them up. What's more important is, why did the killer go to the trouble of bringing her here? The body was bound to be found quickly. Most murderers want to hide their victims. Putting the body here seems almost like a boast. Though...' she regarded the slumped figure once more '...there's nothing special about how it's been placed. No thought put into the impression it would make on whoever discovered it. She was flung

down like a sack of potatoes. It doesn't seem to be the work of a serial killer.'

'Christ, I hope not.'

She frowned. 'But this doesn't fit the brief for a domestic murder either. It's a strange one.'

'By the way,' said Will, 'the dog walker didn't just happen across the body. Someone was chasing her when she found it.'

'What? Why don't *I* know that?'

'Sergeant Parker asked me to tell you. She said she forgot to mention it when she called. The witness was in shock and wanted to go home, but she's coming in tomorrow morning to give her statement.'

The fact that Will and Sergeant Beth Parker were an item was no secret at Cambridge Central.

'Is there anything else I should know?' Shauna asked. 'Has the murderer handed himself in and is waiting for us at the station?'

Will kept quiet.

She took a deep breath in and let it out. The threatening text messages she'd been receiving had set her on edge. Parker's omission was probably an innocent mistake. 'The person chasing the dog walker could easily be our perp.'

'Could be,' Will replied, 'and she had a lucky escape.'

'So someone was running after her when she stumbled across the victim, but then he left her alone?'

'Maybe he was trying to scare her away and inadvertently chased her toward the body. When he knew she'd seen it, he scarpered. But the archaeological team will be back in the morning. They would have found it then anyway.'

'That would be hours later,' said Shauna, 'when he'd had time to cover his tracks. Maybe he simply couldn't carry the body any farther. After dumping it, he saw a random walker who might see it and phone the police before he'd left the vicinity so he decided to scare her away.' But even she was unconvinced by this reasoning.

'It would have taken some effort to get it over or under the tape,' said Will, echoing her doubts. 'If he couldn't carry it anymore he would have picked somewhere easier to leave it. Out here...' He

looked into the darkness. 'The murderer could have planned on burying his victim somewhere nearby, thinking that disturbed ground near an archaeological dig would be less noticeable. People would assume it was part of the work. But then he changed his mind.'

'Yeah, maybe,' said Shauna. 'But why?' The more she thought about the case, the less sense it made.

2

No missing person reports matching the victim had been filed by the time Shauna arrived at Cambridge Central the following morning. No more threatening text messages had been sent to her phone either—not that she'd slept any better for it.

As well as Will, her team consisted of the detective constables who had worked with her on the Scott & Edwards case: DCs Connor Payne, Jas Singh and Alfie Hepplethwaite. No doubt DCI Bryant felt they could emulate the same success as before. She certainly hoped so. In her years of investigating murders, there was something about last night's that particularly bothered her. Despite the lack of classic signs of a serial killer it had a random feel about it, as if the young woman on the fen could have been anyone and she'd just been in the wrong place at the wrong time. There was never any good reason for murder but this one seemed especially unjust. It was a wrong that needed to be made right.

'Thanks for coming in early everyone,' she said to the four expectant faces. She outlined the scant details they had on the case. 'As of this moment our victim remains unidentified. In the interests of putting a name to her, DCI Bryant has decided to go public if we don't hear anything in the next two hours.'

'Not the nicest way of finding out what's happened to your missing daughter,' Jas commented.

'No,' Shauna agreed, 'but the sooner we identify the victim the sooner we can catch her killer, which I'm sure her family will appreciate. DC Payne, I want you to run a search for recent and historical mispers matching the victim's description, age range 15 to 35. DCs Singh and Hepplethwaite, you're to go out to the fen and canvass everyone who turns up at that car park. Did they see or hear anything unusual yesterday, notice anyone loitering, etcetera.'

'What, now?' Alfie asked.

'I'm sorry?' Shauna was too taken aback to reprimand him.

'I mean, it's barely daybreak. There won't be anyone around.'

Recovering her composure, she said evenly, 'People walk their dogs at all times of day and night, DC Hepplethwaite, you might be amazed to know.'

'And it'll be daylight by the time we get there,' said Jas, elbowing him. 'We'll get right on it, DC Holt.' She stood up, hissing at Alfie, 'Come on.'

'Coffee?' asked Will as they left.

Shauna hesitated. Only the truly desperate drank the station's coffee.

'A Costa has opened up down the road.'

'Oh, in that case,' she replied, 'I would actually kill for one.' Had she even slept at all? She wasn't sure.

'I hope our perp had a better motivation to commit murder,' Will commented, putting on his coat. 'Connor?'

'No, thanks. I've started drinking green tea. My mum says it's much healthier.'

Will stared at him blankly. 'Okay.' He asked Shauna what type of coffee she wanted.

While waiting for him to return with her fix, she looked up information on the archaeological dig. The nature of the hole in the ground was the one thing she'd managed to discover about it last night. Though it might not be significant it seemed a lead worth pursuing, considering they had nothing else to go on.

What she found was surprising. The dig was at the site of a World

War Two military plane crash. She hadn't known archaeologists investigated events so recent. She looked up the lead archaeologist's office number and called it. Predictably for the time of day, the phone went to voicemail, so she left a message asking the scientist, Kapherr, to call her back.

Will returned with the hot coffee and a pastry. 'You looked hungry,' he explained, sliding the paper bag across to her.

To her surprise, she found she was. 'Thanks.' Before she could eat, however, her phone rang.

It was Kapherr. 'I thought I would hear from you lot soon,' the woman said.

'You already know your dig is a crime scene?' asked Shauna.

'Oh yes. Nothing stays a secret around here for long. I must say, I was shocked when I heard a body had been found. How awful. Poor woman.'

Shauna was tempted to ask how she'd come to know so much but she bit her tongue. She didn't want to sour relations, or at least not yet. 'Do you know who it might be? We were wondering if the victim might have been working at the site.'

'That was my immediate fear too,' replied Kapherr, 'but I've contacted everyone and they're all safe and sound, thank the Lord. Do you know how long the investigation will take? I would rather like to reopen the dig as soon as possible. We only have a certain amount of funding, you see, and so a finite amount of time.'

'We're still gathering evidence but I expect it won't be more than a day or two. You'll need to speak to Detective Chief Inspector Bryant. It isn't my call to make.'

'I understand.'

'Dr Kapherr, could you tell me about what you're doing?'

'Oh, do you think it's significant?'

'All avenues of investigation are open right now. I read you're digging up an aeroplane that crashed during World War Two.'

'That's right. A Spitfire went down during a training exercise, killing the pilot. Look, would you like to come to my office? I'm based at Duxworth for the duration of the dig. I can explain better here,

where I can show you the documents. Now that I don't have much else to do I'll be in my office all day. Come along whenever you like.'

While she'd been speaking to Kapherr, Will had taken a phone call. He was waving at her.

'Thanks for your time,' said Shauna. 'Perhaps we'll meet later.'

When she'd hung up, he said, 'A mispers report just came in. Gemma Hendricks, aged twenty-four, didn't come home last night. Her mother phoned a few minutes ago. Says her daughter isn't answering her phone and it's completely out of character for her to disappear.'

Though in one sense it was good news, Shauna's heart sank. She hated being the bearer of bad tidings.

'Okay,' she said heavily. 'Let's go and see the family.'

3

Sue Hendricks tipped the saucepan of boiling water against the inside of the sink, emptying out the water but retaining the cooked egg. She popped the egg into an eggcup, cut a slice of buttered toast into fingers, and poured a cup of tea. After placing the three items, a teaspoon and a salt shaker on a tray, she picked it up and turned to leave the kitchen.

Her husband, Peter, stood in the doorway, tightening his tie. Noticing the tray in her hands, his features creased in disgust. 'What on Earth are you doing? He's perfectly capable of coming downstairs and eating breakfast at the table. He could make himself breakfast. He could make *everyone* breakfast if he ever felt like doing something useful. Whatever happened to the notion of earning your keep? It seems to have gone out of fashion.'

Avoiding making eye contact, Sue said, 'Could you move, darling? This is getting cold.'

Peter lifted an arm and propped himself against the door frame, peering at the tray more closely. 'Egg and soldiers? What is he, five? How much longer is this going to go on? I mean, I thought it was a temporary arrangement. You implied it was. Until he gets over his grief or whatever.'

'Could we have this conversation tonight? If you don't leave soon you'll miss your train.'

'It suits you to have him here, doesn't it? Another ally.'

Sue rolled her eyes.

'Talking of which,' Peter continued, 'is the lovely Gemma back yet? I didn't hear her come in while I was getting ready.'

'No,' Sue replied tightly. 'She hasn't answered her phone either.'

'Dirty stop out. Still, it isn't the first time.'

'It's the first time she hasn't called or texted. If she knows she won't be coming home she always lets me know. I'm worried about her.'

'I know,' Peter drawled. 'That's the fourth time you've told me. You didn't phone the police like you were threatening, did you? We don't want a lot of drama over nothing.'

She shifted her weight from one foot to the other. 'Please, Peter, let me give Dad his breakfast, then we can talk, all right?'

He checked his watch. 'No time. *Some of us* have jobs to go to.' He walked down the hall, picked up his briefcase and left, slamming the front door.

'Have a lovely day, dear,' she murmured.

She mounted the steps to the guest room. 'Dad, are you awake? I brought your breakfast.'

Sue's father was taking clothes out of a drawer, still wearing in his pyjamas, a white-and-blue striped dressing gown tied around his waist. 'Aw, that's kind, love. You needn't have bothered.'

'It's no trouble. I like to spoil you. Jump back in bed and I'll put it on your lap.'

He climbed under the covers. 'You'll stay, won't you? We can have a chat. Has Peter gone to work?'

The question sounded innocent, but he must have heard the door slam. The entire street must have heard it.

She perched on the edge of the bed. 'Yes, just now. He should make the train if he hurries. How are you feeling? Did you get much sleep?'

'Some. I'm not sure, but I must have dozed for a few hours.' He tapped the egg with the back of the teaspoon, cracking the shell, before slicing off the top.

His eyes were bleary and red-rimmed, but at his age that was only to be expected.

'Maybe you can catch up today with a nap or two. No need to get dressed. Take things easy.'

'Absolutely not. As soon as I've eaten I'll have a wash and a shave. Maybe go for a walk. Would you like to come?'

'I would but I have to stay here.'

An eggy finger of toast poised halfway to his mouth, Dad lifted his eyebrows. 'Too much to do? Or do you have to wait in for a delivery?'

'Gemma didn't come home last night.'

He put the toast on the plate. 'Where did she go?'

'She never tells me where she's going these days.'

He gave a snort of disapproval. 'In my day youngsters—'

'Dad, please don't. Things are different now.'

His lips worked as if he wanted to continue in the same vein, but instead he said, 'I'm sure she'll be home soon.'

'I hope so. I-I called the police.'

'You...? Isn't that a bit premature? She's probably overdone things and spent the night at a friend's house.'

'I know. I mean, you're right. That's probably all it is. But I can't help feeling something terrible has happened to her.'

'In Cambridge? This isn't Soho, you know.'

'I know, but bad things do happen. There was that murder last year, remember?'

'Yes, but it was the man's wife who did it, or paid someone to do it. It's always someone they know, and Gemma doesn't have any enemies. She's a lovely girl, too nice if anything.'

Sue shook her head. 'Something bad's happened. I can feel it.'

The doorbell rang.

She started and locked gazes with her father. Gemma had a key.

'It's probably just the postman,' he said. 'Did you order something?'

'No.'

'Aren't you going to answer it? I'm in my dressing gown.'

A great reluctance had seized her, as if by not answering the door

she could prevent harm from coming to her daughter. It didn't make any sense but the conviction was so strong it was hard to overcome.

'Don't be silly, Sue. Go and see who it is. It's probably someone selling something or the Jehovah's Witnesses.'

'Then I definitely don't want to answer it,' she joked, her voice high and strained. She took a deep breath and let it out. 'You're right. It's probably nothing.'

The doorbell rang again.

She trotted downstairs, forcing nonchalance into her steps.

It's nothing. Everything's fine. Maybe Gemma lost her key.

It wasn't Gemma. Two shadowy figures stood behind the panel of frosted glass.

Jehovah's Witnesses, then.

Readying her *Sorry, I'm not interested* she opened the door.

The callers were a woman in her mid-thirties with shaggy black hair and a man perhaps a few years younger wearing a pea coat.

'Sorry, I'm—'

'Mrs Hendricks?' the woman asked, revealing a police badge.

Sue blinked.

She swallowed and her grip on the door tightened.

'Yes?' Her voice sounded quiet and distant, like someone else speaking from the end of the corridor.

'I'm Detective Inspector Shauna Holt and this is Detective Sergeant Will Fiske. Can we come in?'

'Is this about Gemma?' she whispered. Of course it was about Gemma. Why else would two police officers be standing on her doorstep at seven-thirty in the morning?

'It's better if we talk inside,' said the detective.

The strength in her legs was disappearing and numbness crept over her body. She stepped back to allow the two visitors into her hall and closed the door behind them. The noise of it shutting was much quieter than Peter's leave-taking yet it sounded like a death knell. 'The living room's this way.'

The female police officer sat on the sofa while the man remained standing. Sue sat on the edge of an armchair.

'Mrs Hendricks, you called to report your daughter missing this morning,' said the woman.

'That's right.'

'I don't want to alarm you unnecessarily, but a body was found last night of someone who appears to be roughly Gemma's age. We're here to find out if it could be her.'

Sue inhaled sharply. 'No, no, no!' She wailed and clasped her hands to her face. 'I knew it! I knew it. I knew something terrible had happened.'

Dimly, she heard the woman saying, 'I'm very sorry, Mrs Hendricks, but we haven't established the deceased's identity yet. If we could ask you some questions?'

'What's happening?' Dad had come downstairs.

'It's Gemma!' Sue blurted. 'The police are here about Gemma.'

'Nonsense,' Dad said. 'She only went out for a drink with a few friends. She can't be in any trouble. She isn't the type.'

'They found a b-b-body!'

'A body? Whose body? It can't be Gemma's. What's this about?'

'You're the missing woman's grandfather?' asked the woman. 'Could you help us with a description? We can't be certain of anything until we know a little more about what your granddaughter looks like.'

The male detective gave a small cough. 'Excuse me, but is this Gemma in these photographs?'

He was looking at the framed photos on the mantelpiece. There were three: a professional shot of her and Peter's wedding with Gemma as a bridesmaid, one from a holiday in Spain, where they'd gone the summer Gemma had finished sixth form, and a picture of her as a baby.

'Yes,' Sue confirmed. 'That's her. She's an only child.' Her voice broke. 'Sh-she *was* an—'

'I'm certain the body that's been found isn't hers,' said the man. 'DI Holt?'

The other detective checked over the photographs and then turned to Sue. 'Mrs Hendricks, the deceased definitely isn't your daughter. We didn't know about Gemma's arm.'

'It's not her?' Sue asked in a wavering tone.

'Gemma was born that way,' said Dad, 'with part of her arm missing. We're so used to it, it's easy to forget.'

'The body that was found has both arms intact,' the female detective said. 'It can't be her. I'm sorry for worrying you.'

'Oh, thank God!'

'Why didn't you mention her missing arm to the police?' Dad admonished. 'You could have saved yourself a lot of worry.'

'I don't know. I wasn't thinking. Like you said, it's easy to forget.'

'We'll continue to keep an eye out for Gemma,' said the female officer. 'Hopefully, she'll come home soon. Could you let us know if she does?'

'I will,' said Sue, 'though I'm still worried about her. It isn't like her—'

'A young woman might have many reasons for going missing for a few hours.'

'That's what I've been saying,' said Dad. 'I'm sure she's right as rain, wherever she is.'

There was the sound of a key being inserted into a lock and the noise of traffic briefly increased as the front door opened and closed.

'Talk of the devil,' Dad said.

'Gemma!' Sue called out. 'Is that you?' She ran out of the living room. As soon as she saw her daughter she grabbed her into a hug. 'Where have you been? Why didn't you answer my messages?'

While she was berating her daughter, the two detectives quietly left.

4

'Back to square one,' Will commented as they walked to their car.

'It's nice to not have to deliver bad news for once,' Shauna replied, 'but you're right, we're left none the wiser about the victim. Maybe Connor will come up with something.'

'Life wasn't meant to be easy.' Will said, unlocking the doors.

Her mobile buzzed in her pocket. Tensing, she took it out. As she read the text, she relaxed. 'The woman who found the body has arrived at the station to give her statement.'

'She's bright and early.'

'Probably wants to get it out of the way. It'll take us ages to get back there now the rush hour's started. I'll ask Connor to do it. Should be straightforward. Let's pay the archaeologist a visit. She said she's at Duxworth. I'm not sure if it's a village or—'

'It is a village, but if she's digging up a downed Spitfire she must have meant the air museum. Haven't you heard of it?'

'I'm not really into museums.'

Duxworth Air Museum occupied a large space in the South Cambridgeshire countryside. Huge hangars stood in a line visible from the road. As they pulled into the visitors' car park, an aeroplane rose into the sky.

Shauna commented, 'You said it was a museum.'

'It is,' Will replied. 'It's also a working airfield. They hold a few air displays a year. I can't believe you don't know about it. That, by the way,' he added, nodding at the plane quickly rising into the sky, 'is a Spitfire.'

'Is it? I thought they were bigger.'

Will rolled his eyes. 'They were fighter aircraft. I thought you were interested in things that fly.'

'I prefer the feathered ones.'

They had called ahead, and when they arrived at the reception and showed their badges, Dr Kapherr came out to meet them. A middle-aged woman wearing jeans, a jumper and glasses, her grey hair in a bun, she shook their hands warmly.

She led Shauna and Will out of the reception area and into a hanger. Aircraft filled the massive space, dotted over the floor and suspended by wires from the roof. Shauna had never seen so many planes in one place all at once. The military craft spanned the range from old, propeller-driven models to modern fighter jets and heli-copters. Information panels stood next to them, some bearing portraits of pilots.

Will lingered at a panel, hastily scanning the text, before he was forced to leave it to catch up.

Kapherr led them through a door with Staff Only sign. As they entered the small office she said, 'I'm very lucky. I'm not employed by Duxworth but they've given me a place to work. Saves me trans-porting documents to and from the university.' She added conspirato-rially, 'Actually, the powers that be don't want the papers to leave the premises, or they might not be so accommodating. Please, sit down.' She gestured to two empty chairs next to a desk.

Stacks of the documents she'd mentioned sat on the desk, giving off a musty odour. The room was too cramped for the large desk, three chairs, filing cabinets and bookcases. A tiny window allowed in

meagre light and Kapherr had supplemented it by turning on the single bare light bulb though it was already mid-morning.

'Would you like some tea?' she asked, moving toward a kettle and mugs on top of a low cupboard.

'Not for me, thanks,' said Shauna.

Will shook his head.

As Kapherr busied herself with her tea-making, the rumble of planes taxi-ing and the roar of them taking off came from outside. She said, 'I'm not sure how I can help you, but please feel free to ask me anything. There's no secrecy about what we're doing on this dig. I'm an open book. And you can examine any of the documentation around it too. Nothing is classified. I've collected it all in that central pile.'

The stack was several inches high.

'The only thing I ask is that you don't take anything with you. As I said, Duxworth doesn't want any papers leaving the place. It's understandable. These things have a habit of going missing, rather like borrowed books. You're welcome to take photographs of anything you think may be relevant.'

She fished a teabag out of the mug with a spoon, deposited it on a saucer and sat down with the drink.

Shauna asked, 'Can you tell me what happened at the dig site yesterday?'

'It was an entirely normal day,' Kapherr replied. 'We uncovered the first pieces of the plane so the mood was good as we finished not long before sunset. We packed everything away, covered up the site and left.'

'No one noticed anyone hanging around? Anyone who shouldn't be there?'

'Not that I'm aware of. *I* certainly didn't.'

'Would you normally see anyone else at the site?'

'Occasionally members of the public might wander up and ask us what we're doing, but as I recall no one did that yesterday.'

'What about your team? Has anyone been acting strangely?'

Kapherr gave a short laugh. 'No more so than usual. We archaeol-

ogists can be a strange bunch, but, Lord, I'm confident no one on my team is a murderer.'

'You'd be surprised what some people are capable of,' said Shauna. 'We'll need a contact list of everyone involved.'

'That's no problem. I expect they're waiting to hear from you, but you're going to hit a dead end there, I'm afraid.'

Shauna eyed the many pages of documents. 'Could you tell us a little more about what you're doing?'

'That's easy. We're excavating a Spitfire that went down on a training exercise in 1942. There was an attempt to recover the pilot's remains soon afterwards but it was unsuccessful. They tried but extracted just a few pieces of wreckage. The area was a lot boggier then, the plane had sunk deep and it was wartime. Resources and manpower were in short supply. The general site of the crash has always been known but it was only recently that funding became available for a dig.'

'Have you recovered the remains yet?' asked Shauna.

'Not yet. We'd just reached the top of the wreckage when this dreadful murder happened. I expect we'll find what's left of it soon once we're allowed to resume work. Then the poor man will have a decent burial at last.'

Will said, 'I wonder if anyone will attend. It's been eighty years.'

'The RAF will attempt to contact his living relatives. They may find them. Hunt wasn't married but there might be some distant family members who would like to pay their respects. It's surprising how important these things can be to people, even eight decades later. We hold our war heroes in high esteem. The pilot was twenty when he died. By then, they were in such short supply that was their average age.'

'Hunt,' Will said, writing in his notebook. 'Do you know his first name?'

'Oh, yes. The records are all complete. It was Douglas, and he was the brother of the airfield commander. I can't imagine how the man must have felt knowing he'd sent his own flesh and blood to his death.'

Kapherr's eyebrows lifted as she watched Will write. 'Do you think it's related to the murder?'

'We're keeping an open mind,' Shauna replied. 'It seems an odd place to dump a body. Can you think of any reason the site might be significant today?'

'I've thought about it,' said the archaeologist, 'but I can't, sorry. It was all so long ago. I imagine it's just a coincidence. Call me morbid, but I find it fascinating that there are now two deaths linked to the place. That little patch of ground seems steeped in tragedy. Though the family of the victim has my deepest sympathies, naturally. Have they been informed? I haven't seen the murder mentioned on the news.'

'We haven't identified the victim yet. Can I ask how you know about it?'

'A little bird at the council told me you'd been enquiring about the site and why.'

'I see.' Shauna surveyed the stack of papers again. 'I don't have any more questions for now. Could someone photocopy the documents for us?'

'Absolutely. I'll arrange for the copies to be left at reception. Are you sure there's nothing else I can help you with?'

'I don't think so,' said Shauna. 'Not at the moment, but if you think of anything...' She handed her card to Dr Kapherr.

'I certainly will.'

5

'I don't think I've ever had so many dogs poke their noses in my crotch in my *life!*' Jas exclaimed as Shauna pushed open the door to the incident room with her shoulder, encumbered by the pile of photocopies.

The young constable's mouth snapped shut.

'Been having fun at the fen?' Will had apparently also heard Jas's comment.

Alfie sniggered.

Turning pink, Jas said, 'We, er, didn't come up with anything at the crime scene. No one we spoke to remembered seeing anything out of the ordinary.'

'Never mind,' said Shauna. 'I'm sure the dogs got a lot out of your presence.'

Jas turned pinker.

'I'm kidding,' Shauna said. 'Connor, how did the interview with the witness go?'

'Okay. I've submitted her statement. She said she saw one other vehicle at the car park, a dark-coloured van, but that's all she could say about it. I found a few possibles for ID-ing the victim on the mispers database, but nothing that leapt out. They're all cold cases. I've forwarded them.'

'Thanks.' Shauna plonked the papers in front of him.

His jaw dropped.

'They're historical documents relating to the dig. See if you can find anything that might be important.'

Nodding glumly, he slowly lifted the first sheet.

She continued, speaking to the room, 'We need to check recent reports of assaults, too, stalking and so on. It's possible something escalated and no one's reported the victim missing yet. And start pulling the CCTV footage from the town centre from five pm onwards that night. We might spot her in the streets. And security recordings from local DIY shops.'

'DIY shops?' Alfie echoed.

'The victim had parcel tape over her mouth, remember?' She ignored the barely audible groans. There would be thousands of hours of footage to watch. The crime reports and CCTV were barrel scrapes but they had little else to go on until the report from Forensics arrived.

She settled down in front of her computer screen. After reading the statement DC Payne had taken she said, 'Not being funny, Connor, but this reads very jumbled.'

According to the account, the witness had been trying to catch her dog, which had run off into the undergrowth, when she'd seen a strange figure watching her. She hadn't been able to make out if it was a man or a woman in the darkness. When she'd moved away, the figure had followed, but after that the narrative became vague.

'Yeah, sorry,' Connor replied. 'I tried to pin her down on exactly what she saw, but it was all shadows and noises. She found the dog, or it found her, then she *thinks* she saw the stranger again. She got scared and ran, and that's when she fell over the safety tape and saw the body.'

'So did she see anyone after the initial encounter or not? Was she actually being chased?'

'She thought she was but it was dark and from what she said she was petrified, understandably, so...' Connor shrugged. He added, 'I think there probably was someone else there at first. The rest could

be her imagination and stumbling across the murder victim was pure chance.'

Will commented quietly, 'The more we find out the less we know.'

'You can say that again.'

A reliable sighting of the murderer near the crime scene would have been a godsend, but the witness hadn't even seen the person's face. The stranger could have been just another walker acting a bit creepily.

'Let's see what James comes up with,' Shauna said. The pathologist should be able to tell them a rough time of death and if the victim was murdered there or dumped later. 'Talking of which...' She opened her emails. Yep, there it was. Bryant had asked her to attend the post-mortem. It was last year's case playing out again. And the PM was taking place in two hours. He hadn't even told her to her face. 'Shit.'

'What?' Will asked.

'I have to go to the hospital. It looks like I'm the go-to person for watching corpses being cut up these days.'

He grimaced. 'Have fun.' He turned to the group. 'By the way, everyone, Sergeant Parker's holding her birthday party next weekend and you're all invited.'

Anxiety clamped down. Shauna was reminded of the first time she'd gone to the pub with Cambridge Central staff and Will had propositioned her. They'd moved past the faux pas but all her life she'd seemed to attract awkwardness like it was going out of fashion.

He said, 'You're all coming, right? Jas? Alfie? Connor?'

'Oh yeah,' Alfie replied.

'Of course,' said Jas. 'Wouldn't miss it for the world.'

'Connor?' Will repeated.

'He won't come,' Alfie snickered. 'His mum won't let him.'

'Actually,' Connor retorted hotly, 'I *am* coming *and* I'll bring my girlfriend if that's all right.'

Will replied, 'I'm sure that's okay.'

Alfie was murmuring something in Jas's ear. She pushed him away from her with a frown.

'DC Hepplethwaite,' Shauna said. 'I want you to observe the post-mortem with me.'

Alfie stammered, 'B-but—'

'It's important to become familiar with all aspects of detective work. Unless you're not up to it?'

He cleared his throat. 'It's fine. Happy to do it.'

Jas smiled and covered her mouth. Connor had returned his attention to the photocopied pages.

ALFIE WAS silent as Shauna drove them to the hospital. She guessed he already knew he was being reprimanded for his low-key bullying of Connor so she didn't push the issue. She'd caught him making fun of DC Payne on another occasion, but she'd seen enough disciplinary procedures enacted at the Met to last her a lifetime. If she could avoid getting embroiled in that nonsense it would save her a lot of headaches. Maybe forcing him to attend the post-mortem would be enough of a warning that things would escalate if he didn't start behaving professionally.

'Have you always lived in Cambridge?' she asked.

'Nah, I'm from Essex. Chelmsford.'

Now she thought about it, she had noticed a difference between Alfie and Will's accents. Alfie spoke with the same nasal Estuarine twang she hated in herself, whereas Will's speech held hints of a rustic burr.

'I thought I'd climb the ladder a bit faster around here,' Hepplethwaite added. 'Smaller force, more opportunities.'

'Makes sense.'

So he was ambitious. He might think he was a cut above everyone else and that was why he liked putting Connor down. Alfie was the last type of police officer she wanted to see rising through the ranks, but he was still young. He could still change or at least tone down his aggressive style.

She said, 'Attending a post-mortem will be good work experience.'

'Yeah, looking forward to it,' he replied nonchalantly while tightly gripping his knees.

When they arrived at the pathology room, James commented, '*Two* audience members today. I am honoured. I assume it's your first time?' he asked Alfie. 'Would you like a seat? There's no shame. It can take some getting used to.'

Alfie snorted dismissively and folded his arms over his chest. 'I'm not bothered.'

James surreptitiously raised his eyebrows at Shauna and she began to question her choice of punishment.

The naked body lay in utter stillness on the steel table, skin the livid pallor of death, curly brown hair spread out. The victim had been wearing eye make-up and it had smudged into panda eyes, as if she'd spent a night on the town and gone to bed without washing her face. Despite the violent manner of her passing, the woman's expression was peaceful, as if relieved to be released from life.

James started his work.

After a while he said, 'She put up a fight, I'd say.' He lifted one of her hands. 'Grazed knuckles and torn nails. And she has scratches on her neck.'

'Self-inflicted?' Shauna asked.

'The fingernail scrapings will tell us. Lots of material under them for us to work with.'

'Let's hope we get the perp's DNA too.' A match with a known criminal would be perfect, but in her experience things were rarely so simple.

'She has pinpoint haemorrhages on her face and eyes,' James commented.

'So asphyxiation due to strangulation?'

'It's never wise to get ahead of oneself, but the signs are here.'

'Any idea what might have been used?'

'If I had to hazard a guess, I'd say a cloth ligature of some kind rather than manual strangulation. There's no finger-shaped bruising, though that isn't particularly unusual, but the scratches all end along a line. That implies something soft was wrapped around her neck and she tried to tear it off.'

Shauna grimaced and peered over the top of the body's head. 'Yes, I see,' she said, though actually she didn't. The light hanging over the table was so bright it washed out details in her untrained vision. She also didn't want to look too closely.

She gave a shiver. She had always been like this. It was why forcing Alfie to attend too had popped into her head as a punishment. She could view murder scenes without skipping a beat, seeing them as pieces of the puzzle she had to solve. But maintaining emotional distance at post-mortems was hard. James's comments had conjured an image of the terrified young woman fighting for her life against a shadowy assailant. Post-mortems made victims and their struggles real.

James went on, 'Clear evidence of strangulation is often scant, but I think you're lucky in this case.'

'Are the blood results in?'

'Not yet. The lab's backed up, but they said they'll get to them later today.'

'What about signs of a sexual assault?'

'Nothing visible. I've taken swabs.'

James's answer lessened the horror of the murder slightly but threw up more questions. If the motive wasn't a rapist's desire to silence his victim, what else would cause someone to take this young woman's life?

Her phone buzzed.

She took it out of her pocket. The black cloud that had been hovering for days slid back into position over her head. This time, the text said: *I know where you live.*

'Bad news?' James asked, clearly reading her reaction.

'Nothing to do with the case.' She deleted the message.

The texts had all been variations on a theme. They were short, no more than seven words at most, often only four or five, and they never gave anything about the sender away, nothing giving a clue about who the messenger was or how he—she presumed it was a he—knew her.

Given her job, any number of criminals could have it in for her, or it could be a crank she'd encountered along the way. She hadn't told Bryant or anyone else. She didn't want to invite drama into her

working life and she had no doubt the texts were sent from burner phones and not traceable.

'I take it you noticed the tattoo already?' James asked.

Jerked from her ruminations, she blurted, 'Tattoo?!'

The pathologist lifted an arm. Pale blue ink in a writhing pattern marked its length from elbow to wrist.

'I must have missed it.'

'Easily done,' said James kindly. 'The colour doesn't stand out well against the skin.'

She remonstrated with herself. She needed to pay better attention and actually *look* at the body, no matter how much it disturbed her. Stepping closer, she said, 'I can't make it out properly. Can you see what it is?'

'It looks like...' he turned the arm gently, exposing the rounded lines to full light '...half a dragon.'

'*Half* a dragon?'

'Yes. See the scales and small wing? The lines cut off at the edge of her arm, as if they carry on somewhere else. She has the dragon's tail.' He bent the elbow, where a triangle tapered to a thin point. 'I imagine someone else has its head.'

'Fantastic.' Finally, they had something to work with. Tattoos were often unique and this one had to be. If they found the artist who had created it he or she might remember the customer.

'*The Girl With the Dragon Tattoo*,' said James.

'Huh, not quite.' Not much international drama at Cambridge Central. Only plain, methodical, grim police work.

'At least you aren't up to your elbows in dead people every day. Time to open her up.' He lifted a scalpel. 'Oh, there he goes.'

Shauna had forgotten about Alfie, who was standing a little behind her. She was no match for the big man's full weight but she managed to protect his head as he hit the floor.

Penelope Carew replaced the telephone receiver. The chef had confirmed he would arrive at four tomorrow, bringing with him all the dishes that could be made off-site. The dinner party preparations were going well. The only fly in the ointment was that she still didn't know if Lauren was coming.

She unscrewed the lid of a bottle of prescription medicine, took out a pill and swallowed it without water. Then she walked from her study across the hallway and down a short flight of steps to the kitchen, where her housekeeper, Janet, was putting away the recently delivered groceries.

'Did you take any messages this morning?' she asked.

'No,' Janet replied with a note of irritation. 'I would have passed them on immediately, as you requested.'

'Well, if my daughter phones, come and find me. I want to speak to her personally.'

'Yes, Mrs Carew. Of course I will.'

Leaving the kitchen, Penelope made a mental note to advertise for another housekeeper. Janet's impertinence was becoming insufferable. A simple 'no' to her inquiry about messages would have sufficed.

She passed through the lounge and opened the French doors to the garden. The neat squares of box running down to the yew hedge

looked dark and sharply defined in the soft, early spring light. The weather was mild for March, but she pulled her cardigan tighter. The sound of a petrol lawnmower could be heard in the distance. The noise her guide, she stepped between the lines of box, through the arched gap in the yew, and out onto the wide expanse of grass beyond.

Stately trees dotted the sward, and navigating between them was Michael, the gardener, on a ride-on mower. As she approached he noticed her, stopped the machine and turned off the engine.

''Morning, Mrs Carew,' he said, removing his cap.

Michael knew how to show proper deference. He'd been working for the family all his adult life. But he was getting on. How old was he? At least seventy, maybe older, though long years spent outdoors must have aged his skin prematurely. Perhaps he was only in his sixties. He hadn't mentioned retiring yet, thank goodness. She didn't know how she would find an acceptable replacement in this era of 'worker's rights'.

'Good morning. You're doing a wonderful job. The lawn looks lovely.'

'Thanks, but, like I said before, the grass doesn't really need cutting at this time of year.'

'I know, but we haven't seen the Carter branch of the family for so long. I want everything to be absolutely perfect.'

'I remember their last visit. When was it? About fifteen years ago? It was late summer. I cut dahlias, roses, gaura and sweet peas for the house, and I harvested a few veg for the kitchen, too, if I recall rightly.'

Penelope said sadly, 'It's a shame we had to replace the vegetable garden.'

'Yeah, but with my arthritis...'

'No need to apologise, Michael. It can't be helped.' Despite her words, she secretly wished she did have home grown produce to serve their guests. 'I was wondering about flowers, though...'

'Not much in bloom right now.'

'I know, but I thought some narcissus would look wonderful in the drawing room and perhaps you could find some sprigs of winter honeysuckle and daphne for the lounge?'

'I'll see what I can do. Well, I'd better get this finished,' he hinted.

'Of course. I won't hold you up any longer.'

'Have a nice time at your dinner party, Mrs Carew.'

She returned to the house. Janet had finished putting away the groceries and was nowhere to be seen. There were no notes on her desk and as her housekeeper hadn't come to find her she presumed Lauren hadn't phoned. Frowning, she scanned the desk again as if a message might suddenly appear. Then an idea occurred.

She'd left so many voice mails on the landline number she had for her daughter she'd assumed Lauren would reply in the same way. She picked up her handbag and searched it for her mobile phone. She hated the things. They were such a distraction. People didn't seem to want to talk to each other anymore. Everyone had their heads down, their gazes glued to the screens like idiots watching freak shows.

She pressed the button to light up the screen but it remained black. The phone was dead, its battery flat. She tutted and searched for the lead to charge it. After plugging it in, she was forced to wait.

This had to be how Lauren had replied. It was her generation's preferred form of communication. Why hadn't she thought of it before? She hoped Lauren had accepted the invitation. She'd given her plenty of notice. Surely she would want to see her American cousins?

The screen lit up.

There were no texts.

She ripped the cord out of the socket and shoved the charger and phone into the bureau, slamming it shut.

She'd put up with Lauren's worsening behaviour for years, but this really was beyond the pale. If she didn't want to come to the dinner party they could discuss it. But to simply not respond to the invitation was incredibly rude.

Why had her daughter turned out like this? Where had things gone wrong? Lauren had attended the best private schools and received an excellent education. Didn't they teach manners, too, at those places anymore? She'd attended a Russell Group university, where she'd rubbed shoulders with students like herself and their families, the elite of British society. She'd been given every opportu-

nity money and connections could provide. Yet somewhere along the way, for some unknown reason, it had all gone wrong.

After everything that had been done for her, was expecting her attendance at a social event too much to ask? Penelope didn't think so. And the Carters would be so disappointed not to see how the little girl of fifteen years ago had grown into a beautiful, accomplished young woman.

She couldn't allow that to happen. Lauren *had* to come to dinner. She would not accept no for an answer, and she certainly wouldn't accept no answer at all. If she didn't hear anything by this time tomorrow, she would insist on speaking to her.

She opened the bureau.

Where was Lauren's new address?

Sue softly knocked on Gemma's bedroom door. 'Tea's ready, love.'

No answer.

Was she asleep? It was six thirty in the evening, but her daughter slept at all kinds of times of day. Sue was sure she heard her moving around the house in the dead of night at times, wide awake while the rest of the household slept.

She knocked again.

When there was no reply for a second time, she asked, 'Can I come in?'

Silence was the only response.

She decided not to push her luck. When Gemma was in a bad mood, forcing contact made her worse.

Sue descended the stairs, stepping softly in case Gemma really was asleep.

Peter waited at the dinner table, his food untouched. 'Well?'

'Well what?' She took her seat. 'Eat up, dear. It's getting cold.'

She'd made a lamb curry, one of his favourites.

His lips thinned to a line before he growled, 'Don't play silly buggers. Is she coming down or not?'

'I think she's having a nap. I'm sure she'll be down soon, or I could—'

'You're *not* taking her dinner up to her again. I told you last night was the final time. She's a big girl now. Twenty-three years old. She's too big for sulks and tantrums, and I'm telling you I won't put up with it any longer!' While he'd been speaking, his voice had grown louder until in the end he was nearly shouting.

'Please don't raise your voice,' Sue said. 'You don't want to wake her up.'

'Oh, but I do. I *do*.' He picked up his fork and thrust it into his curry. He ate several forkfuls quickly, barely chewing the food before swallowing it.

Sue's sense of taste seemed to have disappeared. She'd added all the usual spices to the curry, gently frying them beforehand exactly as you were supposed to. Yet the meal tasted like cardboard. It didn't matter. She wasn't particularly hungry.

Peter's fork clattered to his plate and he pushed the half-eaten dish away. Resting his elbows on the table and steepling his fingers he said, 'We need to have a serious talk.'

A heaviness settled over her.

'Sue, you know how much it pains me to say it, but your daughter is work-shy and lazy. As far as I'm aware she's never even *applied* for a job let alone held one. She has three perfectly good A levels and attended a very good school—which, I might point out, *I* paid for.'

'You've already pointed it out,' she murmured. 'Many times.'

Continuing as if he hadn't heard her, Peter went on, 'Even if she didn't have good qualifications, she should have made connections at her school that would open the door to any number of careers. You know how it works. *Someone* should be willing to give her a hand up. She doesn't have any excuses.'

'Peter, love, you're forgetting she's disabled.'

'And you're forgetting I've known her most of her life. She manages perfectly well. She's grown up like that and doesn't know any different. She copes just fine. And, besides, workplaces have to make accommodations for disabled people these days. Hell, most

companies would be falling over themselves to employ her so they could boost their diversity statistics.'

'It isn't just her disability that's a problem. She's also clinically depressed.'

He waved dismissively. 'Stuff and nonsense. She has a loving, secure home life and she's had a privileged upbringing—at my expense. People with mental illnesses have troubled backgrounds. That isn't the case with her. She plays on this depression rubbish to avoid growing up and getting a job.'

'Well, her doctor seems to think she's ill. She's been diagnosed and she's on medication.'

He slammed the table, making Sue jump.

'Sorry,' he said, 'but this situation would tax the patience of a saint. How much longer is it going to go on? Is Gemma going to be 'ill' for the rest of her life?' He said the words sarcastically, making quote marks in the air with his fingers. 'Are you expecting me to support her forever?' He leaned closer. 'It's been twenty-one years. When I took you both in, I didn't expect I would be on the hook for the rest of my life. Murderers get shorter sentences.'

'I'm happy to go out to work. I could find something part time if it would help.'

'No. You're needed here. Someone has to look after the house. Your fully grown, perfectly healthy daughter, on the other hand, could certainly get herself some gainful employment and then, preferably, move out, like a normal child would eventually. It would do her the world of good. I'm sure she doesn't like being a burden.'

'My daughter is not a burden!' Sue exclaimed.

She snatched her and Peter's plate from the table and stalked into the kitchen. Noisily scraping the remains of the meal into the bin, she sniffed and swallowed. After rinsing the plates under the tap she shoved them in the dishwasher and thrust the forks into the cutlery basket.

When she returned to collect Gemma's untouched plate, Peter was relaxing in his chair, his hands in his lap. He seemed calmer, almost happy.

And so it went. Around and around. The same dance, for years and years.

'We haven't finished,' he said. 'There's more we need to talk about.'

Sue's shoulders slumped and she sat down. Gemma's dinner was cold now anyway. It would need to be reheated before she took it up, assuming Peter allowed it. He hadn't gone as far as attempting to starve his adopted daughter out of her room just yet.

'What?' she demanded. 'This is about Dad, right? Let's get it over with.'

'Of course it is. It's refreshing to see you face up to facts. You know the old codger's a problem as well as I do.'

'Please don't talk about my father like that.'

'I'll talk about him however I like. Where is he, by the way? I'm surprised he isn't here. It isn't like him to miss out on a free meal.'

'He's at the Legion tonight.'

'Meeting his fellow old codgers, naturally. Sue, your dear old dad has been taking up our guest room for nearly three months. Has he mentioned going home yet?'

'He hasn't said anything.' She had a feeling Dad would like to live with them permanently, but she didn't know how to broach the subject with Peter. 'He's still grieving. Mum's death broke his heart.'

'I can tell. He's so heartbroken he needs to go for a drink with his pals. I understand. Sympathetic though I am, he can't live here forever. I already have one good-for-nothing to support. You can't seriously expect me to take on another one.'

'Dad has his pension. He isn't destitute. He's been giving me money to help pay for food and bills. He isn't costing us anything extra.'

'That isn't the point.'

'He and Mum were married forty-five years. You don't get over a loss like that quickly. I hate to think of him all alone in the house they lived in together for so long.'

Peter placed a warm hand over hers. 'As I said, I'm not unsympathetic.'

You certainly sound it.

'But everyone has their limits. Don't you think it would be nice to have *our* house to *ourselves* and not share it with people perfectly capable of standing on their own two feet? Wouldn't you like the freedom of caring for one person instead of three?'

The change of tack was familiar. He would go on the attack, then pretend to offer an olive branch. She'd fallen for it in the past, before she'd learnt.

'I don't see it as a burden. Dad and Gemma are no trouble. They mostly look after themselves. To be honest, I'm glad of the company while you're at work.'

Peter moved his hand away. 'Well, I *do* see it as a burden. A financial burden as well as an imposition on my goodwill. And I won't put up with it forever.'

And yet, you will.

He needed her. He needed someone to control, to harangue, to feel superior to. She wasn't even sure he didn't need Gemma and Dad too. Their presence gave him something to complain about. He loved to feel hard done by.

From the hall came the sound of a key being inserted into the front door. Dad was home.

'How timely,' said Peter.

Sue rose and went out. Her father was taking off his coat to hang it on the hook.

'You're back early.'

'No one was there tonight. No one I know anyway.'

'That's a shame. There's beer in the fridge if you'd like one.'

'Hardly anyone's left alive now,' he went on. 'Nearly all of them have passed on.' He looked sunken and defeated. He'd attended a friend's funeral last week and he'd been down ever since.

It was hard to know what to say. 'You still have us, Dad. You still have family who love you.'

He threw a glance at the dining room door, where Peter sat, silent and invisible. 'I know, but it isn't the same. You'll understand when you're older.'

'You've been saying that to me since I was three.'

'And it's always been true. Is Gemma in?'

Sue sighed. 'Yes, but she didn't come down for her tea.'

'I'll go up and see how she is.'

'Thanks. I'd be grateful.'

Her daughter and father had a special relationship, forged not long after Gemma's birth. She guessed Dad had seen it as his duty to protect the little girl born missing her left arm below her elbow. He'd done a good job, making sure she never went without and buying her things Peter wouldn't fork out for. As she'd grown older he'd always been ready to listen to her teenage complaints and give her a fiver or a tenner whenever she asked. But no one could fully protect her from all the world's cruelties.

She followed him up the stairs. If Dad managed to get access to Gemma's room, she might get inside too. Peter had been permanently banned long ago.

As soon as Dad spoke through the door, Gemma opened it.

'Pops!' She hugged her grandfather.

She seemed to have been awake all along, just not answering. Her bed was made and the room was tidy. Gemma's depression didn't manifest in the same way as it did for many people, in mess and dirty habits. Sue had been truthful when she'd told Peter her daughter was no trouble. In fact, the paintings and drawings she did when she was particularly down brought an artistic beauty into the house, not that Peter would ever admit it.

'Your tea's ready,' Sue said. 'Do you want me to bring it up?'

'Will he let you?'

Gemma rarely referred to Peter by name. She'd stopped calling him Dad years ago.

'He's probably watching telly. I can sneak it past him.'

'Get the girl her food,' said Dad. 'If your husband has anything to say about it I'll have a word with him.'

'Please don't start an argument. If he gives me any trouble I'll handle it. Back in a minute.' As she turned to leave, Sue noticed Gemma's latest painting sitting on the easel.

A woman's face stared out at her. The neck and shoulders were absent, and in place of her hair were long dashes of black. Her eyes and lips were vivid red and her mouth opened wide as if screaming.

Shauna had never wished so much that Cambridge was car-friendly. It seemed every tattoo parlour they visited was miles from a car park or unrestricted street parking. If they hadn't been using a police vehicle she might have been tempted to risk a fine for the sake of saving her tired legs, but if she got a ticket Bryant would never shut up about it.

'I never knew Cambridge locals liked tattoos so much,' she commented to Will as they made their way to the tenth establishment on her list. 'There must be more places to get a tattoo than pubs.'

'There's no way that's true,' he replied. 'But it isn't the locals so much as the students who love them.'

'Cambridge uni students? I find that hard to believe.'

'There's more than one university around here, and getting some ink is trendy these days.'

'Do you have any?'

'Tattoos?' He snorted a laugh. 'No. You?'

'God, no. Too painful.'

'You don't fancy a bird of prey swooping over your shoulders? Blue tit on your ankle?'

She rolled her eyes. 'I think that's it over there.'

Sketches of designs and finished work filled the tattoo parlour's

window. An old, discoloured, striped barber's pole decorated the exterior, clearly a legacy of the previous ownership. The door stood open, and as they approached along the crowded pavement, a young man in jeans and a T-shirt descended the two steps, a patch of transparent material covering a fresh tattoo on his upper arm.

Inside the shop, the reception area was dimly lit, the window display blocking out most of the daylight. The buzz of a tattooist's needle emanated from the open doorway at the rear, and an antiseptic smell filled the air.

Three of the line of cheap plastic chairs were filled by waiting customers. The heavily pierced receptionist eyed them from her perch on a stool behind the desk. She put on a bright smile. 'Can I help you?'

When Shauna and Will showed her their badges she didn't appear surprised. 'We're fully licensed.'

'We aren't here about your licensing,' Shauna replied. 'Can we speak to the owner?'

'He lives in Dubai, so that would be no. I can give you his phone number.'

'Is the manager here?'

In answer, she stood and leaned through the doorway. 'Mordecai! The cops want to talk to you.'

Mordecai?

'That can't be his real name,' Will whispered.

The buzzing sound cut out.

A man in a leather vest and Mohican haircut appeared. Tattoos covered every visible inch of his skin except his face. 'Yeah?' He looked them up and down. 'What do you want?'

'We're trying to find the artist who did this,' Shauna said, taking her phone out of her pocket. She opened the screen, revealing her photograph of the murder victim's arm.

He gave it a brief glance. 'Sorry, I don't—'

'They aren't in any trouble,' said Shauna. 'We want to identify someone.'

The manager peered closer. 'Someone dead?'

There was no denying it. This man worked with skin all day long.

'Yes, someone who died. Do you recognise the design?'

He shook his head. 'Nope.'

Damn. Another dead end. They'd visited nearly every place on the list. Perhaps the tattoo hadn't been done in Cambridge.

'But I recognise the style,' the manager added. 'Nice bit of work, that. Come through.'

The back room contained two padded chairs, a washbasin, and equipment Shauna presumed was used for tattooing. A woman sat facing backwards on one of the chairs. She wore a skirt and a sports bra. From her shoes, hairstyle and make-up, if a large, half-finished butterfly hadn't covered one of her shoulders, Shauna would have said she worked in an office. Tattoos were definitely becoming more respectable.

Mordecai had disappeared through a second doorway.

'Sorry about this,' Shauna said to the woman.

Will was looking pointedly away from her.

'Don't worry about it,' she replied.

Mordecai reappeared. 'You'll have to...Shit, sorry, Natalie.'

She waved dismissively. 'I don't mind, but can you hurry up? I'm on my lunch break.'

'Dave's out the back having a fag,' said Mordecai. 'You can talk to him out there.'

A narrow alley ran along the back of the shops. Wooden fences blocked off the gardens of terraced houses on the other side of it. Dave leant on one of them. He was an older man with a shaven head, wearing black trousers and a black shirt. His newly started cigarette hung between two fingers.

'Let's have a look,' he said.

Shauna lifted her phone up.

He squinted then nodded. 'Yeah, that's one of mine.' He looked closer and grimaced. 'What happened to her?'

'Do you remember her name?' Shauna asked.

'Give me a sec.' He looked down and took a long draw on his cigarette. Turning his gaze upwards he breathed out a cloud of smoke. He shook his head. 'Sorry, it was too long ago.'

'How long ago?' Shauna asked.

'Five or six years maybe, if I had to guess.'

'So you do remember doing it?'

'Oh yeah, but people come and go, you know? And I'm not good with names. I don't think they came back for any more work either.'

'They? Two people had this tattoo.'

'Obviously. It's a split design, right? It was for a woman and a bloke but the woman came up with the idea.'

'So they were a couple?'

'Nah, I'd say they were good friends, or maybe brother and sister. Not lovey dovey.'

'Would Mordecai have a record of the work?'

'If I'd done it here, probably. But I did it somewhere else. That place closed down three years ago.'

Great.

'What about the man?' Shauna asked. 'Can you describe him?'

'He was skinny. His arm wasn't much thicker than hers.'

'Do you remember his face? Hair and eye colour? Was he tall or short? Anything like that.'

'No idea, sorry. I only really remember doing the work.'

Shauna put away her phone. The victim's tattoo had seemed such a solid lead. She was unwilling to let go of it. 'There has to be something else you can tell us. You can't think of anything at all?'

He shrugged. 'Not sure if it's useful, but there's one more thing I do remember—they were posh as fuck.'

The dirty grey concrete façade of a small block of flats confronted Penelope. Why in the name of God had Lauren chosen to live here? If she was so intent on not living at home she could apply to her trust fund for money to buy a house.

The place had a rank smell, no doubt from communal rubbish bins. The horrible car park shrubs growing in front of it hadn't been pruned in years. Gritting her teeth, she stepped up to the entrance. Before trying the door, she pulled the sleeve of her raincoat over her hand. The door was locked, but she spotted the security panel on the wall. Using her knuckle, she pressed the buzzer next to the correct number.

She checked her watch. Would Lauren be here at ten-thirty in the morning? Perhaps not.

'Hello?'

The voice over the intercom was tinny but clearly male.

Lauren had a boyfriend? It was the first she'd heard of it. Hurt welled in her stomach. Moving into her own place, getting a job, beginning a relationship—all the milestones her daughter had passed without sharing them with her parent. 'This is Mrs Carew. Is Lauren home?'

Silence.

The voice burst out again, crackles, distortions and breath sounds muddying its clarity.

'Pardon?' she asked. 'What did you say?'

The voice repeated the same noises, louder.

A buzzing sound blared accompanied by a snap as a lock opened. The door jerked loose from its frame. Penelope elbowed it the rest of the way open, careful to avoid touching the smudged glass. The interior was dim and clammy. The odour here, though equally pungent, was different from the outside. She couldn't place it and didn't want to try.

Four doors led off the ground floor on each side of the metal staircase. Number sixteen had to be on the top floor. She mounted the steps, one hand clasping her handbag strap tightly, the other hanging loose at her side. When she reached the top, the door to number sixteen was already open. A skinny man in his twenties stood waiting, his brown hair and beard long and untrimmed. He was barefoot and his jeans were ripped. A young woman hovered behind him in the shadows. Penelope's heart rose briefly before she realised the woman wasn't her daughter.

Forcing a smile, she said, 'I'm sorry to disturb you. I'm here to see Lauren. Is she here?'

'Shit,' said the man. 'You're her mother, right? I can see the resemblance. You'd better come in.'

She stepped over the threshold and followed him into the living room. Unsurprisingly, the flat was poky and badly in need of redecorating. It also held the same strange smell as the stairwell, but stronger.

Turning, the man said, 'I'm Cam. You should probably sit down.'

Penelope stared at the sofa with its worn, sagging cushions.

The woman held out her hand. 'Chris.' Her hair was short, spiky and the kind of unnatural red that came from a bottle.

Penelope shook the offered hand lightly by the fingertips. 'I'm only here to see my daughter. I assume she isn't home. Do you know if she'll be back soon?'

If she had to wait, she would prefer to wait in her car.

'Please, sit down,' said Cam, giving Chris a look.

His tone and the couple's attitude were beginning to alarm her. She lowered herself onto the sofa's edge.

Chris sat next to her. 'Mrs Carew, there isn't a good way to put this. Lauren hasn't been home for two nights and we don't know where she is.'

'She...' Penelope looked at her and then up at Cam. 'Are you sure?'

'When we didn't see her yesterday morning,' Chris replied, 'we didn't think anything of it at first. We thought she must be having a lie in. But then I noticed her shoes were missing from the hall. We went into her room and saw her bed hadn't been slept in. It was then we realised she hadn't come home the previous night.'

Cam said, 'We've been phoning and texting her ever since but she hasn't replied, which isn't like her.'

In Penelope's experience it was exactly like Lauren to not reply, but she didn't mention that. 'Do you know where she went? Could she be staying at a friend's place?'

'We've tried everyone we know,' said Chris, 'but we don't really have the same friends. No one we contacted has heard from her.'

She wondered how these people knew her daughter. It didn't seem as though they'd gone to university together. These two were not the type of people Lauren typically mixed with. She was tempted to find out how they knew her daughter, but a sudden shame seized her. She should know Lauren's friends. Why didn't Lauren keep her up to date with what was going on in her life?

All she could think to ask was, 'Where did she go on Tuesday night?'

'That's the problem,' Chris replied. 'We don't know. She went out without telling me, leaving a note on the kitchen table to say she was meeting someone for a drink, but that was it. Nothing else. No name, nothing. I mean, she's a grown woman and everything, but she's never done anything like this before.'

Dread and panic began to creep over Penelope. 'You really have absolutely no idea where she could be?'

Chris shook her head. 'We thought she might have gone to stay with her parents, but now you've turned up, so...'

Cam said, 'There's probably a rational explanation. Lauren doesn't have to keep us informed about where she is.'

'It isn't like her to not let us know where she's going,' Chris retorted sharply, 'and you know it. You're downplaying it because you're worried, the same as me. You know how dangerous it is for women out at night by themselves, even these days.'

Cam threw up his hands and walked over to the window.

'Sorry about that,' said Chris. 'We don't mean to worry you, but—'

'No, no,' Penelope replied softly.

It was too much to take in. She didn't know what to think. She couldn't think. Images were flashing into her mind: Lauren being attacked by a strange man, Lauren running down a dark street, tripping and falling, Lauren in a ditch.

A buzz shattered the quiet. Penelope gasped.

'That must be her,' Cam said.

'But wouldn't she use a key?' Penelope asked.

'She forgets it all the time.' Chris replied, trotting into the hall.

'What a relief,' said Cam. 'I *was* worried, just didn't want to admit it. I'm going to make her wear that damned key on a string around her neck.' He chuckled.

Chris returned, her expression solemn. 'It's the police. They're coming up.'

Penelope rose to her feet and then sat down again. 'The police? What are they doing here?'

Chris glanced at Cam before replying gently, 'Didn't you see the news report about a...?' She shifted uncomfortably and went on, 'I reported Lauren missing half an hour ago. Cam didn't think I should. Not this early. But I thought it wouldn't hurt. I thought she might have had an accident and wasn't able to get help.'

The sounds of footsteps mounting the stairs drifted in through the open door. It was like Death himself was drawing nearer. The police had only heard about Lauren thirty minutes ago and they'd come straight here without even phoning back.

It meant bad news.

A dreadful weight settled on her. She was locked in place, frozen. She saw the two plain clothes police officers enter the living room and

talk to Cam and Chris as if watching them on a television screen. They didn't seem real. The female officer homed in on her. She was saying something, asking her a question, but her voice was muffled and indistinct.

'I'm sorry?' Penelope whispered.

'Could you describe your daughter?'

Penelope swallowed before squeezing out a few words in answer.

'Did she have a tattoo of a dragon on her arm?'

This shook her out of her fugue somewhat. 'A tattoo? Certainly not.'

The two police officers chatted quietly, and then the female one asked if she had a photo of Lauren.

Her fingers numb, she took her purse from her handbag and retrieved the small copy of her daughter's graduation photograph. The detective looked at it and said something but the sentence made no sense. It sounded like a record played backwards or a cartoonish distortion.

'I'm sorry?'

'Mrs Carew, I have reason to believe the body we found could be your daughter's.'

10

'**B**loody hell,' Will murmured as he drove through the gates at Penelope Carew's address. He crunched up the chocolate lime sweet in his mouth and swallowed before adding, 'I thought the name Carew was familiar. I must have heard about this place when I was a boy.'

A large mansion stood at the end of a long driveway flanked by trees.

'Maybe she only works here,' said Shauna. 'She could be a live-in housekeeper or cook.'

'What do *you* think?'

She recalled the stiff, reserved woman in expensive clothes at the flat yesterday. 'No, you're right. I wonder if Bryant's made the connection. He's going to be breathing down our necks even more than usual when he finds out we're working with royalty.'

Will smirked. 'Not *exactly* royalty, but if they're anything like most of the toffs around here this lot came over with William the Conqueror. Yeah, Baldy'll be on us like flies on shit.'

It would be an added pressure but at least things were looking up on the case. Mrs Carew had visited the morgue and they finally had an ID for their victim. And the preliminary forensics report had come through this morning. As Shauna had suspected, the soil on the soles

of Lauren Carew's boots didn't match that of the place where her body was found. She hadn't walked there. She had been transported to the fen after death. The DNA from the fingernail scrapings was only her own, but they now had the contents of Lauren Carew's bedroom to sift through. The pieces of the puzzle seemed to be moving into place.

Shauna's phone rang.

DCI Bryant wanted to speak to her. She raised her eyebrows at Will as she took the call. 'Yes, sir?'

It was exactly as they'd predicted. She took in the words *tread carefully* and *a very delicate matter* and *please use your utmost discretion and sensitivity* before interrupting, 'Sir, I'm always sensitive with the families of murder victims. I have been doing this for a while now.'

She was overstepping but his attitude was condescending and irritating. Did he think she was going to go in there and start grilling people or describing how the victim died?

'Yes, yes,' Bryant replied. 'Point taken. I'm sure I can rely on you and DS Fiske to be completely professional. Let me know how it goes.'

The line went dead.

'What did he say?' Will asked.

'He's wetting himself. The Carew family must be really big around here. What do you know about them?'

'Not a lot. I don't move in those circles.'

'But you're a Cambridgeshire lad?'

'From peasant stock. Three or four generations back we were farm labourers.'

'Will Fiske, you've come up in the world. Your parents must be proud of you.'

He gave her a look she couldn't read and pulled up outside the house steps. Applying the handbrake, he said, 'The question is, will I be allowed in the front entrance, or will I have to go around the back with the rest of the servants and tradesmen?'

Shauna yawned.

'Late night?'

'Something like that.' In fact, she'd tossed and turned until the early hours, barely sleeping.

A woman appeared at the side of the house and waved at them. They crunched across the gravel to meet her at the side of the steps.

'You're the detectives?' the woman asked.

Shauna confirmed as they showed her their badges.

'If you wouldn't mind coming this way?'

'And you're...?' asked Shauna.

'Oh, sorry. I don't usually bother introducing myself. Visitors aren't here to see me. I'm Janet Stourton, housekeeper.'

They were walking down the side of the house in its shadow, where the sun hadn't yet melted the frost on the expansive lawn.

'Did you know Lauren Carew?' Shauna asked.

'No, I never met her. Poor girl. What a horrible way to die. And she was so young.'

'You never met Mrs Carew's daughter?' Shauna was mildly surprised. 'How long have you worked here?'

'Two and a half years.'

'Your job must be demanding,' said Will. 'Do you like it?'

'It has its ups and downs,' the housekeeper replied, 'but generally it's all right.'

It was clear she wasn't speaking her mind, but that was only to be expected. She probably had to *tread carefully* when dealing with Penelope Carew's reputation. The fact that she'd been the Carews' housekeeper for more than two years yet had never met Lauren was odd.

They passed under an arched gap in a tall, dark hedge and into a formal garden.

'This way,' said Stourton, leading them towards a plain door at the bottom of a short flight of stairs.

The door opened to the kitchen. Shauna idly anticipated seeing a portly woman in a long skirt, apron and cap, her sleeves rolled up to her elbows, pounding floury bread dough on a wooden table. But the kitchen was a sea of shiny, modern steel work surfaces and equipment.

Next on their convoluted journey to speak to Penelope Carew was a narrow, bare corridor and two small sets of steps. They emerged into

a hall. Oil portraits hung on the walls above a black-and-white-tiled floor. On one side stood the inside of the double front doors they'd seen a couple of minutes previously.

Shauna suppressed a chuckle at the ridiculous palaver. She realised they hadn't even rung the doorbell. The housekeeper must have been watching for them from a window.

After crossing the hall and entering another room, they finally found Penelope Carew. She was sitting on a pink, antique sofa. Similar old furniture adorned the expansive space.

'Thank you, Janet,' she said. 'Could you bring us some tea?'

'There's no need,' said Shauna.

'As you wish.'

Janet withdrew.

In marked contrast to how she'd appeared at her daughter's flat, Mrs Carew was poised and calm, entirely in her element. 'Please, detectives, sit down.'

'Thank you for seeing us so soon,' said Shauna, taking a seat opposite her. 'I understand this is a difficult time.'

'I still can't quite believe it. Why Lauren? She never hurt anyone. Who would do such a thing?'

'I'm afraid we don't know yet but we're doing everything we can to find out what happened. Do you know of anyone who might have wished your daughter harm?'

'What kind of harm?' Carew queried, a tremble in her voice. 'What exactly happened to her?'

'You should know, at the moment there's no evidence your daughter was sexually assaulted.'

Her shoulders dropped a fraction. 'No, I can't think of anyone who would want to hurt her. Lauren was a nice girl. She didn't mix with criminals.'

'The person who did it might not have been a criminal. Most murder victims know their attackers. It could have been an acquaintance, friend, boyfriend or girlfriend. Was your daughter in a relationship?'

'Not that I'm aware of. I thought...' Carew hesitated. 'I don't think so.'

Shauna had the feeling she didn't know any of her daughter's friends either. At the flat, she acted as though she was meeting Lauren's flatmates for the first time.

'How about we turn to the night of the murder?' Shauna suggested. 'Lauren left a note saying she was going out for a drink. Do you know who she was meeting?'

'You asked me that yesterday. No, I don't.'

'I'm sorry. You should understand we may ask you the same questions several times. People often forget things, especially after they've received shocking news.'

Appearing somewhat mollified, Carew reiterated, 'I don't know who Lauren was meeting. I haven't seen her for...' her gaze moved to the view of the garden '...some time. Perhaps the people she was living with might have a better idea who she was going to see.'

The people she was living with? She didn't even know their names.

'How long has it been since you saw Lauren?'

'I really can't recall. Several months.'

Shauna paused, taken aback.

Will asked, 'Mrs Carew, do you have any other children?'

Stiffly, she replied, 'My daughter is...was...an only child.'

'Could you tell us any places your daughter liked to go?' asked Shauna.

'Why? She was found at that dig on the fen, wasn't she?' Carew asked, a catch in her voice. 'Shouldn't you be investigating that area?' When Shauna didn't answer immediately, she continued, 'She wasn't murdered where she was found, was she?'

Penelope Carew might be somewhat aloof, but she wasn't stupid.

'We can't tell you many details about the case at this time.'

A brief pensive look flitted over Carew's features, but then she shrugged. 'I can't help you, and my daughter had no interest in archaeology as far as I'm aware.'

'What would help is a list of Lauren's friends and acquaintances,' said Shauna.

Carew frowned. 'She might have left an old address book in her room. I'll ask Janet to check.'

Shauna asked, 'How long has it been since your daughter left home?'

'She moved into her own place after graduating university two years ago. She was welcome here, but, well, you know young people.'

'What did she do?' Will asked.

'I think she taught classes over the internet. English, to children in China. Such a waste of her talents. She had a First in Linguistics. Such a waste,' she repeated wistfully.

'Forgive me for asking,' Shauna said, 'but is Mr Carew around? I mean, you haven't mentioned her father so I was wondering...'

'My husband died twelve years ago, when Lauren was eleven.'

Shauna had been battling fatigue ever since she'd climbed into her car this morning. It was exactly the wrong time, but a yawn forced its way out.

Carew asked icily, 'Am I boring you, detective?'

'I'm very sorry. Your husband's death must have been devastating.'

'It was a terrible shock. Entirely unexpected. Lauren was away at boarding school at the time.' She added quietly, 'Things were never the same after that.' Her expression hardened. 'Is there anything else I can help you with? I feel as though this is a waste of time.'

Mindful of Bryant's warning, Shauna said, 'We can leave it there for today.' She took a card from her pocket and put it on the polished coffee table. 'In case you think of anything that might be useful.'

Carew picked it up and walked to her bureau to put it away. She must have done something to summon the housekeeper too, for a moment later she appeared.

'Thank you for your visit,' Carew said. 'Janet will show you out.'

'Dismissed like the hoi polloi we are,' Will whispered as they followed the housekeeper across the entrance hall.

The double front doors burst open and a gaggle of children ran in, yelling excitedly.

'Hey, kids,' someone called from outside in a strong American accent, 'keep it down. Show some respect.'

Instantly mollified, the five children of varying ages hushed and then scooted up the stairs, running on tiptoes.

The owner of the voice appeared. A bulky man in slacks, a polo

shirt and baseball cap walked in. 'Hi there,' he said to Shauna and Will. 'Sorry about that. They're a little over-excited. First time in England.'

Shauna replied, 'It's no problem. We aren't related to the family.' Wondering if the man and his children were tourists who had taken a wrong turn, she continued, 'I'm Detective Inspector Shauna Holt and this is my colleague Detective Sergeant Fiske.'

'Oh!' The man's eyes popped. 'The police! You're here about the murder. I'm Gil Carter. Anything I can do to help you catch the son-of-a-bitch who did it, just let me know. Here, take my card.'

Janet Stourton was hovering uneasily in the background.

Putting Carter's business card in her pocket, Shauna said, 'Are you a friend of the family, or...?'

'I'm Penny's first cousin once removed, or something like that. Her late husband's daddy and mine were cousins. Their daddies were brothers.'

'I see,' said Shauna. 'And you're on holiday?'

'You can tell?' Gil Carter joked. 'That's right. We're here on vacation for a couple weeks. First time the families have been together for fifteen years. Awful timing, right? I can't get that poor, sweet girl out of my head. She was eight the last time I saw her. And now some bastard has snatched her away from us.'

'I'm guessing you don't know much about her, considering you haven't seen her for so long.'

'Unfortunately that's so. I would love to help you if I could, but I didn't have any contact with Lauren, only her mother. No, that's wrong. I speak to Rupert once or twice a year too. But that's it.'

'Rupert?' asked Shauna.

'Lauren's brother.'

'Her brother?' Shauna met Will's surprised gaze.

'Yeah, they're twins.'

'Mrs Carew said... Wait, is he still alive?' Perhaps another tragedy had struck Penelope Carew.

'Last I heard,' Gil joked. 'He's doing his thing, you know?'

Shauna didn't know. She was still processing the glaring omission in the mother's statements.

'Aww, damn.' Carter's face reddened. 'I think I've put my foot in it. I didn't know... Shit.'

An uncomfortable pause fell. Shauna waited as it played out into an even more uncomfortable silence.

Janet gave a small cough.

Carter toed a black floor tile like a naughty schoolboy. 'I probably shouldn't say anything but—'

The drawing room door opened.

'Gilbert,' Mrs Carew said. 'I thought I heard you come in. Did you enjoy your walk of the grounds?'

The steadiness with which she utterly ignored Shauna and Will was chilling.

'If you'd like to come this way,' Janet offered.

Back in the car, Shauna slumped into her seat. 'Well, *that* was an experience. I can understand a mother not knowing her daughter has a tattoo, but forgetting all about her twin brother? Let's see what we can find out about Rupert Carew.'

11

When they arrived at Cambridge Central Will stopped at the front desk to talk to Beth. Shauna continued on to the incident room alone.

'I found out some things about Lauren Carew,' said Connor as she went in.

'Great. I'll be interested to hear everything her mother didn't want to tell us.'

'Huh?'

'Did you discover she has a twin brother?'

'Yeah?' Connor frowned at her quizzically. 'Is it supposed to be a secret?'

'It is to Mrs Carew apparently.'

'What?!'

'Never mind. Send me what you have and then see what you can find on Rupert Carew. There's a story there, though I'm not sure if it's relevant.'

'I ran background checks on her flatmates too, like you asked. Both came up clean. They're coming in after lunch for their interviews.'

Shauna read the information Connor had sent. Lauren had

worked online as her mother had said, but not teaching English. She had a Friendly Fans account.

'How on Earth did you find out the victim's source of income?' she asked.

'She was stupid enough to use her real name. It came up in a search, with photos, so...' he flushed 'I recognised her from the crime scene pics. Either that or Lauren Carew has a doppelgänger with the same name.'

What would Mrs Carew—who Shauna was quickly coming to think of as Lady Penelope—make of her daughter's job? Or perhaps she already knew and had lied about it. She certainly seemed comfortable with editing reality.

'See what you can find out about the victim's followers,' Shauna said, 'especially her most devoted fans and the ones who have interacted with her in the last month.'

Connor replied, 'I'm already on it.'

'And find out if anyone would benefit financially from her death.' Money was a popular motivation for murder and the family was rich.

Will arrived.

Shauna was about to tell him about Lauren's work, potentially the source of a homicidal stalker, when she registered the troubled look on his face. 'What's wrong?'

'I bumped into Bryant. He wants to talk to you.'

'I'm guessing he doesn't want to commend me for my excellent work ethic.'

'That isn't the impression I got.'

Her stomach churned as she walked the short distance to the DCI's office. After discovering the importance of the Carew family, she'd imagined the case wouldn't be smooth sailing, but she hadn't thought Baldy would be laying down the law quite this quickly.

He was puce, as red as a stop light from his shirt collar to the top of his head. The silvery survivors of his hair clung to his sweaty, glowing scalp.

'There has been a *complaint*,' he seethed, before she'd even had time to shut the door.

'Who from?' she asked innocently.

'Who do you think?!'

'Lady... Mrs Carew?'

'She says she has never met a more lackadaisical pair of police officers, who seem to have no concern whatsoever over her daughter's murder. She said you put the force to shame. What the hell did you say to her? I warned you—'

'Sir, DS Fiske and I carried out a perfectly standard interview of the victim's mother.' She didn't mention the yawn. It had been unfortunate, but she didn't think a single slip-up warranted Carew's reaction. She had a feeling the woman's ire stemmed from a different source.

'She also said your questions were unnecessarily intrusive.'

'We asked exactly what you would expect us to ask in a murder case. I mean, does she want us to find her daughter's killer or not?' Considering Bryant's fury, it probably wasn't wise to push back, but she was too tired for diplomacy. 'She lied about the victim. She told us her daughter didn't have any siblings, but she has a brother.'

The revelation had no impact on Bryant. His face remained beet-red and stony. She began to worry he would have a stroke or heart-attack.

He replied through his teeth, 'Mrs Carew is demanding I take you off the case.'

'Are you going to?' She held his gaze unflinchingly. 'And is this complaint going on my file?'

Bryant might be angry, but so was she. The idea of an unhinged relative of a murder victim jeopardising her career was infuriating. Was he really going to trust Carew's word over hers, a police officer of fifteen years' service and impeccable record?

Perhaps sensing he'd overstepped and risked losing the input of his most-experienced detective on a high-profile murder, Bryant said, 'I may take into consideration the fact that Mrs Carew is grieving and probably not completely in her right mind.'

'You can check DS Fiske's notebook for the questions we asked and her answers. If you find anything too 'intrusive' I'd be happy to hear your opinion, sir.'

He grabbed the opportunity to save face. 'Good idea. I'll do that. I'll take a look at it over lunch. Tell him to bring it in.'

'Got it. Anything else?'

'No, that's it for now. But please bear in mind what I told you this morning. We must tread extremely carefully.'

Should she tell him about the way Lauren Carew made a living? If that came out in the media, Lady Penelope might try to have them all hanged, drawn and quartered. 'I understand.'

'Good. Let me know as soon as you have any promising leads.'

'I will, sir.'

Back in the incident room, she told Will that Bryant wanted to see his notebook. 'It's nothing to worry about,' she added. 'I just suggested it to give him a get-out clause.'

'No mystery over what the problem was, then.'

'You guessed it. Mrs Carew has taken a dislike to us.'

'But we're so nice and upstanding.'

'Speak for yourself.' Shauna frowned. 'You know what? I think she complained because she knows Gil Carter revealed the secret sibling. I bet she has some more dinosaur-sized skeletons in her cupboard she doesn't want us bringing into the light. She tried to hide an entire person from us! That was no mistake, unless she somehow forgot she pushed out *two* babies, not one. What else is she hiding?'

'She probably had a Caesarian,' Alfie commented.

'What?'

'You know. Too posh to push.'

'DC Hepplethwaite, you have an amazing talent for saying the wrong thing.'

Jas chuckled.

Shauna covered her mouth with the back of her hand as another yawn erupted from her throat.

'Do you want a coffee?' Will asked. 'It's time for lunch. Connor, it's your turn.'

'Yeah,' Shauna replied, 'I do need coffee. But I'll get the lunches. A walk in fresh air will help.'

'I'm not sure how fresh the air is in Cambridge town centre,' said Will, 'but I'll join you.'

'WHAT DID BALDY SAY?' Will asked as soon as they were out of the building.

'That's such a shit nickname. Couldn't you guys think of anything more imaginative?'

'Obviously not.'

'He was really angry, but I think he was just barking. He'll put up with heat from Mrs Carew as long as he thinks we can solve the case. So we'd better do that. I'm interested in Lauren's job. It's the kind of thing that attracts mentally unstable 'fans'. Maybe she agreed to meet up with one of them and things went too far.'

'She was prostituting herself? Seems unlikely, considering her background. You'd have to *really* hate your mother to do that rather than ask for a few quid to get by.'

'Not necessarily prostitution. It could have been a dinner date. It wouldn't surprise me if people with those accounts offer extras for a fee. Maybe the fan expected more.'

The chain coffee shop was only a few minutes away. They ordered the drinks and picked up Alfie's a cheese and pickle sandwich, Jas's vegan salad and Connor's pie. Shauna bought a ham and cheese croissant for herself and Will had his usual sausage bap. By the time they left they were fully laden. When they were outside again, Will said, 'The post-mortem report didn't mention a sexual assault.'

'Doesn't mean he didn't try. Then, when he didn't get what he wanted... Or maybe he'd planned to kill her all along. Oh, bugger.'

A large crowd of teenagers was approaching from the opposite direction. They weren't wearing school uniforms, which meant they were either sixth-formers or from overseas. Either way, they would be on a school trip to see Cambridge's many sites. That was the problem with living in a famous, historic city: you had to share it with numerous tourists.

The ancient pavement was too narrow for the school kids, who were occupying both sides of the street. Half of them were walking on the road, to the annoyance of passing drivers and cyclists.

Shauna and Will halted and moved to the wall, turning sideways

to give the teenagers room to pass. It was a standard manoeuvre for locals—either that or face being mown down.

Then she saw him.

It was the most fleeting glimpse. A man's face in the horde, older than the others. Decades older.

She froze.

A sudden, searing heat rose from her shins, but she couldn't take her eyes from the man. He was looking directly at her.

The next second, he was gone.

Her gaze darted from face to face, but all she could see was teenagers, laughing, joking, fiddling with their phones and ear buds.

Where had he gone?

Had he even been here?

'Shauna!'

Hands shook her shoulders and she found herself staring at Will. 'What's wrong? You're white as a sheet.'

The pain in her shins broke through her trance. She'd dropped her coffee and it had splashed up her legs.

'It's nothing,' she choked. 'Nothing.'

The school group had passed. Will was picking up the coffee cup and lid. The pain in her legs eased as the spilled liquid cooled.

Will stood up. 'Do you want to go back and get another one?'

'No, it's fine. I'll get a drink at the station.'

'Wow, you sure you're all right?' He stared into her face. 'Something's really knocked you for six if you're going to drink the station coffee.'

'Very funny. It isn't *that* bad.' She attempted to force lightness into her voice. 'Come on, we'd better go.'

He tossed the empty cup and its lid into a litter bin and they walked on in silence. The street felt strangely empty now the kids were gone, despite the ever-present traffic.

After a few minutes Will said, 'So you're actually not going to tell me what happened back there?'

'Nothing happened. I dropped my drink, that's all. It's awkward carrying so much stuff.'

'Now that's just bloody insulting.'

His tone was uncharacteristically harsh. He was right to be angry. He'd always been straight with her.

'I'm sorry,' she said. 'It's something private. I can't discuss it. It's nothing to do with work.'

They'd nearly reached Cambridge Central.

'It's not my place to tell you your responsibilities,' Will said, 'but maybe it's something I need to know about. Or if not me, then Bryant.'

'It won't affect how well I do my job, Detective Sergeant. But if you have any complaints, I'm sure you know where to take them.'

She climbed the steps.

Halting at the bottom, Will said, 'You know I didn't mean it like that.'

She went inside.

HER COMPUTER SCREEN faced the window, out of sight of anyone else in the office. While Will was giving out the food and drinks, she closed Connor's summary of information on Lauren Carew and opened a search page.

It had all happened so long ago, and the incident had only made the local news. Would there even be any reports on the web? In all these years, she'd never tried to find out any more information. All she knew was what the police had told her the terrible, terrible day her children's bodies had been found.

Her memory was fuzzy. She knew the place, the date... That was about it. There would be a police record but she wasn't allowed to use the databases for personal research.

It was an excuse and she knew it. If she looked up the information it was very unlikely anyone would ever find out, and if they did she would only get a warning. She just wasn't ready for all the cold, hard facts. Not yet. Perhaps never.

She typed in her ex's name and the town where they'd lived.

Nothing.

She deleted the name—perhaps the media had kept the report

anonymous—and added the name of the river, *drowning*, *suicide* and *children*.

There it was.

Her heart rose into her throat. The newspaper article included a picture. Though many years had passed, she still recognised her ex-husband's car, muddy and wet on the riverbank. Chains used to haul it out of the water were attached to the bumper and the doors stood open.

When the police divers had found the car the doors had been shut. They'd been shut and her sweet babies had been inside. She closed her eyes. She shouldn't be doing this here. She'd already lost it once today.

*

Penelope took her morning dose of medication and stepped from her study out into the garden. The grounds of Windleby Manor softly glowed in the pale sunlight. It was a peaceful, quiet, beautiful scene that Penelope hadn't tired of in her twenty-five years in the ancestral home. It hadn't originally been *her* home, but she'd grown to love it as if it was, and she felt confident she'd looked after it as Bertrand would have wanted.

It was a terrible shame nothing else had turned out so well.

Lauren.

The scene transformed to a summer's day. A little girl sat on the expansive lawn, making a daisy chain. Patches of grass had turned yellow after weeks of no rain and the air shimmered dustily with heat and pollen. The girl's tanned knees poked out from under her skirt. Her head was down as she worked on the necklace, concentrating. Her straw hat had fallen off and hung by its string down her back.

Recalling the frozen image of her daughter she'd seen at the hospital morgue, Penelope shuddered.

Who could do such a thing, and why?

Her chest heaved and a sob threatened to rise up her throat. She bit her lower lip hard, tasting blood. Her palms hurt. Half circles had embedded on her palms where her nails had dug into them.

She must not lose control. She must not give in.

'Penny!'

Gilbert Carter's voice was loud and close. She started and turned. He was right behind her. How had he managed to sneak up without her noticing?

'Sorry, didn't mean to make you jump.' He laid a hand on her shoulder. 'How are you doing?'

She smiled tightly. 'As well as I can be, considering.'

'I thought you might like some company. It can't be good for you wandering around all alone. I'll come with you. Where are you heading? Did you have some place particular in mind?'

Hastily bringing to mind the closest part of the gardens in order to minimise the time spent with him, she replied, 'The glasshouse. If you would like to come along, that would be delightful.'

'Sure. Can't leave my cousin alone in her time of grief.'

They stepped onto the gravel path.

'You know,' said Gilbert, 'if you'd like us to stick around longer, that shouldn't be a problem. My company is very understanding when it comes to family crises. A colleague took off three months last year while his wife was losing her battle with cancer.'

'Is that so? I didn't think American companies were so generous.' The notion of the Carter family extending their visit filled her with horror.

'Depends on the company and the level of the employee. The higher up you get, the better the benefits.'

'How fortunate. I appreciate your kind offer, but I can't possibly ask you to inconvenience yourselves. Your children will miss a lot of time at school.'

'Their schools will keep them up to date. Don't you worry about that. Besides, they're loving their time in England. Hell, they're even talking about wanting to move here.'

Penelope's legs nearly gave way and she had to pretend she'd stumbled. 'Move here? Would that be wise? It would be a huge upheaval. What does Martha say?'

'Oh, she loves the idea more than the kids. She would move to the UK in a heartbeat.'

'Well, that's...' she was lost for words '...something to think about.'

'I'm sorry. Here I am going on about myself and my concerns when you've lost a daughter. Have you heard anything?'

'Nothing. The police sent out a Family Liaison Officer and I sent her right back again. I don't know what they imagine having a stranger lurking in my home could possibly do to help.'

They passed through an opening in the old brick wall, its surface thick with ivy and moss. Beyond it was what had once been the kitchen garden, now laid to grass. The glasshouse remained, filled with leafy tender plants. The glass structure and outer garden wall kept the interior frost-free except in the very depths of winter, when Michael would light paraffin stoves to keep the temperature above zero.

Penelope regretted bringing Gilbert here. The place had become a sanctuary to her over the years. Taking the loud man inside felt like a contamination.

She opened the door. Paint flaked from the cast iron struts. The glasshouse was badly in need of repair but the money wasn't there. Perhaps the glasshouse would be next to go as the estate funds diminished. Bertrand had left a sizeable inheritance in his will but with no further income arriving, she'd been forced to eat into the capital.

'Man, it's like being back in Texas,' Gilbert commented.

The warmth and humidity were indeed high for March. The day was unusually sunny. Yet she doubted the conditions were anything like those in her cousin's home state. He was exaggerating, as he often did.

As they walked the gridded iron pathway among the overhanging plants, he said, more quietly, 'I-I hope you don't mind my mentioning Rupert to those detectives. I didn't know you hadn't told them about him. If I had, I wouldn't have said anything.'

'I'm sure you wouldn't. Please don't concern yourself. It can't be helped. It was just a misunderstanding. As you know, my relationship with my son has been rather strained. I didn't tell the police about him because I saw no point in bringing him into the mess. Rupert has nothing to do with Lauren's death. I don't want the detectives complicating things. I want them to focus on catching the murderer.'

'Of course you do. Can I ask, does he know yet?'

Penelope turned her gaze from the middle distance to the ironwork under her feet. 'He may. I suppose the police will have informed him.'

Gilbert made a small choking sound, as if he were suddenly surprised or confused. 'Y' didn't tell him yourself?'

'I don't have his contact details. I would rather not discuss the matter further.'

A pause.

'Whatever you say.'

'Do you mind if we sit down?'

'Sure.'

They sat on the old metal bench. Like the rest of the glasshouse, it had been here since Victorian times. How many other Carews had rested in this exact spot, where a gap between subtropical ferns gave a view of the high garden wall? The other three walls supported espaliered pears and fan-trained apricots and peaches, but this north-facing one was home to a vast climbing hydrangea. The fruit trees that survived were overgrown and barely gave crops, but the hydrangea continued to thrive. Penelope was reminded of herself, remaining strong and resilient as the Carew estate crumbled around her.

'It's a great spot,' Gilbert remarked, spreading his weight comfortably across the hard surface while Penelope squeezed into a corner. 'We go back a long way, right?' he continued.

'Yes, you could say so.'

'I remember spending summer vacations here from when I was a little thing, maybe six or seven. It was a regular event. Summer in the UK, escaping the heat. Long days playing with my cousins out in the meadows.'

'That was before my time.'

'Yeah. You would have liked it. I recall your wedding day too. It was June, wasn't it? We came over early that year, before the schools had closed.'

'It was June, yes. June the fifth.'

'Bertie looked so happy to be getting wed.'

Penelope winced. *Bertrand*. His name was Bertrand.

Shortening a name made it ugly, like an incorrectly pruned shrub.

'And you,' said Gilbert, 'you were a radiant bride. It was a beautiful wedding. I promised myself that when I found the person I wanted to spend the rest of my life with, I would give her the same perfect day you and Bertie had.'

'And did you? I always regretted the fact we couldn't attend.'

'I did. We sent pictures, remember? We missed you, but you had a good excuse. No one expected you to travel so close to having twins.'

He shifted uncomfortably. The narrow bench was probably too small for him. 'Penny, the police called to ask me to come in for an interview.'

'I see.' So *that* was what this was all about. Approaching her while she was alone, accompanying her for a walk, coming into the glasshouse. He could have told her without going to all this bother. 'And you're going?'

'Do I have a choice?'

'Of course you have. You aren't under arrest. You aren't even a suspect. You have the right to refuse.'

'Why would I? I want to see Lauren's killer put behind bars. I wish the UK had the death penalty. That asshole deserves to die for what he did.'

'But what can you possibly tell the police that will be any use in solving the murder? You had only just arrived when it took place.'

'I don't know. I'm not a detective. But if I can help in any way, I want to.'

She faced him. 'Gilbert, please don't. You risk complicating things. I want the focus to be on Lauren and her killer.'

'So do I. The police know their job. If they want to talk to me, they have a good reason.'

'I think you're placing greater faith in the British police service than they deserve. Please reconsider. Don't you think I've suffered enough? I hate the thought of that pair of nosy detectives poking around in my private life.' She grasped his forearm. 'Please don't speak to them. I'm begging you.'

He patted her hand. 'You're overreacting. No one is interested in

invading your privacy, Penny. They just want to catch the man who killed Lauren. I'm sure your police have confidentiality rules, the same as ours. Don't worry about it.'

She snatched her hand away and turned to stare woodenly out of the glasshouse. What could she do to stop him? If she turfed Gilbert and his pack of brats out today that wouldn't prevent him from attending his interview.

He was wrong. He didn't know anything that could benefit the enquiry. He only knew irrelevant personal details about her and her family. She could just imagine the detectives laughing and sneering.

If Gilbert insisted on being so 'helpful' she would just have to approach the problem from the other end. She would speak to the man in charge of the case, Bryant, and persuade him to drop her cousin from the list of people to be interviewed.

'Your name is Cameron Stinnet?' Shauna asked.

'That's right.'

'Just to be clear, you haven't been arrested or charged. At the moment you're just helping us with the investigation.'

'I get it. Is this going to take long? Only this is my prime time for fares.'

In response to Shauna's questioning look, he explained, 'I Uber for a living. Late afternoons are busy. People going home after work or shopping.'

'We'll be as quick as we can.'

'Thanks. I didn't expect to have to wait so long.'

'Sorry about that.' She felt like adding, *These annoying murder enquiries take time.* 'Could you explain your living arrangements with Lauren Carew and...' she checked Will's open notebook '...Christina Blakeney?'

'That's easy. Chris and I are together. It's a two-bedroom flat and we share one of them. Me and Chris can't afford the mortgage on our own so we rent out the spare room. Lauren moved in about...' he turned his gaze upwards and squinted '...eighteen months ago. Had lots of tenants over the years. Lauren stuck around longer than most. I

mean, before she...' He looked uncomfortable. 'What are the chances you'll catch who did it? Do you know what happened yet?'

'What does Chris do for a living, Mr Stinnet?' Will asked.

'What does Chris do?' Cameron's eyes widened. 'Is it important?'

'We don't know what is or isn't important yet,' said Shauna. 'Ms Blakeney told us she doesn't work. That seems odd considering you're struggling to pay your mortgage and you don't have children. Property in Cambridge is so expensive, right?'

'You can say that again,' Cameron agreed.

'So...?' Shauna pressed.

'Right, well...' He flushed. 'She was probably a bit embarrassed to tell you. I'm not sure if she'd like it if I did. But it's nothing to do with what happened to Lauren.'

'Okay,' said Shauna. 'Let me guess. She has a Friendly Fans account.'

'How did you know?' he replied, amazed. 'You guys are really good at your job.'

'You don't mind?' asked Will.

Shauna shot him a glance. Was his question relevant to the case or was he curious, putting himself in Stinnet's shoes?

'Why would I? She never meets her followers.'

Shauna asked, 'Were you aware that Lauren Carew did the same type of work?'

'Oh, yeah. Chris told her about it.' He folded his arms. 'I'd better go back to the beginning. When Lauren answered our ad for a room, she told us she had a job as a dental technician.' He laughed. 'Complete bullshit. But we took her at her word. I mean, we didn't have any choice. We can't afford the vetting estate agents do. Soon as she was settled in, she confessed she didn't have a job at all. Said she was looking and she would have something soon. She was more honest than most. I'll give her that. She could have strung us along for weeks. It wouldn't be the first time a tenant gave us the runaround.'

'If you could get to the point,' said Shauna. For a man in a hurry he was taking his time.

'Chris told Lauren what she does and offered to get her started, show her the ropes, so she wouldn't be completely clueless. She

thought Lauren was a looker and could make a fair bit of money. It was in our interests that our tenant could pay her rent. I say tenant, but Lauren was more like a friend in the end. We all got along well.' He heaved a sigh. 'So that's what my girlfriend does. She shows men her bits for money. Is that all you want to know?'

'Just a few more questions,' Shauna said. 'Please talk us through your movements on March the third.'

'Right.' He rubbed his beard.

He was tensing up.

'There's not much to tell,' he said. 'I worked most of the day. Got home about midnight. Like I told you when you came to our flat, I thought Lauren was back from wherever she'd gone that evening when I went to bed. Chris told me about the note.'

'You drove the entire day and evening?' Will asked.

'I don't usually get up until after midday.'

'Still,' said Shauna, 'a long day's work. Do you have a record of your pickups and dropoffs?'

'I don't keep any records. Just take the money.'

'But Uber should have something?'

'I suppose so. You'll have to ask them.'

'We will. You said your relationship with Lauren was friendly. Have you met any of her other friends?'

'She moved in different circles from us.' He gave a short laugh. 'I never met her friends. They were all hoity toity. Her posh accent was one reason we thought she'd be okay with the rent.'

'If you didn't know her friends,' said Will, 'how do you know what they're like?'

'I'd overhear her chatting with them on the phone sometimes, or she'd talk about them.'

'What did she say?'

'I don't remember exactly. Stuff about jobs, cars, holidays. I got the impression they came from money.'

'Do you remember any of her friend's names?'

'She mentioned someone called Giles a few times. Giles or Guy. And there was someone else.' He frowned. 'Rupert. That's it. She said Rupert had... I'm sorry, it's gone. I never used to pay a lot of attention

to be honest. I just got the impression she'd come down in the world, moving in with us. Found out that was true when we met her mother.' He whistled and rolled his eyes. 'She's a piece of work, isn't she?'

Shauna couldn't help but silently agree. 'Rupert' had to be the victim's brother. 'You're sure you never saw any of these people Lauren spoke to over the phone?'

'I'm sure.'

'Did you overhear any arguments or disagreements?'

'Not that I remember.'

'Mr Stinnet, you say you were friends with Lauren. Was there ever more between you?'

'What do you mean?'

'Was your relationship ever romantic or sexual?'

'No, never,' he answered defensively.

Shauna wasn't certain she believed him. 'What about when she told you she couldn't afford her rent? Did she offer you sexual favours as payment?'

'Huh, definitely not. I wouldn't have accepted if she had. We needed the money and how would I explain to Chris why we couldn't pay the mortgage?'

'So that was all that stopped you? The fact that you would have to explain to your girlfriend why Lauren wasn't paying her rent?'

'No, I...' He reddened. 'I didn't want anything more with her.'

'But you found Lauren attractive?'

'Look, I know where this is going. I didn't have anything to do with her murder.'

'Please answer the question.'

'She was a young, pretty woman. Of course I thought she looked good. But I love Chris.'

'All right. Going back to these telephone conversations you overheard. Are you sure you never heard any arguments or anything like that?'

'No... Oh yeah,' he added, his eyes widening. 'Now I think about it, I did. It was three or four weeks back.'

'Who was she talking to?'

'That guy, Rupert. She was in her room so I didn't catch most of it.

I don't know how long she'd been on the phone. I didn't notice until her voice got louder. She said something like, *You have to tell someone. Tell the police.* Then he must have said something because it went quiet for a bit. Then she said, *Of course there's a point. If you won't say something, I will.*'

'Tell the police?' Shauna echoed. 'You're sure she said that?'

'Yes.' He nodded emphatically. 'That stuck in my head.'

'What else did you hear?'

'I turned the telly up after that. I figured whatever her problem was, it wasn't my business.' He looked worried. 'Maybe I should have said something or told Chris about it. I didn't want to get involved.'

'Many people don't. Could you please push up your sleeves to your elbows?'

'What?!'

It was a long shot but Stinnet was skinny and he could also be lying through his teeth about how long he'd known the victim. They only had his word to go on. Though he wasn't *posh as fuck* there was a chance the tattooist had been mistaken.

'I'd like to see your forearms.'

'Why?'

Shauna gazed at him without answering.

He slowly took off his jacket and pushed up his shirt sleeves.

His arms were bare of tattoos.

'All right,' Shauna said. 'We'll leave it there for today. Thank you for your time.'

Will showed him out. When he returned, she asked him, 'What do you think?'

'The argument with Rupert sounds interesting.'

'He only remembered it after I asked him about his feelings for Lauren, conveniently.'

'I wasn't getting strong homicidal maniac vibes. Seems a bit of a hippy. Probably more interested in smoking weed than killing anyone. His flat reeked of it.'

'But he fancied Lauren.'

'Yeah, but all that says is he's a normal bloke.'

She drummed the tabletop with her finger tips. 'We have no idea

where the victim was attacked, no witnesses have come forward, and
we haven't come up with a motive.'

'You don't think it could be one of her Friendly Fans followers?'

'I suppose so. It turns out Lauren's fans were more cautious than
her about giving out their personal details. Connor hasn't found out
much about them and it'll take a court order to force the company to
give up their IP addresses. Still, it feels weak. There must be millions
of people using that site. This would be the first murder I've heard
about. But Bryant's going to start demanding progress soon. We need
to come up with something.'

The door opened and Beth stuck her head in. 'DCI Bryant would
like to see you.'

'Perfect timing,' Will said.

*

Penelope had retreated to her study to escape Gilbert and his gaggle of noisy children, citing the need to do the household accounts. Why had she ever thought it a good idea to invite her American cousins for a visit? And for an entire month? Mrs Carter had been wise to elect to return home.

If *she* had four unruly children she would have leapt at the chance of a break from them too. As it was, she'd only had two...one...and that had been quite enough. Children could be pleasant at a distance. On the whole, however, they were loud, unkempt, and ill-mannered. Penelope wondered if the sudden illness of Mrs Carter's elderly mother had been real or just an excuse.

Thank goodness for boarding schools.

Yet maybe they weren't always the best thing for families. It would have been nice to have had more time with Lauren when she was younger. She'd been a quiet, pretty thing. No trouble at all really.

Penelope heaved a sigh and swallowed the lump forming in her throat. Had she known her time with her daughter would be so short, if she'd known their relationship would be fraught with difficulties later on, perhaps she would have made more of an effort to be with her when she was young. The years had been more precious than she'd supposed.

All her hopes for Lauren had come to nothing, and now she was alone, her only company a lazy housekeeper and an old gardener—except when the uncouth American branch of the family visited.

There was a tap at the French doors. Michael stood outside. It was very unusual for him to come and see her.

She rose to open the door and speak to him. 'Is something wrong?'

'Mrs Carew, I think I saw a man in the grounds. I wasn't sure if you wanted to call the police.'

It was the obvious thing to do, yet he was asking her for a reason. He didn't mention it but he must have guessed who the man was.

So had she. 'No, I don't think that will be necessary.'

'In that case I'll carry on with the pruning.'

'Thank you.'

She closed and locked the French doors and then returned to her desk to continue working on the accounts. It was a depressing task. She was heavily in debt. No matter how she juggled the figures, there seemed no alternative other than to sell the estate.

She couldn't bear the thought. It wasn't even the fact that she would be forced to live in a miserable little flat somewhere like Hull that bothered her, it was the idea that the Carew family home for generations would pass to new money, or, worse still, be converted into a senior citizens' residence or some such awful communal living centre. The beautiful family portraits, antique furniture and tasteful ornaments would be removed and sold, the walls would be painted magnolia, and the expansive rooms would be partitioned into cramped cubicles.

She'd held out for so long. She'd kept everything going after Bertrand's death. She'd tried so hard to keep the Carew legacy alive. Like her relationship with Lauren, it had all come to nothing.

There was a knock at the window.

She stiffened.

Her back faced the glass. She didn't turn around, knowing full well who stood outside. From the moment Michael had mentioned a man hanging around she'd known this would happen. He wouldn't come to the front door. No, that was not his way. He would peer in

every window until he found her. Thank goodness the Carters hadn't seen him.

A second knock sounded, louder than the first.

She pushed the accounts ledger into the bureau, put her pen in the holder, and pulled down the roll top before rising from her seat.

'If you don't open this door,' said a muffled voice, 'I'll smash it in.'

Loathing coursed through her. She thought she might be sick. But she had no choice except to obey. She couldn't get rid of him without the shame and embarrassment of the authorities turning up and scouring the grounds. That was marginally more awful than facing the person demanding entry.

She turned.

His appearance had deteriorated since the last time she'd seen him. He was gaunter, his hair longer and his exterior even less groomed, though she'd imagined it impossible.

She smiled grimly. He certainly didn't fit the stereotype.

Resignation in every step, she strode to the door and unlocked it. Then she quickly moved back to her bureau, wanting to put as much distance between her and her visitor as she could.

He came inside, leaving the door open. Putting his hands on his skinny hips, clothed in dirty denim, he looked around as if re-familiarising himself with the room before focusing his attention on her.

'Hello, Mother.'

As well as old, stained jeans, the young man wore a thin jacket, a jumper, dotted with holes, over a tartan shirt. On his feet were a cheap brand of ancient trainers. Her former son hadn't done well in the last five years.

'Please leave,' she said.

'Thanks for the warm welcome.' He walked to the bookshelf and ran a hand along a set of spines. 'It's lovely to see you too.'

'Anything you have to say to me can be written in a letter.'

'So you can ignore it?'

One indelible mark of his upbringing was his accent. His voice hadn't changed at all, though it was an odd and marked contrast to his outward aspect. Some benefits of a good education and background were permanent. Considering the kind of society within

which he now moved, she imagined Rupert hated the way he sounded.

She took a deep breath. She would have to speak to him, like it or not. Otherwise, he might do something that would alert Gilbert or his children.

'I have to admit I would be tempted,' she said, 'but I don't want to permanently close the door. You are welcome back, provided you make the necessary changes and admissions. You know what they are.'

'Oh, I know.' Rupert turned his attention from the books to her. 'Deny who I am, act the right way, do the right things, take back my accusations. Play the game, like you did. Like you still do, every day. Tell me, Penny, don't you ever tire of it? The make-believe? The deceit? Or are the heady fumes of superiority too seductive?'

He called her Penny because he knew she hated it. As if his mere presence wasn't enough, he was deliberately provoking her. He wanted her to shout and cause a scene. Did he know the American branch of the family was visiting or was his belligerence general?

'Why are you here?' she asked. 'What's the point of this visit? Do you want money? You know the answer is no.'

'What's the *point*? Christ. You know, I used to tell my school friends you were a refrigerator mother. Now I think I was too kind.'

'You're here about Lauren?'

He must have been following the local news or perhaps he'd heard from a mutual friend.

Rupert replied through his teeth, his eyes narrowed to slits, '*Yes,* I'm here about Lauren. My sister and I might have had our differences, but—unlike you—I'm not a monster. What have the police said? Are they close to catching the person who did it?'

'I haven't heard anything. I phone every day but there's never any new information. They don't seem to have a clue what they're doing. I'm not sure it matters. Even if they find the murderer and put him in jail, it won't bring her back. Nothing will bring her back.' Perhaps her grief broke through or perhaps the stress of the situation caused it, but the sorrow she'd been suppressing so long welled up and overflowed. Burying her face in her hands, she gave vent to it.

She heard nothing as she cried. Minutes later, when she'd regained some control, she looked up. Rupert remained in the same place next to the books, his expression dark and scornful.

'What are you thinking?' she asked. She'd shown weakness and it made her vulnerable and afraid.

'I was just wondering if you'd weep like that if *I* died.'

Jerking her hands to her sides and rising to her feet, she demanded, 'What do you want?'

'I want to kill the man who killed my sister!' He marched up and thrust his face into hers. 'I want to throttle the life out of him, crack his skull open, stick a knife in his heart. That's what I want.' He glowered, his dark eyes challenging her.

She took a step back but came up against the bureau. 'Stop it, Rupert.'

His gaze bored into her soul. She averted her face. In her peripheral vision, she saw him sag. All his anger seemed to suddenly melt. As he moved away, he murmured something she didn't catch.

'What did you say?'

'I said, I want something of hers. Something to remember her by. That's why I'm here. That's all I want.'

'I see. You could have told me that minutes ago. You could have written to ask. I wouldn't have minded sending you something.'

'I'm not sure what to take. I want to look in her room.'

'She wasn't...' Did he know she hadn't returned to live at home after graduating? He couldn't know or he would have gone to her flat.

'She wasn't what? Can I take something or not?'

'You can, but could you come back later? Now isn't a convenient time.'

The Carters were going on a trip at lunchtime. If he returned then, there would be no chance encounters in the house.

'How can now not be convenient? It isn't like you have a job or anything. I'll find something and go. Don't worry, I don't plan on spending any more time here than necessary.'

'No, wait—'

He was already at the inner door, throwing it open. In another second, he'd gone into the hall.

She sank into her chair and listened. Rupert's footsteps were loud on the tiles. When he reached the stairs, they thumped on the carpet as he ascended.

How long would he take?

Lauren had cleared most of her room when she'd left for her final semester at university. She'd snuck in when she'd known the house would be empty and taken almost everything. Would Rupert even find a suitable keepsake?

Voices.

She cringed.

Exactly as she'd dreaded, Gilbert had come out of his bedroom and encountered her former son. The American seemed to have perfect timing. She couldn't make out the words. What on Earth would her cousin make of Rupert's appearance? What would be going through his mind?

When she saw him later she would have to brave it out and pretend Rupert had never been here. Despite his crassness and overall indelicacy, Gilbert probably had the sensitivity to not mention the unwelcome visitor.

The sound of speaking ceased. Heavy footsteps descended the stairs.

She waited, her hands folded in her lap.

15

When Shauna woke it was still dark. She got up. It was time to go out into the wild. She felt guilty about taking a break from Lauren Carew's murder, even on a Sunday, but it would help clear her mind.

Pressures were mounting: Bryant was desperate to close the case and get Lady Penelope off his back—she had 'connections' in the county who could make trouble for him, no doubt—Beth Parker's birthday party was next weekend, and Will had been off with her ever since their visit to the Costa. At least the texts had stopped. She was convinced she'd been mistaken about the person she'd seen in the crowd. The messages must have been from some nutcase after all.

The great thing about bird-watching was it was as simple or complicated as you wanted to make it. She often went out with only a pair of good binoculars, a notebook, a bottle of water and snacks to stave off distracting hunger. Today she decided to take a square of plastic to sit on, too, so the cold of the ground didn't seep into her bones. Others used expensive, high-powered cameras on tripods to capture their sightings for posterity, but she was content with a tick in her book. *She* knew she'd seen the bird in question. She didn't need to prove it to anyone.

The latest in her list of birds she wanted to see was one or more of

the common cranes that had recently become resident in Cambridgeshire. Standing over a metre tall, the long-necked, long-legged birds shouldn't be difficult to spot whether flying or feeding, but she hoped to see the majestic creatures on the wing. There was something uplifting about a beautiful bird in flight.

A flock of cranes had established itself at the Nene Washes, an hour's drive from Cambridge. To see them in the dawn light she had to leave an hour before sunrise.

She drove down the narrow street of Victorian terraced houses and out onto the main road, quiet at this early hour. The homeless person who begged at the entrance to the Co-Op was still asleep. She drove on to the outskirts of Cambridge while her car's interior warmed and a patch of dark, cloudy sky lightened from the approaching sun.

She settled in for the trip.

When she arrived at the Washes the first of the sun's beams lit the horizon and the small car park was empty.

There were few pleasures greater than having a birdwatching spot all to herself. With no houses or farm buildings nearby, casual passersby, hikers or dog walkers were unlikely to intrude on her watching, or at least not for an hour or so. She was far from the noise and bustle of Cambridge, far from Bryant and work. It was just her and the countryside and the birds.

The sky had cleared during her drive except in the east, where rippled clouds were catching the light of the new sun. If there had been a mist over the wet ground it had lifted. Visibility was great, the air almost sparkling with clarity. Conditions were perfect.

She lifted her binoculars from the passenger seat and hung them by their strap over her neck. Climbing out of the car and taking a deep breath of the clean air, she realised she was already feeling better. She set off along the footpath.

As she reached the top of the ridge, a glistening, glowing expanse spread out. The Washes had flooded from the winter's rain. The water was shallow and islands of tall vegetation stood proud here and there, but the general effect was of a vast lake, a mirror reflecting the vivid pink and orange gilding of the cloud overhead.

There were birds everywhere. She put her binoculars to her eyes and swept the view. Waders and other water birds were out and about already, busily plumbing the water for food, calling and bickering. She spotted snipe and black-tailed godwits. No cranes were visible yet. She decided to walk further and find some bushes where she could comfortably sit and watch without being on show to the birds.

As she walked, she couldn't help thinking about the current case. It was a difficult one, to be sure. As well as having little to go on, the investigation was being hampered by the victim's mother. She'd persuaded Bryant that Gilbert Carter couldn't possibly know anything useful and that interviewing him would be a waste of everyone's time.

At first glance, her opinion appeared justified. Carter hadn't even been in the country the night Lauren had been murdered and prior to that he hadn't set foot in the UK for over a decade. What Bryant hadn't known when Lady Penelope phoned was that Carter appeared to be a more reliable source of information on the Carew family than her.

Shauna had explained it to her boss, citing the example of the forgotten brother, but he hadn't budged. He was more concerned about not revealing the skeletons in the Carews' wardrobe than solving the case. She reckoned she was looking forward to DCI Bryant's retirement even more than he was.

She would just have to ask him again. She needed more information on Rupert Carew. The snippet of a conversation Cameron Stinnet claimed to have overheard might not mean anything but it was all they had at the moment. And Carew had priors though not for anything violent, only drug possession. DC Payne had drawn a blank on his current location, but someone like Carter might know it.

She inhaled deeply again and tried to put the case from her mind.

Her phone buzzed in her pocket.

Dammit.

She'd wanted to leave it at home but she had to keep it with her in case of a development in the investigation. She took it out, her buoyant mood evaporating.

This time the text read: *Yes, it was me.*

Icy stillness gripped her.

The message could mean only one thing. It referred to that lunchtime trip to buy coffee with Will. It couldn't mean anything else.

A barrage of realizations hit. Barely maintaining her grip on her mobile, her gaze was glued to the four simple words. If the man she'd seen in the crowd that day was who she'd thought it was, it meant the dead had returned to life. Her past had leapt into her present.

It also meant she hadn't escaped.

Another text popped up: *You've aged a lot.*

It *was* him. It had to be him. The casual cruelty was just his style.

A rhythmic sound invaded her hearing, rough and laboured. She recognised her breathing. She was gasping, panting with shock and fear. The crystal clear day had vanished. The flooded expanse and birdsong were gone. She had flown back fifteen years into a time of darkness and despair.

The bombardment continued. As she reeled from the implications of the first two messages, a third arrived: *I know where you are.*

A quiet whimper escaped her lips.

She looked up, suddenly recalling where she was. The morning sky seemed strange and unfamiliar. The wild landscape appeared threatening. Was someone hiding in the bushes near the ridge? Who lurked in their shadows? Was it bird cries she was hearing or the crying of frightened children?

Could he really know she was here?

If he knew where she lived he could have been waiting in her street and followed her. She hadn't paid much attention to other cars on the road. She didn't know if the same one had driven behind her all the way.

And if he *was* here, what did he plan to do? Did he want to hurt her or just scare her?

The safest thing would be to get away quickly before he had a chance to do anything. No one else was about. If she called for help it wouldn't come in time.

Scanning up and down the footpath, she began to walk back to her car. Regardless of whether her stalker was here or not, she had to leave for safety's sake. The day had been ruined anyway. She couldn't

relax and watch birds now. She would be constantly looking over her shoulder, wondering if he'd crept up on her.

When she reached the car park, she halted. Another car was parked near hers. It seemed empty.

What did it mean? Was it a coincidence that another birdwatcher or dog walker had arrived? She tried to take a photo but her hands trembled so much the pictures were blurred. Instead, she repeated the registration number over and over in her head. She hurried to her car, feeling for the button on the key in her pocket to unlock the doors.

Cursing, she climbed into her car and immediately locked it again, swallowing down tears as she started the engine.

ABOUT HALFWAY ON the drive back to Cambridge, her mobile rang, triggering her jangled nerves and nearly causing her to swerve. She let it ring and go to voicemail, but curiosity overcame her resolve to wait until getting home to listen to the message. At the next roundabout she turned off into a deserted industrial estate and parked in the empty car park.

Her hands were steadier as she pulled out her phone and pressed the key to playback the message.

It was Dr Kapherr.

Whoops, sorry, I've only just noticed what time it is. I hope I didn't wake you. We've found something rather interesting. I thought you might like to know about it. I'll be at the dig site all day if you want to come along and have a look.

The area where Lauren Carew's body had been dumped looked different in daylight, bigger and tamer, but just as lonely. There was hardly anyone about. The murder had been made public days before, and dog walkers and other regular visitors seemed to be staying away.

Pushing her recent shock from her mind, Shauna approached the dig. Even archaeologists were sparse on the ground. She saw two of them until the head and shoulders of a third person appeared, standing up in the hole.

'Ah, detective,' said Dr Kapherr. 'You got my message. Nice to see you again. How's the case going?'

Shauna dipped under the safety tape. 'Still working on it. Where is everyone?' Her DCs had interviewed eight people in the dig team.

'The rest of them will be along later. You can't expect volunteers to turn up at the crack of dawn on a Sunday. Only we professionals do that. Would you mind...?' The archaeologist reached out a hand.

It took Shauna a moment to realise what Kapherr wanted, but then she grasped it and helped the woman out of the hole.

'Thank you. I'm not as flexible as I once was. Years of kneeling in mud will do that to you.'

'What did you find that you thought was interesting?'

'It's more than interesting. It's revelatory. I was downplaying it in my message. I think I was still reeling when I phoned you. I've never come across anything like this in my entire career. Follow me and I'll show you.'

A short distance from the hole stood a rickety table, dotted with muddy objects.

'After logging the positions of our finds,' Kapherr explained, 'we place the small items here. At the end of the day they're all taken away for cleaning and cataloguing.' She frowned at Shauna. 'Did I tell you we discovered the pilot's remains?'

'No, you didn't. Unless you left a message at the station and I didn't get it.'

'Ah, sorry about that. We're in rather a rush, you see, after losing several days to the murder investigation. And it was exciting to find the bones. Surprisingly well-preserved, too. The acidic fen soil usually dissolves them. We lifted them yesterday.'

'I take it they aren't what you want to show me?' Shauna asked, surveying the table's contents. There were no bones and nothing else was recognisable to her untrained eyes. All she saw was dirty lumps of metal and a few bits of wood.

'No, it isn't. I'm sure you've seen enough dead bodies to last you a lifetime. The reason I called you is... Well, it's twofold. When we recover the remains of someone comparatively recently deceased, we must give them over to the family. In normal circumstances, that wouldn't be a problem. Everything we've recovered from the pilot's skeleton is currently in storage, ready to be transported when the dig is over. But what we found this morning has thrown us into a bit of a quandary.'

She picked up a piece of metal that seemed indistinguishable from the rest. The only unusual thing about it was that it was octagonal.

'Do you know what this is?'

Shauna shook her head.

'Have you heard of dog tags?'

'Yes. This is the pilot's?'

'There's no other explanation for it being at the site. It's quite rudi-

mentary as you can see. That's what they were like at the time. The name and service number were punched into the metal and it was worn around the neck on a length of waxed cotton thread. This one was found within the pilot's ribcage yesterday. We were so intent on getting the bones excavated no one looked at it closely until this morning.' She lifted it closer to Shauna's face. 'Can you read it?'

She squinted at the dull surface but she could make out just a few faint lines.

'It *is* hard,' said Kapherr, 'But if I tell you the name you'll see it. It says Jack Muncey.'

'Oh.' She felt deflated. Why had the archaeologist dragged her all the way out here— 'Wait, that's the wrong name!'

Kapherr grinned. 'Well done. You remembered.'

'Who was supposed to have died here?'

'Douglas Hunt, the camp commander's brother.'

'That's it. But it was really Jack Muncey. Or was it? What are the chances they got their dog tags mixed up?'

'Next to none. I've certainly never heard of it happening. People in military service generally want to be identified if they're killed, wouldn't you say?'

'So why...?' Her words trailed to silence as she tried to figure out what the anomaly might mean.

'Your guess is as good as mine at the moment, but we're working on it. Our friends at Duxworth are looking into their archives to discover who Jack Muncey was and why he might be here in place of Hunt.'

'And if Muncey was flying the plane that crashed, what happened to Douglas Hunt?' Shauna asked. 'He couldn't have still been around or everyone would know he hadn't died.'

'All our records say his life ended here.'

'He must have disappeared.'

Kapherr shrugged. 'Or died at the same time.'

'Is it possible the dog tags or bodies were swapped?'

'Absolutely not. The soil we found the bones in was undisturbed. To my mind and, I would say, every experienced archaeologist's,

there's no question the remains we found yesterday were those of Jack Muncey, not Douglas Hunt.'

'Hmm.'

It was an interesting development but Shauna wasn't sure how it might relate to the murder case. The pilot had died eighty years ago.

'Detective?' said Kapherr.

Realising she'd become lost in her thoughts, she said, 'Thanks for letting me know about this. Could you keep me updated on anything else you find out about Muncey or Hunt?'

'Do you think this discovery might be important in your enquiries?'

'I'm not ruling out the possibility though I can't see a connection yet. Can you?'

The archaeologist smiled. 'I'm used to solving ancient mysteries, not modern ones.'

'What happens now? Do you have to notify the RAF?'

'Most definitely. The service records of Douglas Hunt and Jack Muncey may need to be amended. Whether they'll accept that Muncey died here and not Hunt is another question. More proof than the dog tag might be required.'

'Such as?'

'DNA extracted from the bones, perhaps. It could be matched with Muncey's descendants or more distant family members, assuming there are any, to confirm identification.'

'And Hunt? What will his record be changed to say?'

'I'm not sure. Maybe all they'll be able to state is that he disappeared.'

17

Let's pretend we're normal for once, Sue Hendricks silently exhorted her family. It had taken her days to persuade Peter, Gemma and Dad to go to the fair. Peter had explained at length just how much he hated fairs, Gemma had complained she didn't feel like it, and Dad had stated vehemently that he was sick to his eye teeth of *that man,* i.e., her husband, and was buggered if he would spend a second with him more than he had to. Yet by some miracle she still couldn't quite comprehend, she'd managed to get them all to Parker's Piece without a massive argument breaking out.

A rhythmic pop song blasted from the nearest fairground ride, a contraption styled as Roman chariots that whirled customers into the air while simultaneously spinning them at high speed. Similar machines sat at intervals across the crowded inner-city field. A small roller-coaster, a Ferris wheel, bumper cars, a carousel, a Haunted House, a Hall of Mirrors and the little rides for children, including a Mad Hatter's tea party with circling tea cups and a gigantic bouncy castle. There was also a small petting zoo. Sue wondered what the rabbits, guinea pigs and lambs made of all the noise and bustle. She could barely stand it herself.

What had inspired her to bring her little family here? She'd never particularly liked fairs. Just watching the delighted and terrified faces

of the occupants on the chariot ride made her feel sick. She'd felt certain the excursion would help to ease the tension in the house but now she wasn't so sure. Maybe it would only make everything worse.

The noise of the machine competed with others in the field. All seemed to be vying for custom by belting out popular tunes, the bass notes thrumming the ground.

'Do you want to have a go?' Dad asked Gemma, lifting his voice over the noise and indicating the chariots with a nod.

She gave a look of alarm and shook her head.

Gemma had always been reluctant to go on fairground rides. Sue guessed it was something to do with a fear that, with just one arm, she wouldn't be able to adequately hold on. Dad was doing his usual thing of trying to get her to expand her boundaries.

'All right,' he said. 'What about something else? I could drive you around on the bumper cars.'

She shrugged.

Peter said, 'Have a go, Gemma. It'll do you the world of good. Cheer you up.'

She grimaced and didn't answer.

'Leave her alone,' said Dad. 'The girl said she doesn't want to do it.'

'You're the one who asked her!'

'And she said no.'

'She didn't *say* anything. I know because I would have noticed. Gemma doesn't say much these days. It would have been nice to get a word out of her, or even, God forbid, a smile.'

'Will you stop it?' hissed Sue, mindful of the crowds bustling around them. The thought of attracting attention and exposing her dysfunctional family to the world made her cringe.

Peter clamped his lips. Dad looked furious. Sue was about to suggest they give up and go home when Gemma said, 'I wouldn't mind some candy floss.'

''Course you can have some,' said Dad. 'Where can we get it?' He rose onto his tiptoes, attempting to peer over the jostling figures surrounding them.

He was about five foot four or five tall, but he'd loomed so large in

Sue's life she sometimes forgot he was short compared to most men. Not that his height had ever seemed to bother him.

Peter pointed confidently. 'There's a van selling it over there.' Was he rubbing it in that, as a tall man, he had a good view all around? Probably.

Dad took Gemma's elbow. 'Come on. I wouldn't mind a hot dog or burger myself. Feeling a bit peckish. I'll pay. My treat.'

Their little group edged and dodged their way through the fair's patrons, Peter leading the way, until they reached the van. There was a long queue so they joined the end. Sue's stomach burbled and rumbled as the scents from the van and surrounding food vendors wafted over them: the burnt sugar of candy floss and toffee apples, odours of frying meat and caramelised onions, the sharp, acidic tang of artificial vinegar for chips.

The woman serving was young and busty. Each time she leaned down from the van's window to hand customers their food, she offered the world a view of her cleavage.

Peter was instantly distracted.

Sue rolled her eyes.

'Bob!' A man around Dad's age appeared from the throng and walked up to him. 'I didn't expect to see you here.'

'Frank,' Dad replied. 'What a surprise.' His light words belied the expression on his face. He rarely looked flustered but now was one of those times.

'We don't seem to see you down the Legion anymore. Been busy?'

'Uh, let's talk somewhere else. It's too noisy here.' He said to Sue, 'Would you get me a burger, love? Back in a minute' before disappearing into the crowd with his friend.

'Who was that?' asked Peter, the oddity of Dad's behaviour drawing him from the enticing spectacle at the food van.

'Frank, apparently,' Sue replied.

'You don't know him?'

'Peter,' she replied tensely, 'in all the many long years of our marriage, don't you think you've met everyone I know?'

'Keep your hair on. I was only asking. It must be one of the old sod's war buddies.'

'Would you please not talk about my father like that!' Sue exclaimed, her raised voice turning the heads of the people in front of them in the queue. She lowered her volume before continuing, 'Besides, you're not even making any sense. You know he isn't old enough to have fought in the war. He was just a boy then.'

'What difference does it make?' Peter retorted. 'He was in the army, wasn't he? Same thing.'

'I think the men who took part in combat might have a different opinion.'

'It is,' said Gemma.

'What?' Sue asked.

Peter also looked at her questioningly. It wasn't like Gemma to interrupt their bickering.

'It is one of Pops' friends from his service days.'

'How do you know?' asked Sue.

'I've seen him before.'

'When?' Sue asked, flabbergasted. 'Where?'

Gemma looked down. 'I don't remember.'

'Yes, you do,' said Peter.

Gemma gave her head a little shake and folded her arm over her chest protectively.

Peter leaned closer to her. 'You can't offer up a little tidbit like that and not follow through. Who is that man? Where did you meet him?'

She didn't answer.

Peter straightened up. 'Another great mystery, like where you went the other night. I suppose we'll never know.'

'Stop badgering her,' said Sue.

He returned his attention to the server's breasts.

By the time Dad returned they'd reached the front of the queue and Sue had placed their orders. As well as her candy floss, Gemma wanted a hot dog. Peter had stated he would have a burger, uncharacteristically as he usually turned his nose up at fast food. Sue only had the stomach for a portion of chips. She ordered a second burger for Dad. The well-endowed server handed down the food and Sue looked expectantly at her father.

He searched his pockets. 'Sorry, I must have left my wallet at home.'

'Huh,' said Peter. 'Typical.' Stony-faced, he paid.

Sue was surprised. Ever since she could remember, Dad had always carried a wad of bills in his pocket. He loved to bring it out and peel off notes to pay for this or that. It was all for show. He wasn't really that rich.

Leaving the van, they eased through the crowd, which seemed to have grown thicker while they waited. Sue sought out a spot with less traffic where they could stand and eat their food. There was a place in the lee of the Haunted House, so she guided her family towards it. Peter had already half-finished his burger and Dad was steadfastly munching his. Gemma's eyes must have been bigger than her stomach, however, because she hadn't touched her hot dog. or candy floss.

Sue ate her salty chips, wishing her family's mood would lift but not holding out much hope.

Why do I do this?

Why do I make myself responsible for their happiness?

A sob suddenly burst out of Gemma and she dropped her hot dog. Her bag of candy floss wedged under her arm, she covered her face with her hand and wailed, 'I can't do this! I hate it here. I hate it. I hate everything.'

'There, there, love,' said Dad, giving her a hug. 'If you don't like it we can go home. That's right, isn't it, Sue?'

'Oh, great,' Peter seethed. 'Just great. We come all the way out here just to eat some disgusting food and go home again.'

Gemma wept in her grandfather's arms, her shoulders shaking.

'How can you be so uncaring?' Sue demanded. 'Can't you see she's upset?'

'Sorry, but it's water off a duck's back to me. I have what's known in the trade as compassion fatigue. Your daughter has been holding this family hostage to the whims and fancies she calls her depression for the last ten years, and I'm damned if I'm—'

'That's enough!' Sue hissed. 'Not here and not now.' Heat radiated from her face as she felt curious eyes on them.

'Both of you can shut up,' said Dad. 'Listen to you, arguing in front of her again. You should be ashamed of yourselves.'

'I... w-want to go home,' wailed Gemma.

When Shauna woke on Monday morning her bedroom was too bright. Sunlight streamed through the thin curtains of her rented home and the ambient temperature was uncomfortably warm. The central heating must have been on a while. Coupled with morning sunshine through the east-facing window, the room with its closed door had heated up.

Shit.

She snatched her phone off the bedside table. It was nine thirty-five and four text messages had arrived, all from Will.

Shit, shit, shit.

After weeks of barely getting a few hours' sleep per night, her body had forced a repayment of the debt. Her over-active mind usually woke her earlier than necessary so she rarely set an alarm. Her bad habit had come back to bite her.

She hastily brushed her teeth and hair, sprayed deodorant under her arms, threw on clothes randomly from her wardrobe and made it to Cambridge Central in record time, helped by the fact she'd missed the rush hour.

Laughter emanated from the incident room as she opened the door. Will was leaning back in his seat with his feet on his desk, chatting with Jas, who was giggling. Alfie stood by the window, drink in

hand and laughing, and Connor chuckled as he gazed at his monitor.

'Glad you could join us,' said Will as he spotted her. 'Did you overdo it last night?'

Shauna froze, rigid with fury. She glared at him, unspeaking, until he took his feet off his desk and sat up straight.

'I was only joking,' he muttered.

Connor studied his computer screen intently and Jas's face fell. Alfie returned to his seat and slid into it.

Shauna hadn't moved from her position near the door. She closed it carefully and then faced her team. 'In all my years of policing I don't think I've ever seen such a disgusting display. I'd like to remind you all you're conducting a murder investigation. Imagine if I'd walked in here with Penelope Carew, the victim's mother, and she'd seen you laughing and messing around. How do you think she would have felt? What would DCI Bryant say if he saw the attitude I just witnessed?'

She marched to her desk and slammed her bag down. 'A young woman died. Terrified and alone, someone strangled the life out of her. She was younger than any of you. She'd barely begun to live and she had everything snatched away from her by some murderous bastard, someone who could go on to kill again if we don't catch him. And you're all sitting here *joking*? What is there to joke about, DS Fiske? Please explain.'

He had his head down. A painful silence filled the room.

'You don't have anything for me? I'm surprised. You seemed to have a lot to say a minute ago.'

'Sorry, DI Holt,' Jas muttered. 'It's my fault. I was telling Will—'

'I don't want to hear it,' Shauna interjected. 'And it isn't your responsibility. DS Fiske is in charge in my absence. He sets the tone and the standard and today he's miserably failed.'

A tiny voice in the back of her mind told her she was overdoing it, that the poor behaviour of her team wasn't the only source of her ire, that she was also taking out embarrassment at oversleeping and intense stress in her personal life on Will and the others. But she ignored the warning of her conscience. She couldn't seem to hold back.

'I've never seen such poor behaviour and I'm telling you now I will not tolerate it going forward. You all might think it's okay to be a disgrace to the badge, but your conduct reflects on me as SIO on this case, and I'm not going to let you ruin my career with your idiocy. Everyone in this room is to behave professionally at all times, whether in front of the public or behind closed doors. Do you understand?'

'Yes, DI Holt,' Jas said meekly.

'Yes, ma'am,' said Connor, echoed by Alfie.

Will nodded. 'Got it.'

She paused, swallowed and continued in a marginally softer tone, 'DC Payne, have you read all the documents relating to the Spitfire crash?'

'Uhh...' he turned pink 'not yet. I was side-tracked by—'

'There's been a development. The archaeologists discovered yesterday that the identity of the pilot who died was probably different from the one recorded. It's still a long shot because it was so long ago, but it's bothering me. Focus on those papers today.'

His shoulders slumping, Connor dragged the stack on his desk closer and picked up a photocopied sheet.

'Um, ma'am,' Alfie said. 'I think you should see this.'

'What?' Shauna snapped. She'd barely begun to come down from her angry state, and DC Hepplethwaite hadn't offered anything more useful to the case so far than fainting during the post-mortem.

'I've been reviewing the CCTV footage from the local DIY shops like you asked, and there's this bit here from B&Q...'

'What?!'

'It's best if you watch it.'

Silently cursing, she crossed the room to his monitor.

The video was black and white and grainy. It showed a view of three checkouts. Two were empty but at the one nearest the camera a tall, thin man was buying something. He was wearing a pale-coloured hoodie, the hood up. He paid in cash and the sales assistant gave him his change and a receipt. When he stepped out of view Alfie stopped the video.

'He was buying parcel tape,' he explained. 'The victim's mouth

was sealed with it.'

Exasperated, Shauna tried to temper her response. 'That's good, but lots of people must have bought parcel tape on the day of the murder. We can't arrest them all. We need a bit more than that.'

Alfie smirked, and she held back her urge to slap him.

'There *is* more,' he said, reversing the video to the original starting point. 'Look again.'

Hepplethwaite was always cocky but there was something in his attitude that made her pay closer attention.

'Bloody hell,' she breathed as she saw it. 'Stop the recording.'

Alfie froze it as the man reached out with a paper note in his hand. The sleeves of his hoodie were pushed up to the elbows. Though the image wasn't great quality, the markings on his arm as he gave his money were unmistakeable. The tattoo completed the half-dragon that had adorned the murder victim.

She said, 'I'd bet good money that's Rupert Carew.'

While she'd been watching the footage Will had joined her. 'Why him? Why not an old boyfriend? He could have found out about the victim's Friendly Fans account and got jealous.'

'The tattooist said they didn't seem like lovers, more like good friends or brother and sister. And they're twins, remember?'

'Fair enough, but we can't see his face. We'll have to get a positive ID from the checkout operator.'

'We'll have to find him first,' Shauna said. 'Alfie, track down the woman who served him and get a close up of that tape he bought. We need to check with Forensics if it's the same one that was used on the victim.'

'Uh,' said Connor, 'I heard back from the Carew family solicitor. Now Lauren Carew's dead, her trust fund money goes to her brother.'

'Right,' Shauna announced, 'I'm going to speak to Bryant. Penelope Carew isn't going to tell us anything useful about her son but Gil Carter might.'

'Maybe that was why she didn't mention him,' said Will. 'She might have suspected he did it and she's protecting him.'

'We'll see. Bryant has to let us bring Carter in for an interview now, no matter how much it rocks the boat.'

Rows of clothes on hangers faced Penelope in the walk-in wardrobe, divided according to type. Coats and jackets occupied the section nearest the door. Next came dresses, then skirts, followed by trousers and tops. On the other side of the door hung nightdresses and pyjamas. Stacks of neatly folded knitwear occupied the central shelves and her underwear, tights and socks were out of sight in drawers.

Some of her clothes were decades old: expensive designer gowns now too small for her that she'd never been able to part with; items Bertrand had bought as presents—some of them rather racy— garments long out of fashion; well-loved, comfortable day-to-day clothes now too worn to wear except on the rare occasions she joined Michael in the garden; attire bought on a whim and later regretted. A lifetime of clothing.

The closet was a roomy space and everything fit comfortably, yet somehow the assembled textiles oppressed her. Perhaps it was time to go through it all and sort out some things to give to charity or throw away. Janet could help.

Then she recalled she'd given her housekeeper her two weeks' notice. A heavy feeling settled in the pit of her stomach. The woman hadn't appeared surprised. If anything, she'd seemed relieved.

Was working at Windleby so terrible?

Had it been a mistake to let Janet go?

Probably not. It didn't make any sense to pay non-essential staff when the estate was in financial straits. She could manage perfectly well by herself. How hard could it be to cook and do a little cleaning?

And now Lauren would never come home...

A great weakness seized Penelope and she grabbed the door frame for support. She recalled why she had come here. How could she have forgotten?

Her vision blurred and her eyes became wet. She pulled a handkerchief from under the cuff of her sleeve and dabbed at them. Then she blew her nose and tucked her handkerchief away again. She had to be strong. Bertrand would want her to be strong.

She stepped to the dresses. The organisation of her clothes extended to types only. The colours, fabrics, and intended seasonal wear were jumbled. Pale yellow, cotton, summer frocks hung next to sapphire blue, jersey, winter wraparounds. She ran a hand along the hanging clothes.

'Penny,' said a voice. 'Found you at last. I was wondering where you'd got to.'

Her back stiffening, she turned to face Gilbert. 'Yes, you found me. Is there something I can help you with?'

He looked at her doubtfully, as if finally hearing the iciness in her tone. She'd been longing for her cousin and his brats to fly away home for days, ever since the news of Lauren's murder. But he was too obtuse to pick up on the signs. Paradoxically, he apparently had the impression she wanted and needed him around at this horrible time. The reverse was true, but she didn't know how to convey her feelings to him without telling him outright. That would be unconscionably rude and it might sever her family's ties with their American branch forever, something Bertrand would not have wanted.

'I, er...' He took in the wardrobe. 'You're busy and I interrupted you. Sorry.'

'No need to apologise, but you're right, I *am* rather busy, so if you wouldn't mind...'

But he didn't leave. 'Are you…looking for something to wear for the funeral?'

His words resonated like a tolling bell. 'Yes,' she replied tightly, 'I am.'

'I don't want to intrude but could I speak to you for a moment?'

'Now isn't a good time, Gilbert.'

'Please? Indulge a relative and, I hope, an old friend.'

The last thing she wanted to do was to speak to this silly American but she couldn't think of a polite excuse to refuse him. She was barely functioning as it was.

On each side of one of her bedroom windows was a chair. She and Bertrand had often sat in them on summer evenings, looking out over the garden as twilight fell and the stars appeared.

She sat down and Gilbert took the other seat.

'Penny,' he began.

A muscle in her jaw twitched as she inwardly screamed *Penelope!*

He continued, 'I have to confess I'm worried about you. You've suffered a devastating loss. I cannot imagine what you're going through. To lose a child, especially in such a horrible way…' he shook his head. 'If that happened to me I don't know what I'd do. I want to let you know I'll be here to support you for as long as you need me. I've talked to the CEO of my company and he's agreed to let me work remotely for as long as I want. It's amazing what can be done these days with technology. I won't have to miss any meetings or anything.'

'There's really no need,' Penelope murmured, reeling. Would she never be rid of this man?

'But there *is* a need. There is. You're here practically by yourself. You shouldn't be alone at a time like this. Bertie would never forgive me if I abandoned his widow and let her suffer all by herself.'

She didn't know what to say. She didn't have the energy to fight him. She was exhausted to the depths of her soul.

'I've booked flights for the kids. The airline will look after them. They're great at that kind of thing. Then I'll leave my departure open-ended, and that's that. I won't hear another word about it.'

'Then there's nothing more to say,' she replied weakly.

'Exactly. Except there is one thing.' He looked sheepish. 'The

detective working on Lauren's case contacted me a couple of hours ago.'

She tensed. 'What did she want?'

'They changed their minds about interviewing me. She wants me to go to the station this afternoon.'

'Did she say why?'

'No. I guess they just want some general background information but they don't want to bother you, considering what you've gone through. I thought it was funny they cancelled my first interview. Or maybe they have a lead they want to follow.'

'But we already talked about this. They can't possibly learn anything useful—'

'That's for them to decide, right?'

She wanted to argue with him, to fight this invasion of her privacy, but she was too tired, too weak. Everything was falling apart and she didn't know if she cared anymore.

'Very well,' she muttered, adding a bitter 'Do what you want.'

The sound of a telephone ringing floated up the stairs and through the open bedroom door.

'Is that your phone?' asked Gilbert.

'Janet will answer it.'

They waited but the ringing continued.

Her housekeeper had begun to neglect her duties prior to her departure.

'I'll get it,' said Gilbert.

He must have reached the study before the caller rang off because a minute later his heavy footsteps ascended the stairs.

'It's the police. They want to talk to you.'

Penelope fully expected the call to be about the murder case, but it was something entirely different. The police wanted to enter the grounds and perform a welfare check on Michael, who hadn't been seen in the village for several days, hadn't collected this month's pension at the post office and wasn't answering his phone. His little cottage sat within the estate. As it was on private land the authorities couldn't enter it without permission from the landowner.

The conversation with Gilbert had befuddled her brain but she

managed to grasp all this and reply, 'I'll check on him myself. He's worked for my family most of his life.' She felt a sense of duty towards the old man.

'If that's what you'd prefer,' said the police officer. 'He's probably just a bit under the weather and doesn't want to bother anyone. Old folks are like that. Assuming he's all right, could you ask him to give us a ring and confirm it?'

'I will.'

As she hung up, Penelope tried to remember the last time she'd seen the gardener. He generally kept to himself and did whatever was needed. After all these years he didn't require direction or supervision. She didn't think she'd seen him since he'd come to tell her about Rupert's arrival.

'Everything okay?' Gilbert asked.

'Yes, fine. I just have to go and see Michael. Some of his friends are worried about him.'

'I'll come with you. He might have that nasty cold I heard was going around.'

THE DOOR to Michael's cottage was made of thick, solid wood. The building was as old as the manor house, roughly three hundred and fifty years. A tiny two up two down, it had been the gardener's home since he'd come to work on the estate as a teenager. Penelope had only been inside once, when, as a soon-to-be new wife, Bertrand had taken her for a tour of the grounds. Michael had generously invited them both into his humble habitation. She couldn't remember much about it except that it was dark and confined.

He didn't answer her knock.

'Maybe he can't hear you,' said Gilbert. 'He's probably gone deaf.'

There was no rapper.

She stepped away from the door and gazed up at the leaded windows, all closed. 'Michael! Michael! Are you here?'

'Has he gone away somewhere?' Gilbert asked. 'He could have gone on an emergency visit to a sick relative and forgot to tell you.'

'He would never have left without asking my permission. It would be entirely out of character for him.'

'Could he be working somewhere in the garden?'

'Possibly.' Penelope bit her lip and looked at the reflections of surrounding trees in the upper storey windows. She stepped to a ground floor window and cupped her hands around her eyes as she peered in. She saw a tiny living room, a worn armchair, two-seater sofa with sagging cushions, threadbare carpet and old-fashioned hearth.

But no gardener.

She knocked again.

After another silence Gilbert said, 'We should probably check the grounds.'

It would take hours to search the acres of parks, woodlands and meadows.

She'd brought the spare key to the cottage just in case. She took it out of her skirt pocket but held it, hesitating.

'I guess it wouldn't hurt to take a little look inside,' said Gilbert. 'He might not be able to come to the door.'

'I agree.' She inserted the key into the lock.

A musty, unpleasant odour wafted out as she opened the door.

'Man needs to air his house,' Gilbert exclaimed.

The hallway was dark and silent. Michael's jacket hung on the single hook.

'He isn't at work,' she said. 'It has to be very hot for him to not wear his jacket.' She called his name again, but again no answer came.

'I have a bad feeling about this,' said Gilbert. 'We should call the police.'

'I've had enough of them snooping around,' she replied, though she shared her cousin's presentiment. 'Michael!'

The close walls and ancient wallpaper snuffed out her shout.

'All right,' Gilbert said with resolution. 'If you want to do this we will. But you wait here.'

The door to the sitting room she'd already looked into was on the

right of the hall. The door to the kitchen was at the end, beyond the
stairs. Gilbert walked down the hall and opened it.

'Oh, God! God, no!' He staggered backward.

Penelope caught a glimpse of Michael's legs, hanging in mid air.

20

Gil Carter was, Shauna guessed, in his mid-fifties. He hadn't taken off his baseball cap but minimal, white hair showed beneath it. He was either bald or had an American-style crew cut. He was clean-shaven and his broad face held the puffed, pale shine of heart problems probably brought on by being over-weight most of his life.

'Thanks for coming in to speak to us, Mr Carter.'

'It's not a problem. Call me Gil.'

'Can we get you anything to drink? Tea? Coffee?'

'No, thanks. Is this interview about Lauren or Mike? I was supposed to come in yesterday but I guess your investigation has moved on since then.'

'I still want to ask you about Lauren Carew. We had to postpone yesterday's appointment for obvious reasons. But while you're here, it would be helpful if you could give a statement about finding Mike Battersby's body too.'

'Sure. I'm here to help all I can.'

'Shall we start with Mr Battersby?'

She listened while he gave his account. Jas took notes.

When he reached the part in his story where he'd found the body,

he became emotional. 'Seeing that old guy just hanging there... I've never seen anything like it and I hope I never will again.'

Shauna said, 'It must have been very distressing for you. Can you tell me what you did then?'

'Well, I-I tried to save him. I grabbed his legs and lifted him up while Penny called for an ambulance. But he was cold, stiff, you know?'

'You'd arrived too late.'

'Do you know why he did it? Did he leave a note? I didn't see anything. To be honest, everything after we found him is kinda hazy.'

'I can't tell you anything about Mr Battersby's death while it's still under investigation, I'm afraid.'

'You're investigating it? So it wasn't suicide?'

'All sudden or unexpected deaths are investigated. As I said, I really can't tell you any more.'

'I understand.' Carter's features twisted with pity. 'First Lauren and now the gardener who worked for the family all his life. Penny's really taken some hits lately. But she never shows it. You Brits really do have that stiff upper lip.'

'On the subject of Mrs Carew, you probably noticed, when we met at her house, that the fact Lauren had a brother came as a surprise to me and DS Fiske. I don't think it's a secret that Mrs Carew didn't tell us about him. Why do you think that might be?'

His large chest rose and fell and he looked down. 'Okay, this is it, right? This is why you asked me here. I feel kinda bad. Penny doesn't want me to reveal the skeletons in the closet. She's a very private woman, and nervous, highly strung. But I know it won't do any harm, and you guys have to do your job.' He met Shauna's gaze. 'About a year after she married my cousin, Bertie, Penny gave birth to twins, a boy and a girl. They never had any more children. She wasn't a-a, what you might call a *natural* mother. It didn't come easy to her. Maybe that's why they stopped after two. Personally, I love 'em. I'd have more if Martha would agree.' He chuckled.

'You were around the Carew family a lot? I thought you lived in the US.'

'I usually visited every summer, regular as clockwork, and stay for

about a month, but after Bertie died the invitations dried up. I didn't want to push it. I guessed she was grieving. But we stayed in touch. This is the first time I've been back in years.'

'Gil, do you know why Mrs Carew didn't tell us about Rupert?'

'She, uh...' He cleared his throat. 'She never talks about him. Acts like he doesn't exist. Even though he came to the house the other day—'

'He's been to see her?'

'Yeah. I bumped into him on the landing. Had a chat. He looked a little rough. He gives a certain...impression, you know? But he's a nice kid, deep down. Anyway, I can't tell you for sure why Penny's erased him from her life. She's never told me to my face, but according to Rupert it's because he's gay.'

Jas blurted, 'That's all?!'

Shauna gave her a look and she returned her attention to her notes.

'Crazy, I know,' said Gil, 'but not the first case I've heard of. Some parents have high expectations of their kids. Going to an Ivy League college, having a high-flying career, kids, a big house, foreign vacations, the whole caboodle. Not that you can't do all that when you're gay, but I'm guessing Penny includes heterosexuality in the mix. Rupert and Lauren were never big on conforming. If I was to be uncharitable I'd say it was because Penny and Bertie put too much pressure on them. They rebelled and went off the rails, though Lauren straightened out in the end. I learnt from my cousins' experience. As long as my kids are working hard and treating others with respect, I don't hassle them. All I want is for them to be healthy and happy.'

'Lauren and Rupert Carew had a troubled childhood?'

'That's a good way to describe it. They were nearly kicked out of their school several times for various offences. Drugs, bullying, that kind of thing. I think it was only Bertie's influence that kept them there. I don't know a lot about it. Penny used to vent to me in her emails but then she stopped. She seemed to close down.'

'How old was Rupert when she disowned him?'

'Poor kid was just eighteen. He came out to her and she kicked him out, just like that.'

'That's what she told you?'

'That's what *he* told me. I tried to keep in touch with both kids after Bertie died. I figured they needed a father figure. Rupert responded to my emails. Lauren not so much. Nowadays I don't even hear from Rupert very often but he sends the occasional text or calls me.'

'Do you have his phone number?'

'I haven't, sorry. That's the funny thing. He always keeps his number private. I'm not sure why, except he doesn't want me to call him.'

'What about his address?'

He shook his head. 'Never had it. I get the impression he doesn't stay in one place very long. He, uh...' Gil looked uncomfortable and then smiled with embarrassment. 'I'm really spilling the beans today, aren't I? I think Rupert is an addict and has been for a long time.'

Shauna said, 'Another reason for Mrs Carew to not want to have anything to do with him, perhaps.'

'I guess so. She isn't very forgiving. Gee, it must sound like I hate her. But she grew up on the wrong side of the tracks so she's had her own struggles. Then with Bertie's death and everything, life hasn't been easy for her. She must be barely holding on.'

'The wrong side of the tracks? What do you mean?'

'Oh, she has humble beginnings. Very humble as far as I understand. There's plenty who frowned at Bertie for marrying down.'

'But,' said Shauna, confused, 'her accent...'

'She didn't always speak like that. When I met her she sounded more like you. It's Cockney, right? She changed the way she spoke after she got married. She might have been trying to fit in with Bertie's relations and friends.'

'You're kidding,' Shauna said.

'No way. One summer she sounded like Dick Van Dyke in Mary Poppins, the next she could have passed for the Queen. It was quite the transformation.'

She chewed on this revelation but she didn't know what to make

of it. Dismissing it for the moment as probably unimportant to the case, she asked, 'What was Rupert and Lauren's relationship like? Did they get along?'

'They were thick as thieves, pretty much. I'd say the conditions at home pushed them together.'

'Has Rupert mentioned any recent falling out between them?'

'Nope. He was really cut up when I saw him the other day.'

'Are you absolutely sure?'

'If they did have a fight he didn't tell me. And, anyway, they would forget about it and move on.'

As with the news about Mrs Carew's background, Shauna felt as though she was reaching an impasse. 'Did he mention anything about his current whereabouts?'

'Not a word. Maybe he's staying with friends? He's lived around here all his life. Probably knows lots of places he can stay.'

This was her guess too, but they couldn't search every squat and drug den in the city. 'If Rupert contacts you again, could you let us know?'

'Sure, but why are you so interested in talking to him? You can't think he had something to do with his sister's murder.'

'We have reason to believe Lauren might have been planning to speak to us about a criminal matter involving her brother. Does that mean anything at all to you?'

'Whoa, no, nothing. That sounds screwy.'

'We've also discovered that now his sister is dead, her trust fund money becomes his.'

Carter took off his cap and threw it on the table. ' Look, I understand you're just trying to do your job, but if you think Rupert had something to do with Lauren's death, you're wrong. That's all I can say. Do you want to ask me anything else?'

'I think that just about wraps it up, but if you do hear from Rupert, it's very important that you tell us.'

'I'll remember.' He moved his seat back as if preparing to stand.

'One more thing, Gil,' Shauna said. 'Do you know of any links with the RAF in your family background?'

'The RAF? That's the British air force, right?'

'Yes. Do you know if anyone in your family fought for Britain in World War Two?'

'What an odd question. Why do you want to know? What could that have to do with Lauren's murder?'

'If you could just answer...'

He cleared his throat. 'I'm not sure. I'd have to do some research.'

'If you wouldn't mind, I'd appreciate it.'

'No problem. Are we done?'

'I think we're finished for today.' Shauna kept her tone neutral but her nerve-endings were tingling. The question had been an afterthought based on the notion there might be a remote connection between the murder and the mis-identified dead pilot. 'DC Singh will write up a statement regarding Mr Battersby's death for you to sign.'

After Jas had shown Gil Carter out and returned to the interview room, Shauna asked, 'Did you notice his expression when I asked him about family ties with the RAF?'

'Not particularly.'

'That's a shame, because it was exactly how someone looks when they're lying.'

_____

On the day of Lauren Carew's funeral the weather was appropriately cold and dark. Rain threatened as the mourners gathered around the Carew family plot in the local churchyard. The headstones in this section were modern and included Bertrand Carew's, bearing the inscription: *Fond father and loving husband. Much missed.* Elsewhere the graves were marked by time-worn, lichen-covered stones standing askew. Some didn't stand at all but lay flat on their fronts as if felled by divine judgement. Yews loomed at the borders of the unkempt, damp spot.

The service in the Norman church had been brief, religious and formal and probably unlike anything Lauren would have wanted. Shauna had attended with Will, sitting together at the back. Now she stood with him some distance from the open grave and watched.

Shauna was glad of the distraction of work today. It was Naomi's birthday. She would have been seventeen.

Sifting through the facts of Lauren's short life and the detritus she'd left behind, it had been hard to get a handle on her and the service had left Shauna none the wiser. The information gleaned from her rooms at Windleby and the grubby flat she'd shared had told them—among other, very ordinary things—that she'd been captain of her school's hockey team, volunteered at an animal rescue

centre and interned at a Swiss finance company during a summer holiday while at university. It all felt vague and meaningless. The vicar had concluded his comments with a remark on how God had taken her into his bosom at a young age and how mysterious were his ways.

The story of the real Lauren Carew had not been told and perhaps never would be.

Shauna couldn't help with that. All she could do was find her killer, and she was feeling confident she'd done it.

She scanned the people clustered at the grave. The extended family had turned up for the occasion. Middle-aged and elderly men and women in expensive clothes stood solemnly in a group. Had the Carews come over with William the Conqueror as Will had joked? It wasn't beyond the bounds of possibility. A few ancient families had survived the turmoil of history—endless wars, the Reformation, the Civil War, the Restoration—and retained their wealth if not their power. Perhaps the Carews were among them.

Though the ancestral blood didn't flow in Lady Penelope's veins she certainly knew how to play the part. She stood with the rest of the family, wearing a black wool coat, understated but stylish, and a hat with a fine widow's veil. The look was so archetypal it could have been comical but she pulled it off. Gil Carter stood beside her. His children were absent. A second group of people, younger than the family members, huddled on the opposite side of the grave. Lauren's friends from school and university? Shauna recognized Lauren's flat-mates, standing a little apart from everyone else. It was as Cameron had stated—they had not been a part of the deceased's usual social circle.

The vicar stood over the grave and spoke the rites as attendants lowered the coffin, paying out the lengths of straps beneath it. Mrs Carew slipped a handkerchief under her veil to dab at her eyes.

As if the clouds had been turned on by a switch, rain began to fall. A sudden icy squall hit and the funeral attendees hunched and cringed as they fumbled for umbrellas and hoods. Will began to unfurl a large black umbrella.

'Don't do that,' said Shauna. 'We need to be ready.'

He re-furled it and leaned it against a tree.

The vicar continued his speech without reaction as drops pattered on his bald pate, his voice droning on through the sound of the rain. He closed his book and bent his head. The mourners joined him in prayer. Cold trickles ran down the back of Shauna's neck.

The service was finally over. The vicar spoke to Mrs Carew and then returned up the path toward the church. People began to drift away.

'Damn,' said Shauna. 'I was sure...' She spotted a tall, thin figure step from out of the shadow of a yew tree on the far side of the graveyard. He'd been here all along, standing in darkness, his black clothes hiding him in the dismal day. 'There he is!'

She radioed the team and then headed for Rupert Carew at a brisk pace. Police officers appeared at all the exits. Carew spotted her, halted and hesitated. He swung his gaze around the churchyard, taking in the officers waiting to prevent his escape.

He ran.

'Damn,' Will exclaimed. 'Where's he going? He can't get out.'

'Yes, he can.' Shauna dashed after him.

Rupert Carew raced over the graves. The mourners had noticed the chase and watched, frozen. The vicar called for calm. Shauna wasn't sure how to block the target. If she sent constables to intercept Carew it would leave the exits unmanned. He could easily change direction.

A low wall, a metre or so tall, ran around the churchyard. Carew's trajectory was taking him toward a section and, beyond it, the opening to a side street. If he made it down there he could escape into the warren of little alleys and walkways threading the old village.

The rain hissed down harder, spattering her face and turning the air grey with moisture. She wiped water from her eyes.

He reached the wall. In one smooth movement he vaulted it, his long legs carrying him over with ease. A second later, she reached it too. She scrambled over, ungainly and awkward, hands sliding on the sodden, mossy surface. Carew was already over the road.

She cursed but carried on running. The sound of Will's feet hitting the pavement came from behind but kept her focus ahead.

There was still a chance they might catch him, even on his home turf. The constables had done the sensible thing and left their posts, spreading out to intercept the suspect.

She remained on Carew's heels. He darted down an alley. Radioing his change of direction, she followed and turned into the opening. The ancient bricks of a medieval house rose high on one side. On the other ran garden fences in various states of repair. There was no sign of the suspect.

Had he gone over a fence? Was he lurking in one of the gardens, planning to wait it out until they gave up the search?

She slowed her pace. The rain hammered down, plastering her hair to her scalp. It was impossible to hear footsteps over the noise of drops smacking into the ground.

Where had he gone?

An unexpected exit from the alley appeared to her left. Dwarfed by buildings on each side, the dimly lit passage ran thirty or so metres to a bright opening onto the main street. Carew was belting towards it.

But a figure stepped into the rectangle of light.

Will.

Carew put on the brakes and turned. Then he saw Shauna.

'You can't escape,' she called. 'Don't make this harder for everyone.'

He looked over his shoulder at Will and then back at her.

Putting down his head, he ran at her.

She was clearly the less imposing obstacle. She had two seconds' grace to update the team before he made impact. Bracing herself, she held out her arms, feebly hoping this killer wouldn't use violence to evade capture.

He batted her down like he was swatting a fly...and ran directly into Alfie Hepplethwaite. The larger man's chest stopped him dead. Hepplethwaite grabbed Carew's arm, twisted it behind his back, slapped a handcuff on his wrist and then grabbed the other arm to secure the suspect.

Meanwhile, Shauna got to her feet, shook mud and rain from her coat, and then said, 'Rupert Carew, I am arresting you on suspicion of

the murder of Lauren Carew. You don't have to say anything, but it may harm your defence if...'

HE HAD THE JUNKIE LOOK. Shauna had seen it so many times over the duration of her career. Pasty skin, jutting cheekbones, dull hair, dead eyes. Despite all the terrible crimes she'd known addicts to commit, she retained a modicum of pity for them. In the time following her children's deaths she'd come perilously close to going down that road herself. To this day she didn't know what had stopped her. Maybe it had only been poverty and lack of easy access to hard drugs.

That would not have been so in Rupert's case. There were some downsides to wealth and privilege.

She started the recorder and made the required statements. When it was Rupert Carew's turn to state his name he said nothing so she gave it for him, adding that Mr Carew had been offered legal representation but had not accepted it.

'Would you like a hot drink?' she asked.

He shook his head.

He wore jeans, a tartan shirt under a threadbare jumper and a jacket, too thin for the time of year.

'You must be cold. We all got soaked in that downpour, right?'

He wouldn't look at her.

'When was the last time you used?'

Silence.

'You'll be feeling the effects of withdrawal soon enough. Getting something warm inside you now will help.'

He shot her a venomous look. Wrapping his arms around his body, he shifted on his haunches as if trying to make himself comfortable on the hard plastic chair. He was little but skin and bone and probably wasn't comfortable anywhere anymore.

'Could you please show me your forearms?'

He frowned at her questioningly.

'Mr Carew, you don't want to be manhandled again, do you?'

He pushed up his sleeves.

There was the tattoo, similar to Lauren's but different. As the pathologist had said, Rupert's half of the dragon bore the head.

'Thank you. You can put your sleeves down.'

She could see his resemblance to his sister in his face though her body type had been different. His curly hair flopped over his eyes in the same way but Lauren had been short and on the plump side. He took after his mother physically. Perhaps emotionally too. He was shutting down, withdrawing. She knew the feeling too well.

She was so tired. If he would just confess they could get the interview over with. It wasn't like any of them wanted to be here. Mentally sighing, she forged ahead. 'Mr Carew, can you tell us your whereabouts the afternoon and evening of the third of March?' The parcel tape had been bought at 4.23 pm, according to the CCTV footage and Forensics had confirmed it was from the same production batch as the one used to seal his sister's mouth.

Carew opened his mouth to speak and her ears pricked up.

'No comment.' His accent was exactly like his mother's, clipped, upper class, the 't' clearly enunciated. It also dripped the same disdain.

'How about the afternoon of the fourteenth of March? What did you do that day?'

Mike Battersby's post-mortem results implied the death was suspicious. The man had died by strangulation due to hanging but his body bore the signs of a struggle. Nothing in the little kitchen had appeared disturbed so whoever had fought with him had tidied the place up. There was no forced entry into the cottage either, meaning Battersby had almost certainly known his attacker well enough to let him in. As the family gardener for decades, Rupert Carew would have been a familiar figure to him.

'No comment.'

'When was the last time you saw your sister?'

He looked down and shook his head.

Shauna said, 'For the recording, the suspect indicates he doesn't wish to answer. Mr. Carew, are you responsible for the murder of Lauren Carew?'

'No.'

'Can you tell us about your involvement in her murder?'

'No comment.'

'We have reason to believe Lauren intended to speak to us about something and you didn't want her to. Does that mean anything to you?'

'No comment.'

'Did you argue with your sister and things got out of hand? Did you not mean to do it?'

Silence.

'Isn't it true that you benefit financially from her death?'

A shrug.

'Mr Carew,' said Will gently, 'it won't help you to not talk to us. You'll only make things worse for yourself. If you didn't kill Lauren or Mr Battersby, this is your opportunity to defend yourself. If you know who murdered her or you have an alibi this is the time to tell us.'

Shauna took out the still from the recording of Carew buying the parcel tape and slid it over the table. 'Do you have anything to say about this image?'

Since the beginning of the interview, the suspect's features had hardened into an expressionless mask, but as he took in the picture shock shattered it.

'That isn't me,' he whispered. 'It can't be.'

'You can see the time and date stamp,' said Shauna. 'If you're certain this isn't you, where were you when the recording was made? Do you remember? Where you with someone who can vouch for you?'

But from then on, their suspect appeared determined to not answer a single question. Shauna tried going back to the siblings' childhood, their relationship with each other, their mother, their father, the family's gardener, even Gil Carter. She tried asking him about his school days, where he'd been living since leaving home, every avenue she could think of to bring him out of his shell and get him talking, but nothing worked. He wasn't going to make it easy for them.

'Rupert,' she said testily, 'you don't seem to understand. We have

strong evidence linking you to the murder of your sister and you haven't given us an alibi. '

The frustrating silence of the last two hours rang out once more. Her head was thrumming. She could see Lauren Carew's cold, blue body cut open on the post-mortem table. Mike Battersby's purple face and distended features thrust into her vision.

Something snapped.

'Why would you do such a thing?' she demanded. 'Why would you kill your own sister? Your twin? Didn't she mean anything to you? Didn't her life mean anything?' She could hear her voice growing louder and her pitch rising but she couldn't seem to stop. 'And what about Mr Battersby? He was just an old man, a man who worked for your family all his life. He probably didn't have long left in this world. Why snatch that time away from him? What could he have done that was so bad he deserved to die? To be strung up like a dog?!'

Will said, 'Er, DI Holt, maybe we should—'

'Huh,' said Carew, his lip curling in a sneer, 'you remind me of my mother.'

Shauna leapt to her feet and drew back her hand. Will's chair clattered to the floor as he overturned it and she found herself being bundled out of the interview room.

s Shauna stood on the doorstep of the block of flats, waiting to be let in, she was already regretting agreeing to go to Beth's birthday party.

Will's words of encouragement echoed in her head. *It'll do you good to let your hair down now we've made progress on the case. Beth will be disappointed if you don't come.* Shauna seriously doubted that. Will's girlfriend and their shared colleague was friendly towards her but she was friendly towards everyone. She was the type of person who got along with most people. They weren't friends.

Just show your face. Stay for half an hour. Otherwise, tomorrow everybody will be asking where you were.

She clung to this last suggestion hard as she gripped the cold neck of the wine bottle, her offering to the BYO booze pool. Besides, it was better than sitting at home alone, dreading hearing a text arrive on her phone or a knock at the door.

In her other hand she held a wrapped present of Body Shop toiletries, a recycled unwanted gift from her mother. Not very imaginative, but she had no idea what Beth liked and most of the shops had been shut by the time she finished work.

Half an hour. She could survive half an hour. Even spending half an hour in the kitchen—her usual haunt at parties—wouldn't look

too shameful. It was already late. She could say she wanted a good night's sleep, that she was working tomorrow. It was the truth.

Why hadn't anyone answered the buzzer?

The music was probably too loud. A faint bass beat thumped somewhere above, accompanied by faint wailing sounds. She hoped the latter was the lead singer and not the emotional meltdown of someone too drunk too early.

She hoped things wouldn't get out of hand, or if they did that she would be long gone. Imagine having the police called on a party where most of the attendees were police officers.

Loud laughter and the tap of high heels on pavement came from behind.

Two women in tight, garish, low-cut dresses approached up the pathway, arm in arm.

Shauna marvelled at their imperviousness to the chill of the spring evening.

'Are you here for the party?' one asked, her gaze on the bottle of wine.

'Oooh, we didn't bring anything,' the other said. 'Should we find an offy? It'll be embarrassing to turn up empty-handed.'

'She won't mind,' her friend confidently stated, firmly thumbing the button. 'People usually bring too much anyway.'

In Shauna's limited experience this wasn't the case, but she didn't say anything.

'What's her name again?'

'Uhh...'

'Beth,' said Shauna, speaking for the first time. 'Her name's Beth.'

'Yeah, that's it.'

Dread was growing in Shauna's stomach. It was going to be one of *those* parties, where the rumour had spread and friends of friends of friends would turn up. People who wanted any excuse to have a good time, whose lives oriented around having a good time and nothing else. The kind of people who kept the police busy on Friday and Saturday nights.

She was about to leave, thinking she could make up an excuse about having an upset stomach, when the door buzzed and the lock

jerked open. She stood closest to the door. She had no choice except to go in.

A wave of noise, heat, and the ripe scent of alcohol swept out from Beth's flat. The party was already in full swing. Shauna guessed the host must have invited all the immediate neighbours or Cambridge Central would have received several noise complaint calls already.

The two strange women disappeared into the melee.

Banners proclaiming Happy Birthday Beth and Twenty-Nine Again overhung the living room.

'DI Holt!' Beth exclaimed, appearing from a throng of gyrating bodies. She grabbed her in a tight, sweaty, overly friendly hug and shouted breathily into her ear, 'Thanks for coming. I had a bet on with Will that you would. He owes me a tenner!'

'You're welcome,' Shauna shouted back. 'Where should I put these?' She held up the wine and present.

'Aww, thanks. You shouldn't have. Kitchen's that way.' Beth pointed. 'But you mustn't hide in there. Come back and have a dance.'

'All right.'

'Promise?'

'Promise.'

Shauna would rather walk naked into Bryant's office and proposition him, but Beth was so drunk she wouldn't remember their conversation five minutes from now.

'Where's Will?' she asked.

Beth looked around confusedly. 'Dunno. Haven't seen him for a while.'

One pop song ended and another began. A hand reached out and pulled Beth back to the centre of the living room, where moving bodies were inexpertly adjusting their motions to the new beat.

Shauna carefully stepped around the dancers and through a doorway from which harsh, bright light spilled into the living room. The noise was just as loud in the kitchen but the reduced number of bodies and their comparative stillness was a relief.

The work surfaces were stacked with bottles, most empty, several lying on their sides in danger of rolling off. Shauna righted them and placed hers in an empty spot.

'Booze delivery!' someone exclaimed, reaching past her and grabbing the bottle.

'Help yourself,' Shauna said to the anonymous back as the man walked off, unscrewing the lid of her wine.

Half an hour.

The alcohol vultures had missed a half-empty bottle of Campari. Campari? Had time wound back to the 1970s? It seemed the only thing on offer. Any remaining drinks were being jealously hoarded in the party-goers' small groups.

She found a clean plastic cup and filled it with the sweet, red liquid and some lemonade and returned to the living room. Time to play wallflower. She squeezed in next to the sofa that had been pushed up against the wall and people-watched.

There was Connor, his arm around the waist of an attractive young woman. They both had their backs to Shauna as they chatted in a group, but even so, she could see the woman didn't look at all DC Payne's type. She would have expected someone bespectacled, perhaps nerdy-looking. But his girlfriend's hair was carefully styled, cascading in curls over her shoulder and she wore a tight-fitting black dress that revealed well-toned legs.

And there was Alfie Hepplethwaite, glaring.

Alfie's face was flushed and he clutched a nearly empty plastic beaker of beer to his chest. He weaved unsteadily through the jiggling bodies to Connor's girlfriend's side. He tapped her on the shoulder.

Uh oh.

She turned and Alfie seemed to introduce himself. Shauna couldn't hear him over the loud music. The girlfriend and Alfie talked for a minute before Connor noticed. When he saw his colleague chatting her up, his expression darkened. He tugged her waist, trying to make her move away. She got annoyed.

Shauna took a sip of her drink and grimaced before returning her attention to the drama. Now Connor and his girlfriend were arguing and Alfie was trying to get a word in too. It was like watching a soap opera. She wondered if she should intervene but decided against it. Connor and Alfie were off duty and they were grown-ups. It wasn't up to her to sort out their differences.

'Are you a cop? I'm Helen.'

A middle-aged woman stood next to her.

'Shauna, Um, yes. What do you do?'

'I thought you were. You've got that look about you. But you're one of the higher-ups, right?'

Two could play the game of not answering questions. 'How do you know Beth?'

'I'm her auntie. I was wondering if you were a cop, 'cause it'll be handy if things get rowdy later.'

'Are things likely to get rowdy?'

'Probably.' Helen chuckled. 'You know what it's like.'

Shauna sadly but silently agreed. 'Still, it's nice for Beth to celebrate. I'm sure she's having a great time. She seems to have a lot of friends.'

That was three platitudes in a row. Shauna hated herself.

How much longer did she have? Twenty minutes? Where was Will? She should probably find him so he would know she showed her face and he wouldn't moan at her tomorrow.

'Yeah, everyone's here,' said Helen. 'Cousins, old school friends.'

She seemed to run out of things to say and Shauna was out of ideas too. She returned her attention to the soap opera. Alfie and Connor were arguing, but low key. She doubted it would come to blows. The girlfriend had disappeared, probably sick of both of them.

She watched the dancers. Helen didn't leave. She seemed to have hit on Shauna as her company for the party. Or maybe she felt sorry for her?

Connor appeared to notice his girlfriend was missing and left Alfie to go and find her.

Helen said, 'Come on, I'll introduce you to some people.'

Horror seized Shauna. 'No, it's okay. I'm leaving soon anyway. Just wanted to...'

Helen wasn't paying any attention. She'd grabbed Shauna's wrist and was pulling on it. Helen was even more inebriated than she looked.

'Really, I...' Shauna resisted.

'Hey, why're you still wearing your coat?' Helen appeared to have noticed the woollen material under her hand. 'You must be hot.'

'I am a bit. Where should I put it?'

'There's a pile in the bedroom. Take it off. I'll take care of it.'

'No, no, I can do it.' Shauna unfastened the buttons and removed her coat, forcing her captor to relinquish her hold. 'It's over there, isn't it?' She moved toward a door as Helen mumbled something incoherent.

'There you are!' said Beth. 'Show us your moves, Detective Inspector.'

'I-I'm sorry. I really have to get going.'

Beth's lower lip jutted. 'But you've only just got here. Can't you stay a little longer? If you leave everyone'll think the party's over and they'll all leave too.'

Shauna seriously doubted it, but she said, 'Okay, I'll stay a bit longer. But no dancing. It isn't my thing.'

'I remember. You like birds. You should talk to my uncle. He's big into fishing.'

Failing to make the connection, Shauna said, 'I'll put my coat away.'

'Yeah, yeah. Bedroom's over there.'

Once more navigating moving bodies, Shauna made her way to the closed door she presumed was the correct room. It was dark inside but light from the living room revealed a bed. Still not completely sure she was in the right place, she felt for the light switch and turned it on.

Two startled faces jumped from the gloom.

'Will!'

He was with Connor's girlfriend. Both were mostly clothed, but it was very clear what was going on. Her surprised shout drew Beth's attention. She was suddenly at Shauna's side, peering over her shoulder.

Her quiet, pained intake of breath was loud in Shauna's ear. 'You bastard.'

Will didn't say anything to Shauna when she arrived at work the first day back after the party. He acknowledged her arrival with a nod, not making eye contact, and returned his attention to his computer screen. She said a general good morning. It did little to break the icy atmosphere in the room. Connor, Jas and Alfie murmured replies.

She said, 'Now Rupert Carew's under lock and key, our next task is to keep digging. The fact that he ran at the funeral tells us a lot, but at the moment the only solid evidence we have is the CCTV of him buying the parcel tape. Hopefully, when the checkout operator gets back from holiday she can pick Carew out of a line up. But, without a confession, we still need more. None of his DNA was found on the victim's body and though Forensics are checking his jacket for fibres from her clothes, they were brother and sister. Any reasonable juror would expect them to have been in contact with each other. If we can find out where he killed her we might find evidence that places him there. Or maybe there's something in his background—a friend or acquaintance he spilled the beans to. Our job is far from over yet.'

Connor gave a small cough and said, 'Ma'am, I came in early this morning to finish checking the documents about the plane crash, and I found this.'

He looked like she felt, as if sleep was just some fancy thing other people did. She stepped to his side to read the paper in his hand. It took a second for the penny to drop but then she breathed, 'Shit.'

'Sorry it took me so long,' Connor said, 'but the accident report was on the bottom of the pile. Whoever photocopied the documents must have reversed the order of the stack.'

She gave the team the news: Lauren Carew's body had been dumped at the dig on exactly the same date as the plane had crashed eighty years ago. She went on, 'This is no coincidence. There has to be a connection, and it could blow this case wide open.'

Alfie asked, 'But why would a druggie in his twenties care about something that happened in World War Two?'

'Well, that's for us to find out, isn't it?' said Shauna. 'We can try Carew again but I doubt he'll tell us. I'll talk to the archaeologist again.'

'Carew must have had a car to transport the body to the fen,' said Will, 'and he doesn't seem the sort to have one of his own. I'll check all the car rental companies.'

Rupert Carew was officially 'of no fixed abode' but he would have needed some form of ID to rent a car.

'Good idea,' Shauna said, searching her purse for Dr Kapherr's contact details. 'Ah, here it is.' She pulled out the card and phoned the number.

When the archaeologist answered, it was clear from the background noises she was outdoors. 'Detective, how nice to hear from you. I heard you'd made your arrest. Congratulations.'

'Thanks, but we're still a long way from a conviction. Dr Kapherr, we've stumbled across something significant and I need your help again. Were you aware the date of the Spitfire crash and the murder are the same?'

'Good Lord, are they? I recall it was March but I didn't realise it was the exact same date. Is it significant, do you think?'

'It may be very significant. It may be exactly the breakthrough we're looking for. What did you discover about the pilot you found?'

'Um, I would have to look at my notes and they aren't here, they're

at Duxworth. This is our last day and we're wrapping up, returning the ground to the farmer.'

'Anything you can remember off the top of your head?'

'Well, as you know his name was Jack Muncey.'

'*Jack Muncey.*' Shauna wrote the name down. 'With an 'e', right?'

'That's right.'

'What else?'

'He was twenty-one when he died. Seems tragically young, doesn't it? But it was the average age at the time. He grew up in Cambridge and lasted two years in the RAF. Now that *was* unusual. He'd survived the Battle of Britain, when the life expectancy of Spitfire pilots was four weeks.'

'Wow. Did he have any descendants?'

'Now that I *do* remember. He was married and had a baby boy, John Robert Muncey. The RAF is working on tracing the son and informing him about our discovery, if he's still alive. Jack was recorded as deserting, probably due to the fact no one could find him. That's how we discovered his family. His wife's application for a pension was denied due to her husband's desertion. Such a shame.'

Shauna made notes. 'Anything else?'

'I think that was about as far as I got. I've been busy with the rest of our findings.'

'What about the man who was thought to have died in the accident?'

'Douglas Hunt? I drew a blank there, I'm afraid, except for discovering that his brother, Ernest, died too, not long after the accident.'

'You said the brother was the camp commander. Did he die in battle?'

'No, it was the flu.'

'Did he have any children?'

'That, I can't tell you. I'm sorry I can't be more helpful.'

'It's fine. You've given us something to go on.'

'When I'm back at Duxworth I'll see what else I can discover.'

Shauna ended the call. The lead was tenuous, but it was there.

'Did you say Jack Muncey?' Will asked.

'Yes, why? Does the name mean something to you?'

'The surname rings a bell.'

'What sort of bell?'

'What do you mean?'

'Professionally or personally?' *Was it some girl you hooked up with?*

He seemed to take her implication and gave her a hooded look. 'I don't know. I'll have to think about it.' He turned to Connor. 'Could you run Muncey through HOLMES? With an 'e'.'

Connor grimaced and didn't reply but tapped on his keyboard.

The door opened.

'Ah, DI Holt,' said Bryant, 'you've arrived. My office, please.'

He closed the door.

Shauna lifted her eyebrows and surveyed the room. Will had his head down. No one would meet her gaze. She went to see the DCI.

He was already pink by the time she arrived. Clearly, they were in for a difficult conversation.

'Please take a seat, Holt.'

A very difficult conversation.

He knitted his fingers. 'I'll come straight to the point. It's come to my attention that you...you...'

'Yes?'

He loosened his tie. 'How are things going?'

'With the murder case?'

'Generally, I mean.'

She sighed. 'If this is about what happened at Rupert Carew's interview, I admit things did get a little out of hand.'

'*Things* got out of hand?'

'All right, *I* got out of hand.'

'You do recall you were being videoed? It was a formal interview. Luckily for you the camera angle makes it difficult to see your exact movements. Nevertheless, Carew's defence could accuse us of misconduct. The judge could throw the case out.'

'But he didn't confess anyway, so they couldn't say it was...' Her shoulders slumped.

'Nearly striking a suspect? What were you thinking?'

She didn't know what to say.

'Concerns were raised about your mental stability prior to the

interview with Carew. I should have acted then and I wish I had. I thought the case was probably getting to you. It's easy for things to get on top of us in our line of work. I didn't want to pull you off it at the time but now, after your alarming behaviour, I don't see that I have any choice.'

You think you don't need me anymore.

'Concerns were raised by who?'

As if I don't know.

'Obviously, I can't tell you that. I want you to take a leave of absence and seek out psychiatric counselling. Have a break, Holt, and we'll monitor the situation going forward.'

She weighed up her options. Should she fight it?

'Do I get a choice?'

He leaned over his desk. 'No, but I do. I *could* suspend you.'

His glare was icy.

Bryant had finally found his spine.

'I heard you're a twitcher. Go find some birds to watch. Step back and take a holiday. Relax. You've done a good job on the Carew case and I'm pleased with your work in general since you came to Cambridge. There's no reason why, providing we address this problem now, you can't continue to excel in your career.'

Her hands clenched into fists and angry tears began to well up, but she had no words to fight him. She stalked from the office and marched to the incident room. Snatching her bag from her desk, she hissed at Will, 'Can I speak to you outside?'

24

'*Thanks*,' she snapped as they walked down the steps in front of Cambridge Central.

'You got suspended?' he asked, putting his hands in his pockets. His gaze was frank and unapologetic.

'No, I have to take a leave of absence.'

His eyebrows lifted. 'Baldy must like you.'

'Of course he likes me,' she muttered. 'I do most of his job for him.' She struggled to say any more, fury, embarrassment and misery warring within her.

Will looked at her pityingly.

She choked out, 'I thought we were a team.'

'Come on, Shauna, what did you think would happen? I don't know how things are run at the Met, but we go by the book here. You can't do what you did in that interview and not expect repercussions. Even if I hadn't said anything, it would have come out anyway. Rupert Carew saw you were about to hit him. He hasn't made a complaint yet but that doesn't mean he won't. And if his case comes to trial someone will review the tapes. You aren't the only person involved here. It would have looked bad for me too if I hadn't reported it, and I'm not the one with the temper.'

He was right. Of course he was right. And in his position she

would have done the same. She would never have put her job on the line for a bad copper. But admitting it was hard, even to herself. She certainly wasn't ready to admit it to him yet. 'This isn't just about the interview though. You'd already raised a flag about me. You went behind my back.'

He shrugged. 'What am I supposed to do when you won't tell me what's going on?'

'You don't have any right to know about my private life.'

'I do if it affects me.'

'How does it affect you?'

'Like you said, we're supposed to be a team. And not just you and me. All of us. If you come in and bite our heads off for a little banter at the office—'

'*That's* what this is about? Because I had a go at you the other day—'

'Not only that. Everyone loses it once in a while. The pressure builds up and then it has to escape somehow. If that was all it was it wouldn't matter. But it wasn't, was it?' He peered into her eyes. 'I knew it wasn't because there's something going on with you. You're dealing with something tough and it's bleeding out into your job. That's why you barked at us and why you acted like you did in the interview. It's a pattern.'

She didn't answer.

'You don't have to let me in,' he went on, 'but if you don't I can't help you. And unless you fix this problem you're having, or at least manage to stop it from affecting your work, it *is* my business.' He paused. 'You're liked here, Shauna. More importantly, we respect you. You're a good detective. I hope you get your act together and come back soon.'

He turned and climbed the steps.

She suppressed the urge to throw her phone at the back of his head. His condescension and audacity were breath-taking. Who did he think he was? As if he, Mr Lothario, had any right to criticise *her* professionalism. *She* wasn't the one caught cheating on a girlfriend at her birthday party like some teenager. *She* wasn't the one ruining the dynamics at work.

BY THE TIME she reached home she'd calmed down somewhat. As it was a weekday it was easy to find a parking space in the little street. She put on the hand brake, turned off the engine and sat for a few minutes doing nothing.

Empty time yawned out in front of her. How would she fill the hours? She couldn't watch birds all day, and since the incident at the Nene Washes, she hadn't felt comfortable by herself outdoors. There was safety in built-up areas, not alone out in the wild where anything could happen.

She recalled Lauren Carew's body on the fen and shivered.

Grabbing her bag off the passenger seat, she got out of her car. The slam as she closed the door was loud in the quiet street. She went into her house.

Time for her routine.

She bolted the front door, mounted the narrow stairs and entered the main bedroom. Her heart thumping, she checked under her bed and inside the curtained alcove that served as a wardrobe. Then she checked the second bedroom, where boxes from her life before Cambridge sat unopened. Nothing, and there was nowhere to hide.

In the bathroom no one waited behind the shower curtain.

She descended the stairs and walked down the hall to the living room. She'd never felt entirely comfortable in this room since the incident with Baram Scott and Phillipa Edwards. Her gaze swept the space. No shadow lurked between the blinds and the window. The sofa was pressed against the wall due to the lack of space.

The kitchen also held no intruder.

She unlocked the back door. The tiny square of lawn with its shared access path to allow her neighbours to put out their bins was empty. She stepped carefully along the rotting wooden walkway to the garden shed, jerked open the door and peered into the dimness, lit by daylight filtering through the dirty, single-glazed window. The scent of damp and ancient paper hit her. No one waited in the web-shrouded gloom.

After returning to the house, she locked the back door and slid the deadbolt home.

She poured herself a large glass of wine from the bottle in her fridge and, carrying the bottle tucked under her arm, returned to her living room. She put down the glass and bottle and sat on the sofa, staring into the middle distance. Then she took her phone out of her bag and checked it. No new texts had arrived since the day at the Nene Washes.

What had he messaged her?

Yes, it was me.

And something about her ageing.

She wished she hadn't deleted all the texts. Maybe if she could study them she might see something, a clue that would...what?

What could she realistically do?

How could she convince anyone she was being stalked by a ghost?

The texts might have helped, she thought bitterly. They were all the evidence she had. There were ways to retrieve deleted ones but it was a specialized task and she'd just cut off her access to the people and facilities that could do it. A brief sighting of a familiar face in the street didn't count for anything and neither did her memories or fears.

She swigged her wine and put the glass on the coffee table.

She'd also cut off her access to the police files that could tell her more about what really happened that dark day long ago.

She took another swig of wine, hesitated, and then poured the remainder down her throat before filling the glass again.

_____

Sitting in her study, Penelope unscrewed the medication bottle and tipped out a pill onto her palm. After a moment's hesitation, she tipped out a second and then a third pill. Three were too many to swallow without help. She crossed the hallway to the kitchen, where Janet was wiping the counter top.

'Mrs Carew, I've been thinking,' she said, moving to rinse the cleaning cloth under the tap.

'Wait a moment,' said Penelope, stepping past her to fill a glass with water. She swilled the pills down. 'Yes?'

'I'd rather not work out all my notice if you don't mind.'

'Oh. What if I *do* mind?'

'I, er, didn't think you would object. I got the impression it would suit you if I were gone sooner rather than later.'

'Well, I don't know where you got that from. If I didn't need a housekeeper I wouldn't have hired one.'

Janet swallowed and then continued with a look of determination, 'Only, with all the Carter children gone and Mr Carter going home tomorrow...'

'He's going back to America?'

'Sorry, I thought he told you. He said this morning his boss has asked him to go back. It won't be hard for you to manage by yourself

for a few days until my replacement starts work. There won't be a lot to do and there doesn't seem much point in me sticking around any longer than necessary.'

Gilbert was leaving? Considering all he'd said about his flexibility it was odd.

'Do as you like,' Penelope said, 'but don't expect to be paid for days you don't work.'

She returned to her study and opened the accounts book, but the figures seemed to swim before her eyes. She couldn't bring them into focus. She looked out of the window into the garden.

The narcissi were in full bloom and hyacinths were pushing their cones of fat buds through the soil. It would be a good spring. The soil was heavy with winter rain.

She closed the accounts book.

So she would be all alone soon. Lauren was gone. The son who was no longer her son was locked up after exacting a final, decisive, shaming blow on the family.

Had he really killed Lauren?

Her mind recoiled from the notion. It was a blank space, too awful to contemplate.

Gilbert was abandoning her too, after all his fine sentiments about offering support in her time of need. Even old Michael had been taken from her.

Her pills began to take effect, a fuzzy unreality settling on her mind. Perhaps she would go and lie down for a while.

There was a knock at the door.

'Come in.'

'I hope I'm not disturbing you, Penny,' said Gilbert.

'No, I'm not busy. Have you come to tell me you're going home?'

'You heard about that?' he asked sheepishly. 'I'd planned on telling you myself, but I was chatting with Janet this morning and it slipped out. Can I sit down?'

'Of course.'

He settled his considerable frame into a chair. 'I feel bad about leaving so soon after the funeral. I know I said I'd stay on, but my boss decided he did need me in the office after all.'

'I see.'

He was lying, badly.

Did it really matter? Not so long ago she'd ached to have him gone. But that had been before Rupert had been arrested.

She could bear the private grief of losing her daughter, but not the public humiliation of Rupert's arrest. How would she ever show her face again? The news had hit the national media. Reporters waited outside the gates to the estate hoping for a word or photograph, preventing her from leaving.

Gilbert's broad, open face collapsed. 'Penny, I'll be honest with you.'

'It would be nice if you would.'

'That interview I had with the police, it got close to the bone. I thought they were just gonna ask me about Lauren. You know, general stuff about her background. I guessed they, uh, didn't want to bother you with that and I thought I could help. And they did ask me about her, but they also asked about some things I didn't expect. Family history, going back decades, right back to the time when... when...' He squinted at her. 'Did Bertie ever tell you much about his mother?'

'Marcia? Not much. She died before I met him. But why would the police be interested in her?'

'It's a long story and I only know a little. From what I do know, the less *you* know about it the better. The main point is, I wasn't comfortable with where those detectives were going and I would rather not stick around. I hope you understand.'

'You must do as you see fit.' She couldn't imagine how the details he was waffling about could be so serious he had to leave the country. Perhaps he wasn't being as honest as he pretended. He might have just changed his mind about helping her now the situation had become even worse.

He slowly nodded, accepting the sub textual judgement in her reply.

'Has your family history got something to do with Lauren's murder?' she asked.

'I don't see how. It all happened so long ago. I've no idea why the

detectives were asking me about it. It can only be because of where the poor girl was found, but they were barking up the wrong tree.'

There was a silence. Penelope picked at a piece of loose thread in her tweed skirt and asked quietly, 'Do you think Rupert did it?'

'That sweet boy? No. No way. He loved his sister. I know you and he don't see eye to eye, but he's no killer and even if he was capable of such a thing, he would never have touched a hair of Lauren's head. I'm sure the police will figure it out soon enough and let him go.'

'I don't think they would have arrested him if they didn't have some convincing evidence.'

'They've made a mistake, that's all. It's a crying shame he's sitting behind bars, though, when the real murderer is running around loose.' Gilbert frowned and swallowed. 'He, uh...'

'What?'

'Penny, your son could use a friend right now. I feel bad skipping out on him. You know I've never tried to interfere in your relationship. I didn't see it as my business. You had your reasons—'

'Bertrand would never have approved of Rupert's lifestyle. *Never.*'

'That's as may be. I guess you knew Bertie best. Still, you're Rupert's mom, the only one he's got. And as far as I know he hasn't done anything to hurt you on purpose. They say people don't get a choice about these things. Maybe, considering the spot he's in, you might find a small place in your heart for him? Maybe pay him a visit? I'm sure he'd appreciate it.'

Penelope didn't share Gilbert's confidence about Rupert's reaction if she were to turn up to see him. The last time she'd seen him, when he'd come to take a memento from Lauren's room, he'd seemed to despise her. 'I think you're over-estimating how helpful it would be for him. Rupert must have many friends in Cambridge. He was staying somewhere. His kind stick together.'

Gilbert winced. 'Well, I said my piece. My flight's this afternoon and I have to pack.' He rose to his feet. 'I don't know your financial situation and I don't like to pry, but if you need money for Rupert's legal representation, you can always call on me.'

Perhaps it was the triple-dose of her medication or just her grief and anxiety, but Penelope suddenly saw Bertrand's cousin differently.

Before, she hadn't seen far past the gut overhanging his trousers, his ridiculous baseball cap and his annoying drawl. Now, she saw the kindness and simple graciousness behind his eyes. She had misjudged him.

'Thank you, Gilbert. That's very considerate of you.'

'No problem, Penny. Just let me know.'

She also stood up.

He moved in for a hug.

She leaned backwards and lifted her hand to ward him off.

He shook it. 'I'll pop in to say goodbye before I leave.'

S hauna turned over and groaned. Grey light filtered through her bedroom curtains and rain pattered on the window. Slapping a hand on her mobile on the bedside table, she turned it over and, rising up on one elbow, checked the time. Eleven-thirty.

With another groan, she flopped onto her pillow and then grimaced as the movement redoubled the pounding in her head. After her second bottle of wine she'd passed out but then woken up a couple of hours later and spent the rest of the night half-awake, scenes from her past running through her mind, figures looming from the darkness, images of all the murder victims she'd seen and tried to forget leaping back into her consciousness.

Would she become one of them?

Would Will be called to the crime scene and look down on her corpse?

What was it that was paralysing her, preventing her from acting? The course of her life seemed to have taken on an inevitability; her destiny had become fixed. *He'd* killed her kids and he would kill her, too, once he'd become bored of playing and her fear no longer amused him.

She threw back her covers and climbed out of bed. She needed water. Water, eggs and a hot shower. Downstairs, she checked the

front and back doors remained bolted. Then she ran the tap in the kitchen until the water was cold, filled a glass and downed it, then filled another. She used the second one to wash down two paracetamol tablets. Before stepping into the shower, she set two eggs boiling on the stove.

The steaming water pouring over her head helped dispel her headache, but the subject matter of her hours of wakefulness returned in full force. Whether her eyes were open or closed she could see her kids. She saw them playing in the garden, in bed as she read them a bedtime story, on Christmas mornings opening their presents. So many happy memories. But overlaying all them was another, and it wasn't even real.

She hadn't seen her children after their deaths. A family member had stepped in to identify them in order to save her the heartache. She'd been so grateful to not have to perform that task and have that sight be her last memory of them. But in the end it hadn't mattered. In her time as a detective she'd seen enough drowning victims to form a good idea of how Naomi, Charlotte and Liam must have looked. It was an image she couldn't shake.

The warm water washed away her tears, but when she turned the shower off they continued rolling down her face. She climbed out of the stall and wrapped a towel around her wet body. Stepping into the kitchen she turned off the gas under the eggs and then sat on the floor, her knees up, her hair dripping down her back, and wept.

WHEN SHE GREW SO cold her discomfort overcame her misery, she looked up. How long had she been sitting here? The rain had stopped, the clouds dispersed and weak spring sunshine shone through the kitchen window.

Like an unstoppable train her life continued on, regardless of her feelings about it.

She grabbed the edge of the work surface and hauled herself to her feet. The water in the saucepan had gone cold. She poured it out

then put the kettle on to make some tea. The paracetamol had taken the edge off her headache.

She hung the towel over the rail and put on her dressing gown before taking the shells off the eggs and sprinkling salt on them. She ate them in a few bites before carrying her tea into the living room.

More than two hours had passed since she'd woken up. She was sure this wasn't how DCI Bryant had envisioned her spending her free time during her leave of absence. Getting drunk and then nursing a hangover was probably the last thing he'd had in mind.

She tucked her feet up on the sofa and wrapped her dressing gown over her knees. The rest of the day stretched out with nothing to fill it. What should she do? Put on a film? Try to catch up on her sleep? Open another bottle of wine?

Her stomach rebelled at the last option.

After the empty day would come an empty night and then another day. How long would Bryant make her wait before she could go back to work? Would he insist on seeing evidence of a good mental state before he would let her resume her job? She had a vague notion there were protocols to follow in her situation but she couldn't remember what they were. Maybe something would arrive in the post soon.

But mental health wasn't her problem, or, at least, not the root cause of her problems. Her past was an open sore, a cavernous, rotting wound that would never close, never be healed. It was the reason she'd transferred to Cambridge, for a quieter, less stressful life, a life she could manage without dissolving under pressure.

She smiled grimly.

Look how well that had gone.

If he'd left her alone she might have managed it. Working at Cambridge Central—and particularly under Bryant—entailed more of a challenge than she'd anticipated, but she could have coped. She'd survived that other hard murder case last year without succumbing to the stress, despite that horrible echo of her children's deaths she and Will had suffered.

She'd been okay until *he* turned up.

But had he really survived?

Could it be a hoax?

All she had to go on was the briefest glimpse of a face in a crowd and a text message. Well, several text messages, but only one that tied in directly to the glimpsed face.

Was someone messing with her? Someone who knew about her past?

She got up, carrying her tea in one hand, pulled a chair from under the little table and put it next to the window. The vertical blinds allowed her to see out without anyone being able to see in.

If it really was him hanging around and winding her up, he might be outside even now, watching. He could be sitting in a car, leaning on a lamppost or walking slowly up and down the street. She might spot him, get a good look at his face, putting an end to all her doubts.

A mother walked past holding a young child's hand and pushing a pushchair. The wheels rattled on the pavement. None of the cars lined up against the kerb seemed to have occupants, though the sun reflecting on some windscreens made it impossible to be sure. A cyclist sped past.

Laughter sounded from somewhere down the street. Moments later a man and two women appeared, chatting and giggling. They looked young. Probably students.

How nice it must be to be like that. Not a care in the world.

She sipped her tea.

Would any of her children have gone to university if they'd lived? It was unlikely. Her side of the family wasn't academic. They were practical people. And, from the little she'd been able to glean, their father's family was composed of salesmen and secretaries. He'd been estranged from them. Initially, she'd believed his story that the fault was on their side. As time had gone on, she'd suspected it was *they* who refused to have anything to do with *him*.

She yawned and shivered. She hadn't really warmed up since her episode on the kitchen floor.

The students had crossed the road and disappeared down a side street, and now someone else was approaching. No, not some*one*, two people. An older couple. Late middle-aged, they were walking hand in hand. The woman halted, glanced up and down the road, and then

reached up to grasp the man's face and pull him in for a kiss. It was sweet.

The scene was so ordinary it shouldn't have meant a thing, yet somehow it struck her forcefully.

Life continued steamrollering on, regardless of the fact she was crushed and broken. But things also continued in a good way. The good stuff of life, the happiness and love and fulfilment, it all persisted alongside the bad stuff.

Shit.

What had happened to her? Why had she given up? If her ex really was still alive and stalking her, she was playing right into his hands. She was reacting exactly as he wanted her to, shutting down, living in fear.

What was the saying? *The best revenge is a life well lived.*

She put her mug on the windowsill and returned to the sofa, where her bag sat. She took out her mobile, looked up a number and dialled it.

'Hello, Dr Kapherr. It's DI Holt. Are you at Duxworth today?... That's great. I was wondering if I could stop by. I'm interested in finding out more about Jack Muncey and Douglas Hunt.'

I t started with the steak. Sue lifted the piece of meat from the frying pan with tongs and placed it on Peter's plate before carrying both their meals through to the dining room. She wasn't having steak. So much meat all at once always sat heavy in her stomach for hours afterwards. She'd made herself a cheese and tomato sandwich and supplemented it with some of the oven chips Peter was having too.

Gemma and Dad weren't having anything. Dad had taken Gemma out for fish and chips earlier as a treat to cheer her up. She hadn't been right since her meltdown at the fair. She'd withdrawn further into herself, barely saying a word to anyone except her granddad. She stayed in her room and painted more than ever—dark, scary paintings in red, black and purple acrylics.

Sue was worried but she didn't know how to help her. No therapist ever seemed to have a lasting effect and increasing her medication turned her into a zombie. No one wanted that, not even Peter. At least, that was what he said in his rare moments of compassion and understanding.

He cut into the steak as Sue took a bite of her sandwich.

His cutlery clattered on his plate and he shoved it away from him.

'Is something wrong?' she asked evenly.

'You could say that.' He spun the plate around so the cut section of steak faced her. 'Look.'

The meat was brown all through the middle.

'Oh, I left it in the pan a little too long,' she said. 'Sorry.'

'You know I like my steak medium rare. Medium rare! There's no point in eating this. It'll taste like leather. I don't know why you didn't just give me one of your shoes for dinner.'

'Stop exaggerating. I'm sure it's still tasty. Try some.'

'I don't want to spoil my palate with your nasty cooking.'

'Have some chips, then. You must be hungry. You could have a chip butty. Would you like me to make you one?'

'No. After eight hours at the office and a three-hour commute I do not want a *chip butty*.'

Sue took another bite of her sandwich and chewed stoically. She didn't want another argument. She was worried about Gemma and didn't have the mental capacity to deal with toddler temper tantrums. 'I could order you a takeaway. What about a curry? Or maybe some Chinese.'

'I don't want some Chinese. I want the steak I've been looking forward to all day, properly cooked.'

She sighed, put down her sandwich and rubbed her right temple, where a headache was beginning to form. 'Peter, I'm trying my best here. If you're unhappy with my *nasty cooking*, maybe you should do it yourself.'

'That would suit you down to the ground, wouldn't it? After a hard day's work your long-suffering husband comes home and cooks your dinner. The most onerous of your minimal duties done away with. All you would have to do all day would be a little light dusting and putting dirty clothes in the washing machine. Perfect.'

'As I've often told you, I'd be happy to get a job. Something part-time so I could carry on looking after the house. I could bring some money in and we could afford more things. A foreign holiday would be nice. We haven't been abroad in years.'

'We wouldn't need any more money if your daughter wasn't sponging off us.'

'Right,' she said, her jaw tightening. 'Could you make up your

mind what we're arguing about? Is it my laziness and ineptitude or Gemma?'

'I wasn't aware I had to pick.'

'You can't have it both ways. You can't have a go at me for not working and then in the next breath tell me you don't want me to work.'

'I didn't say that.'

'Yes, you have. Many times.'

And so the argument went on, their voices growing louder. Their dinners sat uneaten, the expensive steak wasted. Then a sound came from Gemma's room overhead. Something bulky had hit the floor. Footsteps followed, moving to and fro.

Sue had forgotten her daughter was home. 'Keep it down,' she hissed at Peter. 'Everyone will hear you.'

'You mean Gemma will hear us. Don't tell me you've suddenly giving a shit about what the neighbours think.'

'Is this open season on me? Is everyone allowed to take a pop at my character? Should I see if there's anyone in the street who would like to join in?'

'You're being ridiculous. Can't take the slightest bit of criticism. It's time you got over your sensitivity and grew up. It's easy to see where Gemma gets her problems from.'

'That's it!' Sue leapt to her feet. 'I'm sick of your constant complaints. If it isn't my cooking it's Gemma, and if it isn't Gemma it's Dad, or I don't Hoover enough, or I've ironed a crease in your shirt, or who knows what else. I'm not going to put up with it any longer. If you don't like living here you can get out!'

Peter also stood. He leaned over the table and growled, 'There's no way I'm leaving this house. I'm the one who pays the mortgage. If anyone should be leaving it's you, and you can take your mooching relatives with you.'

Sue was about to throw back a retort when she heard footsteps on the stairs. She swallowed her reply, gave Peter a furious look and then turned her attention to the section of hall visible in the open doorway. 'Gemma? Is that you? Are you going out?'

But it was Dad who poked his head into the dining room. 'I've

asked Gemma to come and stay with me for a few days. I hope that's all right.'

'No, it's…' All her focus had been on Peter and their argument. The sudden switch to this new development was disorienting. 'It's not all right.' She stepped to the door. Her father had two suitcases, the one he'd come with and another she recognised as Gemma's. She looked up the stairs.

Her daughter was perched about halfway up with a deer-in-the-headlights look.

'Gemma?' Sue said. 'Is everything okay?'

She didn't answer. She seemed frightened but Sue wasn't sure what was scaring her.

'Of course everything isn't okay,' said Dad. 'Things haven't been okay for a long time, have they Gem? That's why I think it would be a good idea for her to live with me for a while. It'll give her a break.'

'A break from what?'

'It makes sense,' Dad continued, ignoring her question. 'With your mum gone, I'm rattling around in that old house by myself. Gemma will be company for me. And it'll help her spread her wings. She's lived at home all her life. A change of scenery might do her the world of good.'

'A break from what?' Sue repeated, louder.

'So you two are off?' asked Peter, reaching out a hand languidly to rest on the door frame. 'I think it's an excellent idea.'

'No it isn't,' Sue protested.

'We can just try it for a short time,' said Dad, 'and see how we go.'

'I don't want you to try it.' Sue looked up the stairs at her daughter. 'Gemma, is this really what you want? You want to leave home?'

'She isn't leaving home,' Dad said. 'She's going from your home to mine. And no one's saying it's permanent.'

'Gemma?' Sue persisted.

'It's only for a little while, Mum. Pops invited me. We both think it'll be good for me to get out of your and Peter's way.'

'My and Peter's way? What does that mean? You're welcome to live here as long as you want. You aren't in anyone's way.'

Peter put a closed fist to his mouth and gave a fake cough. Stepping away from the door, he muttered, '*Don't let the door hit you...*'

Sue whirled to face him. 'This is your fault! You're the reason Gemma wants to leave. You've never done anything to make her feel at home, let alone treated her like a daughter. You've done everything you can to make her feel unwelcome.'

'Oh yes,' he replied acidly, 'that's why my bank balance is tens of thousands of pounds lighter. Because I've been so unwelcoming.'

'It's all about money with you, isn't it? That's what it always comes down to in the end. You care more about money than people.'

She heard the front door open. By the time she turned back, Dad and Gemma were already on their way out. She raced into the hall. 'Don't leave, Gemma.'

'It's temporary,' said Dad. 'Let's see how things go.'

A car was waiting at the kerb, its engine idling. They'd called an Uber.

'Dad, I know you're trying to help but this isn't the right way. We need to decide as a family what's the best thing to do. You can't just take my daughter away from me.'

'No one's taking her anywhere. Like she said, we decided this together. And you know you can visit any time. Come over tomorrow if you want and we can talk about it. But I think right now the best thing is to get Gemma out of this environment. It doesn't help her state of mind.'

'This environment?' Sue echoed.

'I think you know what I mean.' He lifted the suitcases over the step. 'Let's go, Gem.'

'Bye, Mum.' She lifted her head to look over Sue's shoulder, perhaps contemplating whether to say something to Peter. She must have decided against it, for she said, 'Why don't you come to Pops' tomorrow?'

'I don't want to...' Despair was rising in Sue's chest. She shouted, 'Don't go, love! Not like this. Please, don't go.'

Peter's sharp tones cut through from the dining room, 'Would you please stop being so dramatic, Sue? What will people think?'

'Shut up,' she hissed, facing him again.

He was sitting down looking at his phone.

'Just shut up!' she repeated.

The front door closed.

They were gone.

D r Kapherr peered over her glasses at Shauna before inviting her to sit down and offering to make her some tea.

'I would like some, thanks,' Shauna replied.

'Alone today?' Kapherr asked as she walked to her kettle. 'I imagine you and the other detective aren't quite as busy now you have your man.'

'DS Fiske does have other things to focus on. There's still plenty for us to do before the suspect comes to trial.'

'I was shocked when I read it was Rupert Carew. Who would have thought?'

'Do you know the Carew family?'

Kapherr snorted a laugh. 'Only by reputation. I don't breathe the same rarefied atmosphere as that sort, I'm happy to say.'

'What *is* their reputation around here? I haven't lived in Cambridge long.'

'Oh, it isn't anything strange or sinister. I don't want to give you the wrong impression. They're just one of the local prominent families, that's all. They've lived in the county for generations. And now, of course, it makes it all the more scandalous that the son killed the daughter. I would love to know more, to be honest, but I realise you

can't talk about the case. So you really think it's tied in somehow with our dig? Sugar?'

'What?'

The archaeologist was holding a teaspoon over a bag of sugar.

'No, thanks,' Shauna said.

Kapherr gave her the full mug and sat down on the opposite side of her desk. 'After you phoned, I gathered all the additional information we've been able to find on Muncey and Hunt. Would you like to see photographs of them?'

'I'd love to.'

What Muncey and Hunt had looked like had no bearing on the case, but she was curious to set eyes on them.

Kapherr leafed through the stack of paper in front of her and drew out two black and white photographs. The portraits of the pilots had been shot in the old Hollywood style. Each gazed off camera, their faces tilted slightly upwards and illuminated by light.

'Muncey was twenty-one when he died?' Shauna asked. 'He looks older.'

'People grew up quickly in those days. As soon as you left school you were an adult, wearing adult clothes and hairstyles. Teenager-hood hadn't been invented yet. In fact, Pilot Officer Muncey was nineteen when this photograph was taken.'

'Nineteen?! Unbelievable.' Shauna studied Jack Muncey for several more moments, recognition dawning, before turning to the other photograph.

'Douglas Hunt was very good-looking, don't you think?' said Kapherr. 'His brother, Ernest, was quite a bit older. He'd been in the RAF since before the war, hence his being the camp commander. He was thirty-one when he died of flu.'

'Still, he was young to be responsible for all of Duxworth.'

'Promotions come fast when your superior officers are being steadily killed off.'

Shauna put the photographs down. 'What else can you tell me?'

'Not very much, or at least not facts pertaining to your case. I realised after you phoned I don't actually have very much for you.'

'I think I'm the best judge of that,' said Shauna without rancour.

'I take your point, but I don't see how the pilots' wages or their number of battle victories could be relevant to someone living eighty years later.'

'At the moment, I don't either, but—'

'So I arranged for you to speak to someone who was here at the time.'

'You...what? He's still alive?!' Shauna blurted.

'*She*,' Kapherr emphasised reprovingly. 'Women worked here too, you know.'

'Yes, of course. That was stupid of me.'

'It's an easy mistake to make. The pilots were the heroes and get all the attention, but did you know there were women pilots who flew the planes between airbases? The Air Transport Auxiliary operated throughout the war, and women died in its service. They weren't trained to fly all the different aircraft, you see, only given a little book of notes. One woman flew two light aircraft, two medium bombers, a Spitfire, a four-engined bomber and a Stirling heavy bomber within 24 hours, based on notes. Unfortunately, sometimes the planes crashed due to engine failure or terrible weather.'

'Really? I had no idea.'

'Most people don't. The person I found for you wasn't a pilot, however. She was a member of the WAAF, the Women's Auxiliary Air Force. I believe one of her roles was as a plotter in Ops.'

'A...?'

'She plotted the positions of the planes on a tabletop map as battles progressed.'

'Oh, I know what you mean.' Shauna recalled seeing the women in uniform pushing models representing squadrons around on a map with a long stick. 'How old is she?'

'Ninety-eight. She lives in an old folks home.'

Shauna was doing mental arithmetic. 'So she was eighteen in 1942. Another teenager doing an adult's job.'

'That's the story of those times. And you should see where she worked. The only protection the Ops Block had against bombs was a brick wall. If the building had taken a direct hit that would have been it for everyone inside. Anyway, I took the liberty of speaking to the

centre where Edith lives. They said you're welcome to try to pay a visit but if she refuses to see you they have to uphold her wishes. You are a complete stranger to her after all. I suppose you could use your police powers to insist—'

'I don't want to be heavy-handed. Couldn't they ask her permission for me to visit when you phoned?'

'They said there would be no point. Her memory is terrible, and she might agree but then refuse when you arrive because she's completely forgotten what she said.'

Shauna deflated. It would have been great to speak to someone who might have known Muncey and Hunt personally but it didn't sound as though this person, Edith Brown, would be able to tell her much.

'I got the impression they were talking about her short term memory,' Kapherr went on to explain. 'I think if she couldn't help you they would have told me so. It's often like that with older people. They vividly remember things that happened decades in the past but can't recall what they ate for breakfast.'

OSBERN HALL RESEMBLED Penelope Carew's mansion except the place was buzzing, if senior citizens could ever be said to buzz. The weather was fine and warm for the time of year, and the staff seemed to have taken advantage of the opportunity to get the residents outside to enjoy fresh air and sunshine.

When Shauna asked at the reception desk about the possibility of speaking to Edith Brown, she was careful to not show the receptionist her badge or introduce herself by her job title. Already, her eagerness to pursue the Carew case while she was supposed to be on leave was beginning to wane. Her behaviour at Rupert Carew's interview had jeopardised her career. If she were caught interviewing a potential source of information in an official capacity that would end it.

'Oh, yes,' the receptionist said. 'We've been expecting you. You're a student from the university, right? Sent by Professor Kapherr.' She picked up a lanyard and ID card.

'No, I'm...studying that period of history and Dr Kapherr is a friend.' It was a relief the archaeologist hadn't gone into more detail about why someone wanted to speak to one of the Hall's residents.

'I see.' The receptionist looked doubtful and put the lanyard down. 'Usually, it's only family members who come to see the residents. I'm not sure...'

'Do the people here get many visitors?' Shauna asked, stalling as she tried to think of a good reason for the woman to allow her in.

'No, they don't, which is a shame because most of our residents love seeing their families,' the receptionist replied.

'Edith might be glad of someone to talk to about her life.'

'I'm sure she would but that isn't a good reason to let you in. I know you've come all the way here but we have strict rules to follow regarding who has access to the residents. They're classed as vulnerable adults. We can't just let anyone in. The person Dr Kapherr spoke to must have got the wrong impression. I'm very sorry but I don't think we can help you.'

'But...' Shauna hesitated, itching to pull out her badge.

'I'm very sorry.'

Kicking herself for not simply lying about being a student on one of Dr Kapherr's courses, she left the reception area.

Outside, she squinted in the bright sunlight. Senior citizens sat on park benches in the grounds, many of them with a walking stick propped beside them. Others made slow progress along the paths aided by walking frames. The staff were easily identifiable by their youth even if they hadn't been wearing uniforms. There weren't many about, just a few attending to some of the frailest residents.

Shauna glanced over her shoulder at the reception. The receptionist was distracted, talking on the phone.

She stepped off the path and onto the lawn. Acting as if she had every right to be in the place, she walked around the side of the building. At the back, a longer, wider garden spread out. Here, the seniors were sparser, dotted over the lawn as they got their slow exercise.

The sound of strained tones drifted toward her. A resident was arguing with a member of staff, who was gently restraining him.

'Help!' the old man weakly called out. 'They're keeping me a prisoner! I want to go home. Let me go. Help!'

The carer's frustration edged her voice as she replied but Shauna couldn't make out what she was saying.

She walked over.

'I want to leave,' the man exclaimed. 'Let me go. You can't do this!'

'Excuse me,' Shauna said to the staff member, 'I'm looking for someone.'

The carer's harassed expression turned darker as the old man managed to free his arm from her grip. She quickly grabbed him again.

'Are you the police?' the man asked. 'Have you come to rescue me?'

'Uh...'

'I'm kind of busy,' the carer snapped.

'I'm here to see Edith Brown.'

'I've been kidnapped,' said the man. 'Phone the police. Please!'

The carer nodded at a small copse. 'Edith's favourite spot. You might find her there.' She returned her attention to the man. 'Come on, Albert. It's nearly time for dinner. Wouldn't you like something nice to eat?' She hadn't checked to see if Shauna was wearing a lanyard and ID.

'I want to go home!'

She set off towards the copse.

An old lady sat alone in the quiet shade underneath the trees. The space was barely large enough to fit the wooden bench she perched upon, her knees drawn together beneath a plain blue skirt. She wore flat shoes and a thick, beige, cable-knit cardigan fastened up to her neck, where scant white hair, curled and bouffed into meagre volume, grazed its edge. The eyes that turned to regard Shauna were china blue.

'Hello?' she asked querulously.

'Hello.' Shauna introduced herself by her first name only. 'Are you Edith Brown?'

'That's me, dear. Is it time to go in?'

'No, not yet. Do you mind if I sit down?'

'I don't mind at all, but you'd better not let your manager catch you.'

Deciding not to correct Edith's assumption that she was a care assistant, Shauna sat next to her.

How to begin? This was hardly a typical police interview.

'Are you new?' Edith asked. 'I don't remember a Shauna. But I'm not good with names anymore. Are you sure it isn't time to go in? I don't want to be late for dinner.'

'I'm sure.' Shauna took in the peaceful spot. Cut off from the rest

of the grounds by tree trunks and shrubs, it could have been anywhere. It was a nice place for Edith to remember what must have been the many events of her long life. 'I can see why you like it here.'

'Can you? Why do you think I like it?' Her tone was mischievous.

'It's secluded, and if it rains the trees will keep it off.'

'Wrong!' Edith giggled like a little girl. 'I come here to hide.'

'To hide?'

'From that awful woman, Mavis. She thinks we're friends. I'm not her friend. All she talks about is her grandchildren. Kevin did this. Diane did that. Who cares? Certainly not me.' She paused.

Her short term memory didn't seem so bad.

'What were you saying, dear?' she asked. 'Have you come to fetch me?'

'I haven't come to fetch you. It's okay. You can sit here for a bit.'

As Edith had been speaking, she hadn't looked at Shauna at all. Ever since Shauna had entered the copse, her focus had been on the middle distance.

She was blind.

'Do you have any grandchildren?' Shauna asked.

'No, I...' Edith looked troubled. Perhaps she couldn't remember.

'How about children?'

'I had a son, but he died.'

'I'm so sorry.' She touched the old lady's arm. 'I didn't mean to bring back bad memories.'

'It's all right. It was a very long time ago, when he was a baby. He died of measles. Children sometimes did in those days. Not many, but some. He was one of the unlucky ones. We tried for more but none came.'

Shauna felt bad. Did she have any right to plumb this frail, old woman's mind? But Edith might hold the answer to why Rupert Carew had killed his sister.

'What was your son's name?' she asked gently.

'George, in honour of the king. There were a lot of Georges that year.'

'He was born in 1952?'

It was the year George VI had died.

'That's right.'

A silence opened out. The similarity Shauna shared with this woman was difficult to contemplate.

In the distance, a bell rang. It was probably the signal that dinner was ready. It was time for Edith to go in, but she didn't seem to register the noise. She continued to stare vacantly ahead, her rheumy eyes moist with the memory of the child from seventy years ago.

'I-I had a baby who died too,' Shauna said, forcing the words out. *More than one.*

'You did?' Edith's head turned towards her though her gaze remained without focus. She felt for Shauna's hand and grasped it tightly. 'Then you know how it feels.'

They sat holding hands without speaking for several minutes as the familiar pain expanded in Shauna's chest. She forced it down again reflexively from long practice. 'Edith, I'm not one of the helpers here. I'm sorry if I misled you.'

'You're not?' She withdrew her hand. 'Then who are you?'

'I'm...I've come to talk to you about things that happened in the war. Would that be okay?'

'Ah, the war. It's strange, you know, but in some ways they were the best years of my life. We were all fighting together against that evil man, Hitler. He got off light. Took the coward's way out. He should have been strung up with the rest of them.'

'You worked at Duxworth, didn't you?'

'Started when I was eighteen. Just a girl, really. My mum and dad didn't want me to do it. They wanted me to join the Land Army. Said it was much safer. But I couldn't see myself digging potatoes in a muddy field. Becoming a WAAF was more glamorous, though I wouldn't have admitted it at the time. We had a smart uniform and we had lots of vital work to do. I loved it, to be honest. Every minute of it.'

Someone was calling a name. It was faint but Shauna could just make it out: *Edith!*

The staff had noticed she was missing.

'Do you remember Jack Muncey and Douglas Hunt?' she asked quickly.

'Douglas Hunt? Of course I remember him. But I wouldn't have dared to call him by his first name. He was the commander's brother.'

'What was he like?' It was a banal question yet, now she had the opportunity, Shauna was muddled about what she should ask.

'He was a good pilot, if that's what you mean. Kept himself together, despite all the pressure he was under. We were constantly losing pilots and planes. It was hard to keep going sometimes but we all did. There was a war on and we all had to do our duty.'

'Edith!' The voice was louder.

'What was Hunt like as a person? And do you remember Jack Muncey too?'

'Well, I don't like to speak ill of the dead—but I don't think I could honestly say anyone *liked* Hunt. He was a...what's that phrase?...a Jack-the-lad. Us women at the base knew how he was and wouldn't have anything to do with him, but he would pick up girls in Cambridge. Young girls. Pick them up and dump them. A different conquest every Saturday dance night, that's what people said. Then there was that nasty business—'

'Edith, there you are.' A care assistant had appeared.

Shauna stood up.

The assistant stared. 'Who are you?'

'Just a relative. I didn't realise visiting hours were over. I'll get going now.' She bent down and kissed Edith's cheek. 'It's been lovely talking with you, Auntie. I'll be back soon.'

Heart thumping, she strode past the assistant and out into the open. The lawn area was empty. Groups of senior citizens seated at dining tables could be glimpsed through the home's glass doors.

'Excuse me,' the assistant called after her. 'Could you stop, please?'

Shauna pretended she hadn't heard, though it was impossible. She marched over the grass, fighting to stop herself from breaking into a run. It would make her look even more suspicious.

What was she doing? If it got back to the receptionist that a strange woman had been found talking to Edith Brown, it wouldn't take a genius to put two and two together. The receptionist knew Dr

Kapherr's name. All she had to do was to phone her up and ask her who she'd sent over.

It was a big mess.

The assistant seemed to have given up chasing her. When Shauna risked a backward glance, she saw her helping Edith towards the building's central entrance.

She'd reached the corner. She stepped quickly behind the cover of the wall and her pulse and breathing slowed. Perhaps she might get away with it.

The area in front of Osbern Hall was empty. Shauna jogged to her car and climbed into the driver's seat. She started the engine. Her fate was in the lap of the gods now. There wasn't anything she could do except leave as fast as she could.

Her mobile rang.

She was tempted to let it go to voicemail, but something compelled her to check who was phoning.

It was Will.

She accepted the call.

'Shauna, what the hell do you think you're doing?!'

The living room of her two-up-two-down terraced house had always been cramped but now it seemed unbearably small. Shauna crossed it in five strides, turned, and crossed it again. She'd been walking the same route for the last half an hour, waiting.

This time when she arrived at the window she peeked out between the blinds. Her living room was dark, allowing her to see outside. Night had fallen and the street lights cast feeble beams, barely illuminating the roofs of the parked cars jammed bumper to bumper. The street's inhabitants were home from work. Soft yellow light from downstairs windows added to the efforts of the municipal lighting, lending the wet pavements a gentle shine.

In a way, the scene was beautiful and, aside from the two rows of motor vehicles, probably not much different from how it had looked every rainy spring evening for the more than a hundred years of the street's existence. There was a beauty to the simple, humble homes, something to do with their age and the rust-coloured, worn bricks.

A figure crossed the pavement in front of her and stepped up to her front door.

Her heart rose into her throat. She clasped her hands tightly.

He knocked.

Three raps of iron on iron echoed through the house.

She watched, her pulse roaring in her ears.

After a minute's pause, he knocked again.

Her feet were glued to the floor. She could only look out at her visitor.

He squatted and her letterbox rattled open.

'Shauna, I know you're in there. Stop pissing about. I'm not going to stand here in the rain all night.'

Still, she didn't move.

'All right. You've got thirty seconds to open this door or I'll phone Baldy.' He pulled a mobile from his pocket and waggled it threateningly. 'I've got him on speed dial.'

That did it. The fear of losing her job, her remaining purpose in life, edged over her other, long-standing fear. She broke from her trance and ran to the door.

Will's face was in shadow but she could just make out his angry frown and glistening hair. He must have come straight from work and didn't have his hat or umbrella.

'Are you going to let me in?'

She took a backward step and turned sideways to allow him room to walk past her. He stopped halfway down the hall.

'You didn't seriously think I was going to let this go?' he asked as she closed the door.

'The light switch is on the wall,' she mumbled.

'What?'

'You can turn on the light.'

He ran his hands over the surface and flipped the switch. 'That's a stupid place to put it.' He looked tired and stressed.

'Do you want a towel?' she asked. 'You're soaked.'

'Had to walk half a mile to get here. Couldn't find parking for love or money.'

'I thought you didn't usually drive in Cambridge.'

'I took the car because it was raining.'

The irony of his situation brought a wan smile to her lips.

He smiled back sadly. 'No, I don't want a towel. Is this your living room?'

She nodded.

He walked in and turned on the light. It was the first time Will had set foot in her home. Last year, after she'd been attacked, he'd offered to stay with her. What a disaster that would have been.

She moved to the doorway. 'Do you want a drink?'

He was taking off his coat. 'Yes. Alcohol if you have it. Something tells me this is going to be a tough conversation.'

'I've got some wine.' She held out a hand. 'I'll take that.'

He gave her his coat and she hung it from a hook in the hall. Then she went into the kitchen, collected a bottle of wine and two glasses and returned to the living room.

Will was sitting on her sofa, the knees of his long legs poking up. She sat on the remaining seat, the armchair opposite him.

'Give it to me,' he said. 'I'll pour. You don't look in a fit state to do anything. Dr Kapherr said you looked a right sight when you went to see her today.' He unscrewed the lid of the bottle.

'Did she? I'm surprised she would notice.'

'She's trained to observe stuff, isn't she?' He handed her a glass of wine before pouring himself one.

She put hers down on the coffee table. Her throat closed up at the thought of drinking it. If she tried she would surely vomit.

He took a sip and rested his back on the cushions, laying an arm expansively over the back of the sofa.

Make yourself at home, Will Fiske.

'I must have been inside fifty of these houses,' he said. 'They're all over the place. I prefer living in a flat. More room.'

She regarded him silently. Small talk was the last thing on her mind though she also dreaded the dialogue he expected.

He sighed, leaned forwards and put down his glass. 'This can't go on, Shauna. It's going to end one way or another, and most likely with you getting the sack. I couldn't believe it when I phoned Kapherr today to chase her up about the dead pilots and she said you'd already been to see her. What were you thinking?'

'I was sure I was onto something. I still am. I went to see—'

'Don't tell me you didn't stop there. Bloody hell. In for a penny, in

for a pound, is it?' He shook his head. 'You went to see who? I might as well hear it all.'

'Kapherr found a contact for us. A woman who worked at Duxworth the same time as Hunt and Muncey.'

'She's still alive?'

'She was a teenager at the time. She's in a home for senior citizens now. I was leaving there when you phoned.'

Rubbing the bridge of his nose with the tips of his fingers, Will said as if speaking to himself, 'Okay, that's two incidents of gross professional misconduct I'm covering up at the moment. *At the moment,*' he added to her. 'If this comes out, I was never here, we never had this conversation. I spoke to Kapherr and then I couldn't get a hold of you. Right?'

'Right.'

'I've got until tomorrow to make a decision whether to report this.'

He gave her a long look.

She wanted to disappear down the crack between the armchair cushions. He was jeopardising his career on her behalf. He had no reason to. They'd been working together less than two years. They got along but they weren't what she would call close, despite the fact they'd almost died together on the Scott and Edwards case. He didn't owe her anything. He was giving her a chance purely out of kindness.

He said, 'I need to hear what's going on with you.'

A black shroud enveloped her, swathing her, binding her tightly.

'There's no other way,' he went on. 'I have to justify this to myself.'

Her shoulders sagged. 'I know. I understand, and I'm grateful for everything, Will. I really am. But maybe you should go ahead and report me to Bryant.'

'You'd seriously rather lose your job, maybe your pension too, than tell me what's wrong?'

'It's...' She swallowed and took a breath. 'It's very hard for me to face. Impossible. I'm stuck and I don't know how to get free.'

'You're stuck where? How?'

'Stuck in my past. There are some things you don't move on from. You can't. I realise that now. I should stop trying.'

He took another sip of wine. 'You aren't making a lot of sense, but

it's a start. This is better than the stonewalling you've been doing ever since we met.'

'I don't want to tell you any more. You should leave. Go home and report me to Bryant. Leave him a message or something. I don't want to get you into trouble.'

'That's my decision. I've said I'll wait until tomorrow and I will. So you've got tonight to tell me.'

'I can't. I just can't.'

'What do you mean? Of course you can.'

She gave a little shake of her head, her back rigid.

'If you can't tell me,' he said, 'can you show me?'

It was an idea she hadn't thought of. If she couldn't force the words past her lips perhaps there was another way to explain to him. Even though it wouldn't save her, he'd earned the right to know.

She left to fetch her laptop from her bedroom. When she returned, she joined Will on the sofa and opened it up. Her hands shook so much it took her a moment to bring up her emails and the link to the newspaper report.

She watched his eyes move side to side as he read.

He turned to her, puzzled. 'What does this have to do with you?'

'Don't be an idiot,' she snapped, her nerves frayed to threads. 'You're a better detective than that.'

'But what *could* this have to do with you?' He peered at the screen again. 'Is it something to do with that time we nearly drowned in Phillipa Edwards' car? Have you got PTSD from that?'

'No.'

He gazed into her eyes, his face creased with concern, and then he returned to the news report.

After a couple of seconds he breathed, *'Jesus Christ.'* He stared at her. 'Those were your kids?!'

She couldn't answer.

'I didn't get it at first,' he said. 'This happened years ago and your surname's different from theirs. So that's why you had all that emergency escape stuff in your car?'

She whispered, 'My children had my first husband's name.'

'The guy in the article.'

She nodded.

'So your ex killed his own kids just to spite you? What a bastard. You *have* got PTSD, not from what Scott and Edwards did but from what happened to your children. Shauna, this can be fixed. You could get therapy or medication, or both.'

'I've tried. What makes you think I haven't? It doesn't work. Nothing works.'

He moved to put an arm around her. She shrank from him, got to her feet, and returned to the armchair.

'Sorry,' he said, 'I was only trying to—'

'I know,' she replied tightly. 'It's okay.'

He drank more wine, watching her thoughtfully. When she met his gaze, he politely looked away and around the room.

'Are you going to tell Bryant what I did?' she asked. 'I wouldn't blame you but I'd like to know.'

'I still haven't decided. There's more to this you're not saying. What you've told me explains some things but not everything. Why have you been on edge the last few weeks in particular? What's in those work texts you keep receiving and deleting? And what happened the other day when you dropped your coffee?'

'I think...I don't know...' It was a supreme effort to squeeze the words out yet also a relief to finally get it off her chest. 'I think it's him.'

'Who?'

She nodded in the direction of her open laptop. 'I think he didn't die and for some reason he's come looking for me and found me. I don't know how. I haven't gone by my maiden name in a long time. Holt's my second husband's name.'

Will read the article again. 'It doesn't state if the father died too, just your children.'

'I know. I always assumed he drowned with them because I never heard from him afterwards. He would never have left me alone by choice. He would have wanted to gloat. I thought he was dead, until now.'

'No one told you what happened to him?'

'They might have. I don't remember. I was in a state.'

'Of course you were. Have you checked the PNC? The case will be on record.'

'I couldn't. All I've done is I looked up the registration number of a car I suspected might be his, but it wasn't. It belonged to an old couple.'

He drained his glass and put it down. 'Now it all makes sense. You think your ex has been texting you, and I'm guessing that time we were coming back from Costa you thought you saw him?'

'Yeah, but it could have been my imagination working overtime. I've been on edge. I'm not actually sure it's him who keeps texting me. It could be some nutcase and I'm reading too much into it.'

'Right.' He paused and took a deep breath. 'Is there anything else I should know?'

'That's about everything.'

'Okay. I understand why you've been bottling all this up. It's even worse than I imagined.'

'What about Bryant? Are you going to tell him or not? About seeing Kapherr today, I mean.'

'I won't—but only if you promise to not pull any similar stunts. You have to stay off the Carew case, Shauna. You were lucky it was me who found out what you were doing. If it had been Hepplethwaite who phoned Kapherr he would have been in Baldy's office faster than a greyhound out the trap.'

'I'll stay home from now on, but could you keep me updated? I can still help, unofficially. I learnt something today that might be significant, in fact.'

'I'll think about it. The most important thing to tackle right now is your stalker.'

'What can we do? It's just a few text messages and I'm not even sure who they're from.'

'First thing tomorrow I'm going to see if I can find out what happened to your kids' murderer. But tell me what you learnt today.'

Penelope leaned on the window of her study, looking out, hugging herself. She was cold. Something was wrong with the central heating. It should have started up automatically at six o'clock so the house would be warm by the time she got up, but it hadn't. The temperature indoors was too low to not trip the thermostat. Usually, Michael would have taken a look at the system, only...

She swallowed.

Janet hadn't worked out her notice. Gilbert had gone home. The house was empty except for her. She recalled the racket Gilbert's children had made running across the hall, stamping up and down the stairs, screeching at the tops of their lungs as they played in the garden. At the time, the noise had been annoying. Now, she almost wished she could hear them again. The silence of Windleby hung heavy and cavernous.

It was time to sell up. Past time, considering her financial state. She'd clung onto the estate so long because it would have broken Bertrand's heart for it to leave the family, but Lauren's murder and Rupert's arrest had made the place entirely unliveable. Reporters would be hanging around for months until Rupert's trial and, regardless of the verdict, there would always be members of the public, true crime aficionados, turning up to gawk.

She would miss it. The distant memories, anyway. The last few years had been difficult, the most recent months horrendous. Where had it all gone wrong? What had *she* done wrong? Since her marriage she'd tried her best to navigate an unfamiliar world and learn its attitudes, behaviour, and language. She'd tried so hard, yet everything had fallen from her grasp. Her husband, the love of her life, had been snatched from her ridiculously young, before their children were even grown. Her daughter had been taken from her too, violently. And her son had transformed into a thing she barely recognised.

He was *not* her son.

He was all she had.

She moved away from the window and rubbed her upper arms. Perhaps she should call a plumber to fix the central heating. She definitely should, but somehow she couldn't motivate herself to do it. Previously, if Michael hadn't been able to repair something, Janet would have dealt with the problem. She didn't know what plumbing service her former housekeeper used to contact. All she'd had to do was to write a cheque in payment. Would the name of the company be on a cheque stub? She hovered near her bureau, unable to open it.

Something drew her out of the room. She stepped into the hall and then climbed the stairs to the upper floor. She knew where she was headed but wasn't sure she wanted to go there. Her legs seemed to carry her forwards without her input or consent.

At the end of the landing, two doors faced each other. Both stood closed. Faint traces of old sticky tape clung to one of the painted surfaces. As a boy, Rupert had taped a sign on his door, stating something like Private, Keep Out or some other nonsense. She'd made him take it down immediately but the damage had been done. She hadn't got around to having the door repainted.

Lauren's room was opposite Rupert's. She hadn't stuck anything to her door. She'd always been the easier child. Not perfect—her school reports were testament to that—but less trouble at home.

She turned the handle of Lauren's door and opened it. Her room was nearly bare. Her wardrobe and bookshelves were empty. A drawer jutted from the chest, also empty. She pulled out the other drawers, but they rattled, hollow in the frame. In her desk a few items

remained: blunt pencils, marbles, rubber bands, paper clips, marker pens, scrunchies, Kirby grips, coins, two grubby troll dolls and a bouncy ball. Whatever Rupert might have found here to take as a memento Penelope couldn't fathom. Lauren had done an excellent job of clearing the place. It was obvious she'd intended to never return.

Her daughter had been lost to her too. She just hadn't been able to admit it.

Why?

Had she really been such a terrible mother?

She turned and left.

Now she was outside Rupert's door. She hadn't been in his room in many years, not since she'd kicked him out at eighteen. One of the former housekeepers had seen to it that everything he hadn't taken with him was either given away or dumped. She'd wanted no trace left of the young man who had shamed the memory of his father. If Rupert had been remotely contrite or conciliatory she might not have taken such draconian action, but he'd been bold, angry, challenging. He'd cursed Bertrand to her face, uttering unmentionable slurs against his character. What he'd said was unforgivable and she had no regrets over what she'd done.

There seemed no point in opening the door that faced her yet she did it anyway.

She gasped.

Scrawled across the wall in giant letters were the words *FUCK YOU, BITCH.*

He must have written it when he'd come to the house after Lauren's murder.

A wave of black hatred emanating from the message washed over her.

Her chin trembled.

Had Rupert even wanted something to remember Lauren by? Or had he come here to purposely insult her, using his sister's death as a pretext to gain entry?

Her vision blurring, she blinked as her gaze roved the rest of the room. Nothing else appeared to have changed. The bare mattress sat

on the bed frame. The furniture held no trace of the boy who had grown up here.

His desk stood at the window overlooking the garden. As a child, he'd sometimes watched her while she was out there picking flowers or talking to Michael. She hadn't known at the time, except one day she'd happened to glance up at the right moment and seen him. They'd exchanged a happy wave and later he'd confessed he liked seeing her there while he did his homework. He would finish it faster knowing he would be able to go out and play. When the children were young she'd insisted they could only play in the grounds if she was there too.

She imagined the little boy, his small frame hunched over the desk, peeking out, pleased at what he saw. The scene was from another time, unreachable.

She crossed the room and pulled out the chair. Sitting down, she looked out of the window. The garden was a haze of green shoots, new growth bursting from brown twigs and pushing up through the soil. The plants had returned for another year. No matter what her mood the arrival of spring would always lift it, but this time she felt nothing. She wondered what Rupert made of his memory of the woman in the garden.

Crossing her arms on the desk, she rested her forehead on her wrists as tears slipped silently from her eyes.

Halfway up the garden path to her parents' front door, Sue halted. She hadn't been back to the so-ordinary, 1950s semi-detached house since Mum died, when she'd collected Dad to bring him to stay with her. The sight of the place she'd grown up in sparked mixed feelings: grief over her mother's death, nostalgia for her happy, simple childhood and fear over what Gemma would say when she asked her to come home.

The garden was overgrown, neglected in the months of Dad's absence. Mum would have been annoyed. She'd always had to push him to mow the lawn and weed the beds. He'd never been much help around the house, always down the Legion with his pals or off 'working'. Mum had been the steady one who'd brought in a regular pay packet every week from her job at the dry cleaners. Dad's income had varied according to whatever scheme had taken his fancy. Some had been more lucrative than others, when there would be a sudden boost in nice food, treats and outings. Then things would be tight and she would see the worry in her mother's face as she handed over money for school lunches.

That was the only way Sue had been able to track the success and failure of Dad's business speculations. He'd never talked about his work, not even to Mum as far as she could tell. Certainly, if Mum did

know more she'd never let on. As she grew up, Sue learnt not to bother asking where her father was or what he was doing. Mum's answers were always vague.

She hadn't cared very much about it except for those times at school when her friends would talk about what their fathers did and she couldn't join in. Otherwise, he'd been a good Dad—when he'd been home. And when Gemma had come along he'd seemed to take a step back from his business dealings to focus on his granddaughter. He'd been more present in Gemma's life than hers. Maybe he'd learnt from his mistakes. She'd pushed aside her minor jealous gripes, grateful to have another loving figure in her daughter's corner.

When she'd married Peter, she'd hoped to add another member to Gemma's team but it hadn't been so. Peter's affection for his stepchild had melted away soon after their wedding day. Gemma had soon joined his long list of things to complain about, though he *had* provided for her. She had to give him that. Her daughter's life had been privileged. She'd grown up in affluent circumstances Sue could never have managed to supply alone. Had the financial support been worth sticking around for? It was impossible to tell.

She stepped the last few metres to the house and rang the bell.

Dad's expression was grave as he answered the door. 'Hello, love. Come in.'

'Gemma's home?' She hadn't phoned to say she was coming over in case her daughter went out in order to avoid her.

'She's up in her room. I'll get her. Make yourself some tea.'

She went into the kitchen, the familiarity of the old Formica-covered units and lino flooring washing over her. In the two days since Dad and Gemma had been living here, while she'd been screwing up the courage to confront her daughter about why she'd left home, it looked like neither of them had cleaned up after themselves. Used mugs, plates and saucepans were piled in the sink and the rubbish bin was on the verge of overflowing with ready meal packaging, tea bags and food packet wrappers.

She filled the kettle and then let the tap run down the side of the washing up bowl until the water turned hot. Then she moved the stream into the bowl and added a squirt of washing up liquid.

'Leave that,' said Dad, appearing in the kitchen doorway. 'I was getting around to it.'

'And how long would it be before you actually did it?'

'I was building up a full bowl.'

'*Dad.*'

'Gemma's in the living room.' He began to wash up.

Sue carried through two mugs of tea and set one down in front of her daughter.

Gemma was wearing her favourite colour: black. Black leggings and socks, and a black hoodie with a skull on the front. She didn't have clothes in any other colour as far as Sue was aware. And she'd also been dying her hair black for years. Her natural colour was a beautiful chestnut brown. Sue had always thought it a shame Gemma covered it up but she'd never said anything, fearful of upsetting her daughter's delicate emotional state. As usual, she also wore an almost-white foundation and outlined her eyes with black eye-liner. Her lips were the only part of her appearance that was not black or white. They were vivid scarlet, like a gash.

Sue was reminded of the disturbing painting of a woman screaming she'd seen in Gemma's bedroom the morning after she'd stayed out all night. Had the picture portrayed how she felt inside? The therapist she'd seen while she'd been at school had said never to prevent or discourage her from creating art because it was an outlet for her emotions. Peter had scoffed, but then he was scornful of most things, especially anything to do with feelings and psychiatric illness.

'How are you feeling?' Sue asked. She didn't want to start by inviting Gemma to return home. She didn't want to put too much pressure on her.

Gemma murmured, not meeting her gaze, 'All right.'

'You're not, though, are you? Or else why would you have come to live with your granddad?'

'It makes sense, Mum. I can help Pops and he won't have to live alone. I've decided to stay here for as long as he needs me.'

Her heart sinking, Sue cast a glance around the living room, which was crying out for a dust and a Hoover. She couldn't imagine

what the house would look like after a few months of the two of them living together.

'It makes *more* sense for you to live with me and your father,' she said, 'where I can look after you.'

'Don't call him that. He isn't my father. My dad died before I was born. Anyway, I'm too big to need looking after. I should leave home. That's what Peter wants.'

'It isn't!'

'Mum, stop lying. He's wanted me out for...I don't know how long. All my life. He doesn't love me. He doesn't even like me.'

'That isn't true. I mean, sometimes he might say—'

'Yes, it is. Do you think I can't hear what he says when you argue? And even if I couldn't he doesn't have to state it. He tells me with every look and sarcastic comment. Sometimes, I think he actually hates me.'

'Don't say that. Of course he doesn't hate you. Or why would he have supported you all these years?' Sue bit her lip. She hadn't meant to let that point slip out. The last thing she wanted was for her daughter to feel like a burden.

'Because he loves playing the victim,' Gemma said. 'He loves having a hold over you and making you feel guilty about keeping me around. It's how he controls you.'

'You're wrong,' Sue replied, more vehemently than she'd intended. 'It's nothing like that. It's complicated. You have to judge people by their actions, not their words. Peter has worked hard for us for all our married life, putting a roof over our heads and food in our bellies. He paid for your education, clothes, holidays, everything.'

Gemma grimaced, disgusted. 'Shut up, Mum. You sound exactly like him. It's disgusting when you parrot his words.'

'I'm not...' Sue's skin prickled and an uncomfortable feeling grew in her stomach. 'Love, it's nice that you want to help your granddad, but this isn't going to work out. You're not your nan. She was used to doing everything for him. It was the way she was brought up. You don't want to tie yourself down looking after an old man. You're young. You have your whole future ahead of you.'

A cough sounded behind her. Her Dad stood in the kitchen doorway, arms folded over his chest.

She flushed. 'Sorry, Dad. But it's true. It isn't fair to bring Gemma here just so she can keep house for you. You'd both be better off at mine and Peter's.'

'That isn't why she's here and you know it. It's time you woke up and admitted to yourself what's going on and what's *been* going on most of your daughter's life. But if you refuse to admit it, I don't care. My granddaughter needs somewhere to go to get away from your— what do they call it these days? Yeah, your toxic marriage.'

'Toxic? How dare you! What makes you think you have the right to criticise my relationship? Do you think Mum had it any better living with you? You were never home, and when you were home you never helped out. She worked a full time job and did all the housework and looked after me. At least Peter doesn't have *me* slaving away all day and night keeping things going while he's off gallivanting, doing who knows what, and only turning up when it suits him!'

Without registering the movement, Sue had risen to her feet during this speech, the words spilling out, bypassing her brain and any conscious thought. She'd come here to help her daughter and suddenly she'd found herself under attack. What a cheek this pair had to cast aspersions on her and Peter.

'Gemma, you're welcome home any time,' she said stiffly. 'Any time at all. And that's from me *and* Peter.' To her father, she said, 'I'll show myself out.'

R epulsion so severe she thought she might be sick flooded
through Penelope as the prison guard searched her,
moving her hands up and down her legs and patting her
sides. If she'd known she would have to go through this she would
never have come here. Her decision had been borderline at best. She
didn't truly know why she'd come, except it was an alternative to
sitting alone in Windleby, listening to the wind rattling the windows
in their frames.

'Step over there, please,' said the guard before moving on to the
next visitor.

The remand centre was revolting. Green and yellow paint like the
vomit of someone suffering a disease was the only adornment of the
bare walls. Dirty, scuffed tiles covered the floor, cracked and broken in
places. Worst of all was the smell: a mixture of disinfectant and
unwashed bodies. She suspected the odour of stale sweat came from
some of the other visitors. Dressed in cheap tat, sporting home hair-
cuts, every other utterance a swear word, they were society's dregs. A
mother with a toddler in a pushchair stood at the end of the queue.
Who would bring a baby to a place like this? The guard was giving the
pushchair a thorough going over, no doubt looking for drugs.

A buzzer sounded and a door unlocked. The visitors filed through

into a room set up with tables and chairs. At each table sat a man. She was surprised to see the prisoners wore ordinary clothes. She'd been expecting them to wear uniforms.

She held back. There was still time to leave. She could tell a guard she'd changed her mind or that she felt unwell. Someone pushed roughly past her. The visitors were zeroing in on the people they were here to see, joining them.

She saw him. He'd already spotted her and reacted with his usual lazy, arrogant, sardonic smile. The urge to leave redoubled. What good could possibly come from this?

Yet she stayed. He could have refused to see her but he hadn't. Was it because he wanted to taunt her with Lauren's death? Did he want to enhance his revenge by seeing the pain in her eyes? Drawn by an irresistible force she weaved through the happily reunited groups to Rupert's table and sat down.

'I didn't bring you anything, I'm afraid,' she said. 'I didn't know what was allowed or what you might need.'

He didn't reply, only stared in silence. He looked almost as bad as he had the day he'd come to the house. His cheeks had filled out somewhat and lost some of their pallor. It was hard to reconcile his appearance with the baby she had birthed two minutes after his sister. His sleeves were rolled up and he had a tattoo of a dragon on one of his forearms. She recalled the detective asking if Lauren had a tattoo.

'How have you been?' she asked.

Still he didn't reply.

'If you've brought me here just for your amusement,' she said, 'I'll leave.'

'No, stay.' He reached out as if to touch her arm but then drew back, slumping in his seat. 'I didn't really believe you'd come.'

'I didn't really believe it myself.'

While the people surrounding them chattered, laughed, bickered, and cried, they sat and stared at each other, not speaking. After her initial statements, Penelope's stock of small talk had dried up. She didn't know how to bridge the gulf of pain, anger and shame that separated her from this young man. She wasn't sure she wanted to try. What would Bertrand think? Surely he would disapprove, especially

considering the accusation against their son and their son's accusations against him.

What kept Rupert silent now, she didn't know. She continued to suspect he was playing with her. Life on remand had to be excessively boring.

'How are you dealing with your, um, addiction?' she asked.

'Pretending to be a caring mother at last?' he sneered. 'It doesn't suit you.'

'Rupert, I'm trying. God help me, I'm trying.'

He curled a lip in disbelief but said, 'They have me on methadone. It isn't the same, but what's a man to do?'

'I'm...sorry. I know it must be hard.'

'Aha,' he said, 'I finally have it.'

'What?'

'I've figured out why you're here. You're lonely. Uncle Gil's gone back to the US. Lauren's dead – not that you had any contact with her anyway. Mike's gone too, and I'm guessing you sacked yet another housekeeper. You're all alone and you've finally figured out you need people, that you aren't quite the self-sufficient, superior person you thought you were. My father's family never did have much to do with you, did they? Except for Uncle Gil. They kind of pretended to like you while my sperm donor was alive but after he died they cut you off like a—'

'Don't call your father that!' she spluttered though quietly, mindful of others in the room.

'What? Sperm donor?' Rupert asked innocently.

'He deserves your respect,' she hissed. 'He loved you very much.' She dreaded making a scene amongst these lowlifes. The very notion of them laughing at her made her skin crawl, but she couldn't allow Rupert to disparage Bertrand.

'I don't disagree,' he said, 'although I'm not sure I would call it *love*. The main point on which we differ is how he expressed it.'

'*Don't.*'

This was what she'd been dreading. Why did he have to bring up this ridiculous allegation again after all these years, when it had

caused so many problems between them? Why couldn't he accept he was mistaken or just let it go?

'Don't what?' he asked, his gaze level.

'You know what. Whatever happened between you two, whatever you think he did, it's in the past now. It's over.'

'No, it isn't.' He leaned over the table, turning paler than she thought possible. 'It isn't over for *me*. And I didn't imagine what he did. I remember it all, vividly. So vividly you wouldn't believe it. You can deny it all you like, pretend it's all a big mistake, but that doesn't make what he did to me any less true. And I'll tell you something else to make your hair curl. I don't think it was only him. I think there were more of them involved. The problem is, a lot of the time I couldn't see, but I'd swear it wasn't only him.' His face twisted in fury. 'I'd bet my *life* on it!'

She stared at him, appalled, and rose to leave.

'Everything all right here?' asked a prison officer.

She started. The officer had wandered up behind her without her noticing.

'Yes,' said Rupert. 'It's all hunky dory here. We're getting along like a house on fire, aren't we, Mother? Best conversation we've had in years.'

She sat down and glared, unmoving, until the officer had walked away.

'You know what pisses me off the most?' Rupert asked. Without waiting for her answer, he continued, 'Your ingratitude.'

'Ingratitude? What on Earth do you think I have to be grateful for?'

'I could have told the authorities about dear Bertie and his little gang. I could have told Uncle Gil or other relatives—though perhaps they already knew or were involved themselves. Any number of people. I could have brought disaster down on our little family, but I didn't. I only told you, at first. And, being the wonderful mother you are, you saw fit to disbelieve me.'

'What do you mean you only told me at first? Who else did you tell?'

'Straight to the most important point, hmm? Don't worry. The

only other person I told was Lauren.' As he uttered his sister's name, pain flitted over his features, a glimpse of his internal struggle flared, then it was gone. The defiant mask descended. 'Everyone else thinks you kicked me out just because I'm gay.'

'Around the time she graduated?' she asked softly.

He nodded once.

'That explains it.'

'She didn't want anything to do with you after that. I'm not sorry, in case you were wondering.'

Penelope looked down at her hands, folded in her lap. At a loss for words, her chest heaved as she fought down a rising tidal wave of emotions. When she had mastered herself, she asked, 'Have you heard from your solicitor?'

'Not today. I didn't have much to say to her, and things have gone quiet anyway. I would thank you for getting me top-notch legal representation but I know it's just because you want to salvage what's left of the family name.'

She replied heavily, 'I'm glad you accepted my help in the end. I won't try to deny I want to save our reputation.'

'Good. Some honesty at last.'

'That isn't the only reason. I don't want you to go to prison, Rupert. I do still care for you, despite everything.' As she spoke, she was surprised to realise she was stating the truth.

'I wish I could say the same.'

His words cut into her, icy hot. Yet she couldn't blame him. He believed his memories of Bertrand's actions were real. He clearly wasn't making it up. He'd suffered more than anyone from his delusions, yet he seemed to continue to add to them, thinking up additional actors in the depravity. It made sense of his addiction and transient lifestyle. In the circumstances, it was no wonder he despised her.

'If it means anything to you,' she said, 'I don't believe you killed Lauren.'

'It's nice to be believed about *something*, but frankly it amazes me you could even entertain the idea. My sister wasn't perfect, but I loved her.'

'I don't understand why the police have arrested you. Do you know what evidence they have?'

'All they've shown me is a picture they have of someone who looks like me buying packing tape the day of the murder.'

'Packing tape?'

His voice thick, he said, 'The murderer put it over her mouth.'

'Oh,' she murmured. After a pause, she said, 'Someone who looks like you?'

'Yes, it has to be, though I can't remember the picture very well. I was still high at that interview.'

'You have to fight this.'

'What's the point? I'm just a useless junkie. Why would the police believe me? They have their evidence and they want to close the case.'

'But you have to tell them the truth about where you were and what you were doing when Lauren was murdered. Do you have an alibi?'

'I don't think so. I can't remember, and, anyway, it would be a waste of everyone's time. I might as well plead guilty. You get three square meals and a place to sleep in prison. And, as I said, methadone isn't too bad. I might get used to it.'

'Rupert, you can't give up.'

'Why not? You gave up on me.'

'I...'

She recalled the little boy at his bedroom window.

Gilbert Carter's words filtered into her mind. *He's a sweet kid.*

Could she have been wrong all these years? Could her son's accusations against Bertrand really be true?

S hauna had to kneel down to reach into the back of the alcove in her bedroom that served as a wardrobe. Pushing aside her hanging clothes, she grabbed the edge of a cardboard box and dragged it out. It contained the detritus of her earlier life before she'd moved to Cambridge: photograph albums, certificates, bank documents, her kids' health care records, so many items. She could probably throw most of them away. Digging through the layers, she found what she was looking for and pulled it out.

She held an old sketchbook from the time she'd begun birdwatching. It contained her attempts at drawing the birds, soon given up when she'd accepted she was no artist. She opened it, leafed through the terrible sketches with a grimace, until she hit clean, plain paper. She tore off a couple of the large sheets and returned the book to its rightful place at the bottom of the pile.

After taking the sheets downstairs she rooted in her bag for a pen. A pencil would have been better in case she made mistakes but that would have entailed a trip to the local newsagents and she didn't feel like going outside. She couldn't shake the feeling she was being watched.

She placed a sheet of paper on her coffee table and wrote two names at the top of it: Douglas Hunt and Jack Muncey. Underneath

each name she wrote the year of their deaths, 1942. She drew a line next to Muncey but couldn't remember the name of his wife so she wrote a question mark. Next, she drew a vertical line descending from the 'marriage' line and wrote beneath it John Robert Muncey.

Had Douglas Hunt been married when he disappeared, everyone at Duxworth presuming he'd died in the Spitfire crash? She didn't know but it shouldn't be too hard to find out. Next to his name she wrote the name of his brother, Commander Ernest Hunt.

Edith Brown had said something about 'that nasty business' involving Douglas Hunt. What had that been about? It was a shame she hadn't been able to talk to her for longer. Maybe Will could get another interview but she feared she'd killed that goose.

Towards the bottom of the page she wrote Penelope Carew, drew a link and then wrote Bertrand Carew. Beneath the two names she listed their offspring, Rupert and Lauren. Next to Bertrand she wrote Gilbert Carter. What names should appear in the blank spaces, across the span of decades, connecting the past and the present? Gil had said his and 'Bertie's' grandfathers had been brothers. Her gaze travelled up to Ernest and Douglas Hunt.

Could it be possible?

The surnames were different but that could easily be explained by marriage. Will had made the same failure to connect her and her children. And Gil had been unsettled by the question about family connections with the RAF.

Her pulse quickening, she picked up her mobile and called Will.

He answered immediately but then told her to wait a minute.

There was the sound of a door opening and closing.

'You can't phone me at work,' he said. 'It's going to look suspicious if I keep ducking out to take calls.'

'Sorry, I won't do it again. Or I'll text. But I think I might be onto something.'

'I think you are. I just got off the phone to Mrs Hendricks.'

'You did? What did she say?'

'You were right. You've pulled an absolute blinder, Shauna. Her father *is* John Robert Muncey, Jack Muncey's son. I don't know how you saw it. I had a look at the photo Kapherr showed you and even if I

did remember that old man we saw at the mistaken mispers, Gemma Hendricks', house weeks ago, which I don't, I would never have spotted the resemblance.'

'He's the spitting image of his dad, minus the hair and plus a lot of wrinkles.'

'You must have a helluva memory for faces.'

'Well, I'm glad I'm right but I still don't know what it means. Except it's an unbelievable coincidence that on the same date Jack Muncey died his great granddaughter went missing and Lauren Carew was murdered.'

'Rupert Carew has to know something.'

'He isn't going to help us. He'll only incriminate himself. We have to figure this out by ourselves.'

'You're not wrong,' said Will. 'He's finally started talking, though only to his solicitor.'

'He agreed to representation?'

'Mummy's bought him the best.'

'Shit.'

'Yeah. Sorry.'

The implication didn't need to be stated. Now Rupert Carew had a member of the legal profession on his side, he surely wouldn't waste any time in filing a complaint about her conduct at his interview. The best she could hope for after the investigation was a slap on the wrist so Cambridgeshire Police could save face. If she kept her job she would never rise any higher. *If* she kept her job.

'The solicitor says Carew proclaims his innocence,' said Will. 'We're going to be facing a hard fight to get him convicted.'

Pushing aside her own problems, she said, 'But this new connection with John Muncey is a start.'

'Yes, and that isn't all. Connor found plenty of results on HOLMES for the Muncey family. That was why the name rang a bell for me. Crime used to be worse in Cambridge, and if this place could ever be said to have had a Mafia—which it really can't—the Munceys were tied up with it. Old coppers used to talk about the family. Bryant might remember them.'

'Pilot Jack Muncey's son was involved in organised crime? Was he ever convicted?'

'He was arrested plenty of times but he always managed to stay out of jail.'

'I wonder if Rupert Carew knows him. Lady Penelope's son mixing with riff-raff due to his addiction.'

'Lady Penelope?'

'Uh, that's what I call Mrs Carew in my head.'

Will chuckled. 'There's something else. I did some more digging around about the family. Jack Muncey's sister died in 1942 as well.'

'What killed her?'

'Sepsis.'

'Gee, they dropped like flies in those days. Thank God for the NHS. By the way, I had another idea. What do you think about the possibility that Gil Carter and the Carews might be related to Douglas and Ernest Hunt? Carter said his and the late Mr Carew's grandfathers were brothers.'

'That's quite a stretch.'

'I know, but it's worth investigating, right?'

'I'll get Connor on it. He's good at tracing people.'

'Connor's speaking to you again?'

A breath of a sigh came down the line, then, 'Talking of tracing people...' Will's tone became more serious when he said, 'Shauna, there's something I have to tell you. Are you sitting down?'

'This isn't about the Carew case, is it?'

'No, it isn't.'

'I'm not sure I want to hear it.'

'I think you should. And I think you should talk to Baldy about it.'

The excitement at making progress in the case drained away, leaving her empty. Dread slowly filled the hollow. 'What did you find out?'

'The report states...' He paused. 'The part you need to know is that when the car was dragged from the water, the driver's side window was open. Divers searched the river for your ex's body but it was never found. I looked him up. Seven years after his disappearance he was declared dead. None of his bank accounts had been accessed

in that time and there had been no sightings of him. Officially, he doesn't exist.'

'Right.' She felt numb. What was she supposed to make of this new information? Was her children's murderer dead or wasn't he? Had it been him she'd seen in the street?

'Are you going to come in and explain to Bryant what's been going on?' Will asked.

'What can I tell him? You just said my ex is officially deceased.'

'That's not the point. It gives a reason for your behaviour.'

'It tells our DCI he can't rely on me. Not until this problem in my life is resolved. And I'm not sure it ever will be.'

'We can retrieve the texts you deleted, make a report about what you thought you—'

'And make myself sound mentally ill. That's the exact opposite of what I need right now. It would be best if I have a few therapy sessions, say something about stress and pretend I'm all better.'

Will asked, 'How is that going to help anything?'

'It'll get me back to work. I'm going insane sitting here at home all day. This is harder than being taunted over text messages.'

'Have you received any more?'

'No, nothing lately.'

'Do you think you might have seen him hanging around?'

'No, I haven't. I'm becoming convinced I saw a few dodgy texts from a perp I arrested once and I've blown it all out of proportion.'

'If you say so.' Will sounded doubtful.

'I do. Let me know what else you find out about the Carew case, okay? I'll keep thinking about it and see if there's anything else I can suggest.'

'All right. Do me a favour, though. Keep your doors locked.'

'I always do.'

After she hung up, Shauna returned her attention to her family trees. She drew a line from John Robert Muncey and wrote Mrs Hendricks. Below Mrs Hendricks, at the end of another line, she wrote Gemma Hendricks. She chewed the end of her pen.

As the detective hung up, Sue had a feeling she'd done something wrong. Why had he wanted to know Dad's name? Yet she couldn't lie. Lying to the police could get you into a world of trouble. So she'd told him her father's full name right away. The man had also wanted to know Dad's address. Should she warn him the police might turn up? Could he be in trouble? He was just an old man. Though he'd caused a lot of upset by taking Gemma to live with him, he hadn't done anything illegal. Gemma was an adult and she'd gone with him of her own free will.

'Who was that?' Peter asked sharply, coming into the living room. He was always suspicious when she took phone calls. Not that she'd ever given him cause. It was just one of his more irritating traits.

'One of the detectives who came here when Gemma went missing.' She was busy texting her daughter, telling her to pass on the message about the phone call to Dad.

'Really? What did he want? She hasn't run off again, has she?'

After hitting Send, she replied, 'She didn't run off the first time!'

'Didn't she? Do *you* know where she spent the night? Did she ever tell you?'

Sue couldn't deny she had no idea what Gemma had been doing that night, but she didn't want to give Peter the satisfaction of hearing

her admit it. 'That isn't the point. She came back the next morning. If she'd run away she wouldn't have come back, would she?'

'It was probably your father who persuaded her to return. He was hatching a plan for them to create a big scene and leave together.'

'That's ridiculous. Why would he do that?'

'So he can complete his plan of turning you against me. He knows if you have to choose between me and Gemma you'll pick your daughter every time. So he persuades her to leave under the pretence I've done something wrong, knowing you'll blame me.'

'You've been telling me she needs to leave home for the last five years! You've got what you wanted and now you're complaining about it. Dear God. Not everything is about you, Peter. You aren't the centre of the universe.' She paused for breath. Pressure was building up inside her. Years of listening to his endless griping and sarcastic comments, putting up with his penny pinching, having to justify every purchase she made with 'his' money.

The dam broke and words flowed from her in a torrent.

'And, for your information, I was already against you. Dad didn't have to do a thing. I try my best to defend you to people. Lord knows why. Maybe I'm just ashamed I'm still married to you. But no matter what I say to anyone else, in truth I'm sick to the back teeth of you and have been for a very long while.'

He opened his mouth to speak. Perhaps he did speak. She wasn't paying attention. She raised her voice to drown him out regardless.

'Do you have any idea what you're like to live with? You're a miserable, endlessly moaning worm. From the moment you wake up until you go to sleep you're constantly seeking out things to complain about. I don't think I've seen you smile in years, let alone laugh. You're a drain to be around. You're exhausting. When you leave for work in the mornings I breathe a sigh of relief. I steel myself for your return at night, and I spend my weekends avoiding you or finding distractions to shut you up for five minutes and give me and Gemma a rest.'

Peter's lips had thinned to a line.

She didn't care how he felt. Now she'd started she had to finish. And when had he ever cared about anyone except himself? 'Gemma said you use your income to keep a hold over me, and she's right.

That's why you never wanted me to get a job. If I had my own wages I would have some control over my life. But you wanted to keep me trapped, beholden to you, forced to listen to the drivel you spout. I loved you once, but now I don't know what I ever saw in you. The only thing I can think is that you were pretending to be nice until I had a ring on my finger. Then you started to show your true colours, when it was hard for me to leave, and next you made it harder by making me dependent on you. Well, I'm not putting up with it anymore. I am leaving you. Now.'

Breathless, she pushed past him and ran upstairs to pack.

Her speech and decision had come in a rush. She hadn't known when she began that it would end with their separation, but it felt right and it had certainly been a long time coming.

She took a suitcase out of the wardrobe in their bedroom and lifted it onto the bed. After opening it she began to throw clothes in randomly, fearful that if she slowed down she might reconsider. Already, a little voice at the back of her mind nagged her, telling her she was doing the wrong thing, that she should talk things out with her husband, maybe go to marriage counselling. But no amount of counselling could change who Peter was and if she didn't leave now she might never leave. Part of the reason she'd stayed so long was because of who *she* was and that wouldn't change either.

'I see your dear father's plan succeeded,' said Peter, leaning on the door frame.

'This has nothing to do with him. This is all about you and me. You've known this would happen eventually. You can't deny it. You can't tell me you expected me to put up with you forever.' She swept dresses, blouses, coats and jackets on their hangers out of the wardrobe, folded them in half in a great lump and pushed them into the suitcase on top of her underwear. Tucking in the edges of clothes hanging out, she closed the lid and zipped it up. She'd left so many things behind but she could come back for them later.

Sliding the suitcase off the bed she stepped towards the door.

'All right,' Peter sneered. 'You've made your point.' He straightened up, effectively blocking her exit.

'I'm not making a point. I'm leaving you. Get out of my way.'

'Don't be stupid, Sue. What will you live on? Your father's pension? That isn't enough to support one person, let alone two additional leeches.'

'I'll get a job.'

He laughed. 'Who's going to give you a job? A middle-aged woman with no work experience and no skills? You've got to be joking.'

'Someone will give me something. Maybe I could work in a complaints department. I have plenty of experience of that.' She pushed up against him, gripping the handle of her suitcase tightly. 'I said, move out of my way!'

'What if I won't?' He leaned down until his nose hovered an inch from hers. 'What are you going to do about it?'

Several scenarios ran through Sue's head. She was dreadfully tempted to bite his nose, sink her teeth in until he screamed. Another possibility involved driving her knee into his groin. But she'd never been an impulsive person. If she had, she would have done this years ago.

'Peter,' she said evenly, 'if you don't allow me to leave I will phone the police. And if you try to stop me, if you lay a finger on me, I will fight back. I will attack your face first and you'll have to explain to your manager on Monday exactly why you're covered in scratches.'

He turned puce and his eyes appeared ready to pop from their orbits. 'You wouldn't...' He paused and his expression softened. 'We should talk about this. There's no need to throw twenty-odd years down the pan. I've been stressed lately. Maybe I have been difficult to live with, but that doesn't have to last forever. I could look for another job, closer to home so I don't have to—'

'Move!'

The idea that she would want to spend *more* time in his company was laughable. Hadn't he listened to a word she'd said?

When he still didn't comply she shoved him aside, elbowing him in the ribs. Her suitcase was too large and heavy to carry down the stairs so she slid it down, descending quickly beside it and almost falling as she reached the bottom.

Peter watched from the landing. 'Sue, don't go.'

The speed of his climb down from arrogant disregard of her feel-ings was spectacular. It wasn't enough for her to stick around, however. She picked up her handbag from the hall stand, slung it over her shoulder, and left.

The suitcase barely fit in the boot of the Yaris. Her car was so much older and smaller than Peter's, but it was all she needed. As she drove from the driveway, she spotted him in the rear view mirror. The scarlet hue had returned to his face, and he must have been beside himself with rage because she faintly heard him scream, '*Bitch!*' after he was out of sight.

Twenty minutes later, she pulled up outside Dad's house. She hadn't let him know she was coming. Despite their disagreement about Gemma, she knew she would always be welcome in her child-hood home. He and her daughter would be glad she'd finally left Peter. She would apologise for how she'd acted, they would make up, and, once the divorce was over, she would begin her new life. She wasn't as confident about getting a job as she'd made out to Peter but maybe she could do a training course. She would be entitled to some of the marital assets. The money should be enough to tide her over for a while.

She pulled the suitcase on its wheels up the garden path and rang the doorbell.

No one answered.

She rapped the knocker.

Still, no one came to the door.

Maybe they'd gone out, but it didn't matter. She had a key.

She unlocked the door, pushed it part way open and called inside, 'Dad! Gemma! It's me.'

The house was silent. They must have gone somewhere.

She hefted her suitcase over the little step and closed the door. Taking out her phone, she texted Gemma, explaining the situation. While waiting for a reply she made herself some tea, and then sat in the living room, keeping watch through the net curtains in case Peter turned up to harangue her. He would guess where she was soon enough.

Peter didn't arrive, thankfully, but neither did Gemma or Dad. Nor

did her daughter reply to the text. It was very strange. She waited more than two hours, sending several more texts as the time dragged out, expecting minute by minute to either see or hear from her father or daughter, before she decided to investigate further.

She went upstairs to her old bedroom, where Gemma slept whenever she came to stay with her grandparents. The room was empty and in disarray. The wardrobe door was open and half-empty drawers jutted out, as if Gemma had left the house in the same hurry she had left Peter.

Sue sat on the bed. Where had her daughter and father gone?

36

When Shauna arrived at Cambridge Central, Will was waiting for her at the bottom of the steps.

'I'm honoured, but there's no need for a formal welcome,' she joked. 'I've only been gone a few days.'

'I wanted to tell you the story DCI Bryant and I agreed before you go in so you don't mess things up.'

'It's DCI Bryant now, is it? What happened to Baldy? Or is the nickname out since you two got so close?' She regretted the words almost before they were out of her mouth, but she couldn't help feeling the pang of professional jealousy that Will had their boss's ear, that he must have stepped into her place as his favourite.

Will gave her a pained look.

'Sorry,' she murmured. 'I am grateful for what you did for me, persuading Bryant to let me come back to work.'

'Call it my self-interest if it makes you feel better. We need you on the team if we're going to get a conviction, and Bryant knows it too.'

'But you didn't have to tell him it was me who recognised Jack Muncey's son. You could have let him assume it was you and taken the credit.'

'It was the main reason he agreed to your return and, besides, you know me better than that.'

'How did you spin it? I shouldn't have been at Kapherr's office or seen the photograph.'

'I implied you'd seen the photo before you took your leave of absence, but the resemblance to Gemma Hendricks' granddad didn't dawn on you until later.'

'Okay, that works. And what did you tell the others about why I've been away?'

'Your mother died and she lived in the US so you had to fly out to the funeral.'

'My mother? That's a bit personal.'

'It had to be serious for you to take so much time off.'

'Fair enough.'

'I also told the DCs you don't want to talk about it.'

'You're a genius. Remind me to never trust you again.'

'I didn't think you trusted me now.'

'I don't, but...about you reporting me to Bryant...'

'Yeah?'

'It was the right thing to do, and in your shoes I would have done the same. You're forgiven.'

They began to climb the steps.

'Thanks,' he said. 'It's nice to have one woman in my life forgiving me.'

'How *is* Beth Parker, by the way?'

'Hasn't spoken to me since the party.'

'I don't blame her.'

'Neither do I, to be honest.'

The automatic doors slid apart and they walked into the reception area.

Before they reached the incident room, Will said, 'Are you sure you don't want to pursue this thing with your ex? If anyone can find out if he still exists, it's us.'

'I know that, but it would mean opening an investigation. I would have to go over everything that happened. I don't think I'm ready to do that yet, if ever. And there's no guarantee anyone would take me seriously anyway. I could put myself through it all again only for some by-the-book superintendent to say no. I just can't face it.'

His hand on the door handle, Will said, 'I think you're making a mistake, but it's your call.' He opened the door.

Alfie, Connor and Jas nodded their hellos, clearly mindful of Shauna's supposed grieving state.

Inside the incident room, photographs of Lauren Carew's corpse stuck out starkly on the display board. One photo focused on her tattooed arm. Next to it stood a blown-up still of the DIY shop CCTV recording, showing her brother's corresponding skin art. Also on the board were pictures of Michael Battersby in death and a snap of him when he was much younger. Someone had obtained copies of Jack Muncey and Douglas Hunt's RAF photos too. Penelope Carew was represented by a media shot of her presenting a prize at a fair. She was standing beside a man Shauna didn't recognise.

Then she saw someone she *did* recognise. 'Well done for finding John Muncey.'

'The Cambridge Times covered a British Legion charity event four years ago,' Connor explained. 'It was hard to locate him at first. The RAF hadn't had any luck. So I tried variations on his name. He goes by his second name, Robert, shortened to Bob.'

Shauna peered at the caption. *Event organisers, from right to left, Bob Muncey...* 'Great work. Did you find out anything else about him?'

'Not a lot. He's a pensioner now. Before that he was self-employed, buying and selling stuff.'

'A Del Boy?'

'Exactly. I've got his address if you want to talk to him.'

'Fantastic. What about the Carews, Carters and Hunts? Are they related?'

Jas cleared her throat. 'I looked them up while Connor was working on Muncey. It was easy to trace the Carew line through marriage and birth registrations. Bertrand Carew's mother's name was Marcia Hunt, daughter of Ernest Hunt.'

'Bingo,' said Will. 'The camp commander.'

'What about Gilbert Carter?' Shauna asked. 'He said his and Bertrand's grandfathers were brothers. Were there any other brothers apart from Douglas and Ernest?'

'The only other sibling was a sister who died as a baby.'

'That has to mean Carter's grandfather was Douglas.'

'There's no record of Douglas Hunt ever having married,' said Jas. 'His death certificate states he died in the crash in 1942.'

'Maybe he had children out of wedlock,' Will suggested. 'It was shameful back then.'

Shauna said, 'Jas, look up birth certificates prior to Hunt's death that state his name as the father. Maybe that's the explanation.' She was convinced Gil Carter had lied in his interview about his family not having connections with the RAF. What she didn't know was what he was trying to cover up, but she doubted it was something as innocuous as illegitimacy.

Will said, 'Bob Muncey can't know his father's body was found at the dig.'

'Good point,' said Shauna. 'Someone will have to tell him, preferably the RAF. Alfie, could you inform Dr Kapherr we've found him? She'll know who to contact. Meanwhile, we need to interview Rupert Carew again.'

'Is it worth it?' Will asked. 'Now he has a fancy lawyer he'll be shut tighter than a clam.'

'We have more facts to throw at him. Even if he doesn't answer any questions we might be able to read something from his reactions.'

RUPERT CAREW FASTENED his gaze on Shauna the moment she entered the interview room. His arms folded over his chest, his eyes followed her as she sat down and opened her file. Will had said their suspect hadn't made a complaint about her previous conduct yet. Perhaps he felt he had some kind of power over her, that he was hanging an unspoken threat like Damocles' sword over her head. Regardless, she couldn't let him make her flustered.

After recording the necessary information at the beginning of the tape, she led with the photos. Taking them out of the folder one by one, she oriented them to the right way up from Carew's perspective, and then slid them across the table to him.

They were all perspectives of his sister, taken at the crime scene

and at the post-mortem. For people unaccustomed to the graphic horror of murder, they were shocking. She doubted the man had seen pictures like this before, even in the course of his day-to-day junkie life.

His gaze broke from hers and travelled from photograph to photograph, silently absorbing the staring eyes, torn fingernails, bruised neck and naked corpse, skin the colour of death.

'Are you actually planning to ask my client any questions?' the solicitor asked sardonically.

'I'm working up to it,' said Shauna.

The solicitor huffed and crossed her legs.

To allow time for the horrible reality of the pictures to sink in, Shauna began with a different aspect of the murder. 'Mr Carew, from the beginning of this enquiry we've been wondering why your sister's body was dumped at an archaeological dig. We've discovered this place was not chosen at random. The date of the World War Two plane crash on the site and the murder are the same, so there's clearly a link. Now we know the link centres on your family. Your great-grandfather Ernest Hunt was the commander of the airbase from where the plane took off, and his brother, Douglas Hunt, was supposed to have been the pilot killed in the crash. It turns out it was in fact another man, Jack Muncey. Does any of this mean anything to you?'

Carew glared at her, then leaned towards his solicitor to whisper in her ear.

She whispered back and then said, 'My client declines to comment.'

'I'm surprised,' said Shauna. 'I would have thought if there was no connection you would take the opportunity to clear your name.'

'It's hard to prove a negative, detective,' said the solicitor. 'Mr Carew has nothing to say on the matter.'

'Perhaps we can come back to that,' said Shauna. 'Rupert, you see this parcel tape over the victim's mouth?' She pointed at the relevant picture.

The anger in his features was replaced by another emotion.

Shauna couldn't tell what he was feeling, but the photographs of his handiwork had unsettled him.

'No comment.'

She said into the tape recorder, 'We know you bought the same brand and batch number of tape. Our forensics team has confirmed it. You bought it at 4.23 pm the same day your sister was murdered, which tells us the murder was planned. We've identified you in this picture by the tattoo on your arm. It matches the tattoo shown in the image. Do you have any comment on that yet?'

Rupert's head jerked downwards as he stared at the still. 'I'm sure I've already told you it isn't me!'

His solicitor placed a hand on his arm. After a short discussion, she repeated, 'My client retracts his previous statement and declines to comment.'

'If you're denying this man is you, which is hard to believe, can you tell us your whereabouts at the time the image was recorded?'

'I wasn't there.'

'Mr Carew...' the solicitor admonished.

'Can you prove it?' asked Shauna. 'Is there someone who can provide an alibi?'

His forehead creased in concentration. 'I don't remember.'

In an exasperated tone, the solicitor said, 'I would like five minutes' recess to confer with my client.'

'Fine,' said Shauna. 'Recording paused at...' she checked the time '...10.04 am.'

The solicitor did her job well. For the rest of the interview, Rupert Carew gave no response to any further questions. He said nothing except *No comment* until the recorder was turned off. But as his solicitor stood up to leave, he leaned over the table and whispered to Shauna, 'Don't worry. I'm not going to report you for trying to hit me. I want to hit Lauren's killer too.'

Somewhat shaken, she didn't know how to respond.

After they'd left, Will said, 'He has no defence to speak of.'

'Right,' Shauna agreed. 'I didn't pick up much from him except he got angry at the mention of his family—not so surprisingly—and when he said he didn't buy the parcel tape he seemed to really believe

it. Maybe he genuinely has no memory of the day due to being off his face. His solicitor's working damage control, stopping him from incriminating himself. If we get him to trial his legal team won't allow him to take the stand. We only have the financial incentive as a motive, and no jury is going to convict him on that, a tattoo and a bit of family history. We need a clearer why and we need more evidence.'

37

'It reeks of bad blood,' Shauna commented as she was driving her and Will to Bob Muncey's house. Cambridge traffic had struck again and they were sitting in a queue, waiting to pass some road works.

'You do mean the case, right?' asked Will, glancing around as if checking she wasn't referring to something going on outside the car.

'Yeah, of course. Sorry, I was thinking out loud.'

'Chocolate lime?' he asked, pulling a bag of the sweets from his jacket pocket.

She tutted. 'You and your chocolate limes.'

'They help me think.'

'Go on, then.'

They weren't going anywhere soon, so she took her hands off the steering wheel to unwrap the sweet. Tucking it into her cheek, she continued her train of thought. 'All this family stuff, going back decades. The pilot who was reported to have died in the Spitfire crash disappeared. The pilot who did die was declared a deserter. They both met mysterious or tragic ends. Then three generations down the line a brother murders his sister and leaves her remains at the site of the crash. It's like there was a family feud. Edith Brown said some-

thing about a 'nasty business' to do with Douglas Hunt. Maybe that was the start of it.'

'None of that explains where Mike Battersby comes in, or the Munceys.'

'Battersby worked for the Carews all his life, don't forget. He was probably as much a part of the family as the twins.'

'I *really* doubt Mrs Carew saw him that way.'

'Maybe he knew something,' Shauna said. 'He would have known all the family's business. Maybe Rupert Carew murdered him to shut him up.'

'If Battersby did know something I wish he'd written it down. The SOCOs didn't find a thing at his house.'

'The same as Lauren's flat. Absolutely nothing to tell us where she was going that night or who she was meeting. She must have had a mobile but there's no trace of it.' Shauna sucked on the sweet, her brow furrowing. 'The answer to it all has to lie somewhere in the past. Something so cataclysmic happened its echoes continued down the years until now, driving Rupert Carew to murder his sister and most likely Mr Battersby too.'

'I'll speak to Edith Brown,' said Will. 'See if I can get her to elaborate.'

'Better you than me. I daren't show my face at that home again.' The line of traffic began to move and she edged the car forwards. 'We need to go back into the past too. We have to look at school reports, medical records, anything we can find on Lauren and her brother. And I want to speak to Gil Carter again. I want to hear it from his own lips that his grandfather was Douglas Hunt. He had two grandfathers. I suppose it's in the realm of possibility he was referring to two different brothers, or he might simply be mistaken.'

'These family trees are making my head spin,' said Will.

'You know what doesn't add up? How could Rupert Carew, a long-time druggie and vagrant, not strong enough to fight his way out of a paper bag, kill two people, carry one of them miles across fenland and string the other one up? And, at the same time, leave virtually no evidence behind. Can you square all that with the Carew we know?'

'I can't. He must have had an accomplice. Someone who knew

what they were doing and masterminded the murders. Someone he wants to protect.'

'Great. Now we have another perp to find.'

Once they were past the traffic jam, Bob Muncey's house was two streets away. Shauna pulled up next to the kerb. An old Yaris sat on the driveway, so it appeared Muncey was home.

The person who answered the door, however, was Mrs Hendricks, his daughter.

'I'm sorry,' she said in response to Shauna's enquiry. 'He isn't here at the moment.'

'Do you know if he'll be back soon?'

'I really couldn't say.'

'Do you know where he is?'

Mrs Hendricks seemed uneasy. 'I-I'm not sure. What do you want to see him about? Is he in some kind of trouble?'

'We were hoping he might be able to help us with a case.'

'What case?'

'It's best if I speak to Mr Muncey in person,' said Shauna. 'Could you give him this?' She handed over her card. 'I'd appreciate it if he would phone me when he has time for a chat.'

'So he isn't in any trouble?'

Shauna peered into the woman's eyes. 'Is there a reason he would be?'

'Oh, no. Nothing like that. It's just it isn't every day two detectives come knocking.'

'I suppose not. Thanks for your time.'

Mrs Hendricks didn't say goodbye, just closed the door.

Shauna had reached the end of the driveway when a niggling feeling made her halt.

Will walked on for a few seconds before he noticed. 'What's up?'

After giving him a look, she retraced her steps to Bob Muncey's door and rang the bell.

When Mrs Hendricks answered she looked even more flustered. 'It's you again. I already told you—'

Shauna interrupted, 'I've been a police officer a long time. Some-

thing's wrong, isn't it? Are you going to tell me what it is? Maybe we can help.'

Mrs Hendricks let out a sob and clasped her hands to her face, moaning, 'They've left! Both of them. They've packed their bags and left, and I don't know where they've gone.'

'COULD WE GO OVER IT AGAIN?' Shauna asked. 'I'd like to be clear about what you're saying.'

Will was doing his usual thing of surreptitiously snooping, peering at photographs on the mantle piece, assessing the general state of the place, looking for anything that seemed out of place or suspicious. They would never get a search warrant on the basis that an old man and his granddaughter hadn't returned home for one night.

Meanwhile, it was her job to keep Mrs Hendricks distracted and preoccupied.

'I'm sorry,' the woman said. 'I'm probably not making much sense. It's just that I'm out of my mind with worry. Neither of them has done anything like this before.'

'Um, didn't you report your daughter missing the other day?'

'Oh, yes.' Mrs Hendricks flushed crimson. 'I forgot. That was different. Gemma has occasionally stayed out all night when she's slept over at a friend's. The only reason I phoned the police that time was because she hadn't texted and I couldn't get in contact with her. I overreacted.'

'And this time you think you aren't overreacting?'

'It's completely unlike my father to disappear. He's an old man. Where on Earth would he go?'

'You're in a better position to answer that question than me,' Shauna said. 'Would you like a glass of water to help calm yourself down? Is the kitchen through here?'

'No, I... Yes, maybe.'

Shauna led her out of the living room and glanced back just in time to see Will tiptoeing up the stairs. 'You said Gemma and your

father were gone when you arrived yesterday. Why had you come over? To pick your daughter up and take her home?'

'I-I've left on my husband and I'd come to stay here for a while until I can get on my feet. We had a big row, and I walked out. Gemma was already living here. Things have been tense at home lately. Well, for a long time. It was all a long time coming.'

'Do you think your separation could be related to your father and daughter's unexplained absence?'

'They didn't know anything about it. Still don't. I haven't had the chance to tell them.'

'So you're certain it was something to do with our enquiry about your father's name and address.'

'It's the only thing I can think of,' Mrs Hendricks said sadly. 'I was at a loss about it until you turned up. Then I realised you must want to speak to him about something serious. I wish I knew why you're interested in him.'

'I'm afraid I can't—'

'Tell me. I know.'

'It's interesting that your daughter went with him.'

'Not really. They're very close. Gemma's father died, you see, and my husband never really took his place. So Dad stepped in. He's been wonderful with her. She was bullied a lot at school and he helped her cope with it.'

'She was bullied because of her arm?'

'You remembered.' Mrs Hendricks smiled wanly. 'Mostly because of that. Children can be very cruel. I considered moving her to a different school but there wasn't another one nearby that Peter thought was up to scratch.'

'Peter is your husband's name?'

'Yes. He was paying, so he had final say.'

'He insisted your daughter stayed at a school where she was being bullied?' Shauna tried but failed to keep an accusatory tone out of her voice.

'It sounds terrible, doesn't it? And it was, I suppose. Somehow, at the time, it seemed like the right decision.' She put her head in her hands. 'What have I done? I feel like I've done everything

wrong and now Gemma and Dad have gone and it's too late to put it right.'

Shauna was getting an impression of the family dynamic that she didn't like. It seemed clear that Gemma Hendricks' mother had been neglectful, perhaps too caught up in her dysfunctional relationship with Mr Hendricks, ignoring her daughter's needs. Or else why would Gemma have run away without telling her mother where she was going?

She usually tried not to be judgemental but, as someone who would have loved the chance to see her children grow up, it was hard. She pursed her lips and then said, 'It's still very early days. Too early for us to draw any conclusions about why they left. It could be something innocuous, like they decided to take a trip on the spur of the moment and neglected to tell you.'

Mrs Hendricks shook her head. 'It's more serious than that. They left in a hurry. I can't think where they could have gone. Apart from the Legion, Dad never goes anywhere.'

Will appeared at the kitchen door.

'I think we've done all we can here,' said Shauna.

'You aren't going to do anything?'

'You said they packed their bags before they left, so wherever they've gone it was intentional, not coerced. As adults, they have every right to do that and they're under no legal obligation to notify you of their whereabouts. If we hear anything and we have their permission to pass on information we'll certainly let you know.' In a softer tone, she added, 'I hope Gemma and your father turn up soon. If they do, could you give me a ring?' She handed over her card.

Nodding, Mrs Hendricks took it.

38

The letters on the wall were obliterated one by one. The paint took out the K, then the C, the U and finally the F. Penelope had worked backwards across the words. The first two coats of paint hadn't covered them properly, leaving Rupert's disgusting message still faintly visible. The writing had to be completely gone before she could put Windleby on the market. Even the thought of allowing the estate agent, or anyone else for that matter, seeing what her son had written made her cringe with shame. No one could know her son was so depraved or that she was so hated.

Had Janet seen what he'd written? Or perhaps Gilbert or his children? All of them had been in the house when Rupert had come here.

She comforted herself with the conclusion that they probably hadn't. No one would have any reason to go into the room. On the other hand, he might have left the door open...

She shook her head. Tormenting herself with what might have happened would only drive her insane. She rolled the roller in the tray to gather more paint and then applied it to the wall. She was doing a terrible job. She'd never painted anything before, except pictures at school. There seemed to be more paint on the old sheets she'd spread out and herself than the walls. But it didn't matter as long as those awful words were no longer on view.

The reason she had little experience of painting was because Mummy had always been very careful about keeping their home clean. Messes were not tolerated in any shape or form. After every meal the dirty plates and cutlery had to be washed, dried and put away immediately. One of Penelope's earliest memories was of her mother tidying up behind her as she played, almost pulling the toys from her hands before she'd finished with them. When she'd grown older, she hadn't been allowed to play indoors at all, only read books or watch television, two activities that created virtually no disturbance to the order of everything. If she'd wanted to actually play, it had to be outside, regardless of the weather.

Penelope had spent as little time as she could at home, and her mother had seemed relieved when she'd married young, no doubt glad she finally had her clinically tidy and clean sanctuary to herself. There had also been a smidgen of glee at the fact that her daughter was 'marrying up'. Mummy had scorned their neighbours and implied she and Penelope were better than them in every way. It had been unfortunate circumstances—namely, Daddy's abandonment of them before she was born—that led them to live among the lower classes.

Now she thought about it, she realised she'd derived her dislike of name shortening from her mother. She'd always called her Penelope, never Penny. She'd told her she was named after a virtuous, loyal wife who had waited twenty years for her husband to return from war.

She sighed. *Her* husband was never coming back, and now even her memory of him was besmirched by Rupert's accusations.

The more she thought about it, the more confused she became. Bertrand had worked so hard in the City, he'd spent little time alone with the twins. Even before they'd gone to boarding school he'd only seen them on weekends. During the week he'd left before they woke up and returned after their bedtimes. Once they'd turned eight and become full-time boarders, he'd seen them on holidays, the same as her.

She'd never pressed Rupert for details about what Bertrand was supposed to have done. She'd refused to even listen to her son after he'd begun to 'confide' in her. Her stomach convulsed at the

memory of that moment. She blocked it out, refusing to bring it fully to mind.

She placed the paint roller in the tray and took a step backward to assess her work. The writing was entirely invisible now, the magnolia colour covered all the walls relatively evenly. It was good enough. Most astute house buyers were more interested in the structure of a property, not its decoration. They would want to put their own stamp on the place.

The decision to sell had been difficult to make. She was glad Bertrand was no longer alive to see it. Perhaps he would have understood her situation was impossible. If she didn't find money soon the bailiffs would be here and further scandal would be unavoidable. As it was, she was already under pressure to pay Rupert's solicitor her retainer.

The distant ring of a telephone came through the half-open door. Penelope checked the soles of her shoes were free of paint, and then descended the stairs and went into the study. The phone was still ringing when she reached it.

'Hello?'

'Hello, Mother.'

'Rupert?' She swallowed. The memory of his slurs against Bertrand still hovered at the back of her mind. 'How lovely to hear from you. How have you been?'

'Your capacity to make my incarceration sound like a pleasant stay in a gîte is quite remarkable.'

'I'm trying,' she said quietly.

'I suppose I have to give you that. I've been about as good as you might expect, though that isn't saying much.'

'Can I bring you anything? I think you're allowed another visit tomorrow.'

'Unless you can smuggle in some smack up your snatch, no.'

'Some smack up my...?' She paused. 'There's no need to be vulgar.'

'Isn't there? I would have thought vulgarity was the mildest of potential responses to my predicament.'

'If you've phoned in order to provoke me, I'd rather not continue this conversation.'

'Naturally you wouldn't, but don't hang up just yet. There is something you can do for me, but I warn you, you aren't going to like it.'

'Will it help your case?'

'It might if you're successful. In fact, it might be the only chance I have.'

'Tell me what it is.'

'Very wise not to commit yourself. After all, you wouldn't want to go *all out* for me no matter what.'

'Tell me what you would like me to do.'

'The day Lauren was murdered, I was in Cambridge—something I haven't admitted to the police yet. It was pure coincidence. Uncle Gil had told me he was here with his kids. I'd travelled down from York on the overnight coach, got in about seven in the morning. Gil wanted to meet up but I chickened out. Didn't want him to see me like this, how low I'd sunk. I ended up crashing somewhere. I think I know where. The rest is a blur, but someone there might give me an alibi.'

'Have you told the police this?'

'There's no way those people will talk to pigs. They can sniff them out a mile off. If those detectives go there, they'll clear the place out in a few seconds flat.'

Penelope was forming an unappealing image of the kind of habitation Rupert was talking about. 'You want me to go there instead? What good would that do? If none of these people will talk to the police, what makes you think they'll talk to me?'

'Because you've got money. They can sniff that out like a bloodhound too.'

If only he knew.

'I can't pay someone to provide an alibi for you' she said. 'That's ridiculous. And if it comes out that I tried I'll get into trouble and it would weaken your case.'

'I wasn't suggesting you pay someone to lie. I just... I don't know. I can't think of anything else that might help me.' His tone had softened and for the briefest moment Penelope heard the voice of the boy she used to know.

'I'm glad you're thinking more positively,' she said. 'Give me the address and I'll see what I can do.'

There was a pause, then, 'Thank you.'

S hauna waited as the international call went through. Gil Carter picked up almost immediately.

'Mr Carter, it's Detective Inspector Shauna Holt. I'd like to ask you some more questions regarding Lauren Carew's murder.'

'How did you get this number?'

'You gave me your business card the first time we met, remember?' It was late in the day for Shauna, the beginning of office hours in the US.

'Right. Could you give me a minute?'

'Of course.' She waited as noises of him moving around came down the line. There was the sound of a door closing.

'Detective Holt,' he said in a hushed tone. 'I can't talk to you right now. Not while I'm at work.'

'I only have a few things I'd like to clear up,' she pressed.

'I already told you everything I know, and it'll look bad if someone in the office finds out I'm talking to the police, even the British police.'

'It won't take long, I promise.'

'I'm not sure I should be talking to you at all.' He sounded cagey.

Shauna was reminded of the end of his interview at the station, when the open, chatty Gil Carter had disappeared and been replaced

by a far more circumspect individual. 'You aren't a suspect, if that's what you're worried about.'

'Hang on a minute.' At his end, drawers were opened and closed. 'Here it is. I'm going to give you the number of my attorney. Anything you want to—'

'Please, let's not make this more complicated than necessary. If you would just answer my questions we can get this over with and you can go about your day.'

'My attorney can deal with—'

'Mr Carter, don't you want to see your cousin's murderer brought to justice?'

'I do, but nothing I can tell you will help with that, and, besides, I don't have any confidence in your abilities, to be frank. You have the wrong man behind bars.'

'If you believe Rupert Carew didn't do it then tell me what I need to know and perhaps he'll be released.'

He gave a heavy sigh. 'It won't help, but go ahead. Shoot.'

'You said your and Bertrand Carew's grandfathers were brothers.'

A heavier sigh. 'I thought it might be about this. It isn't relevant to anything, just some dirty laundry.'

'I think *I'm* the best judge of what's relevant. So you were talking about Ernest and Douglas Hunt?'

'Yeah, my granddaddy was Douglas Hunt. He changed his name to Carter after he came to the States.'

'He...' For a moment, Shauna was lost for words. 'He didn't die in 1942?'

'Something happened. I don't know what. I don't think even his son, my daddy, knew. Something that made him leave the UK in a hurry.'

'So you knew he didn't die in the Spitfire crash?'

'What Spitfire crash? Oh, you mean the place where Lauren's body was found? I'm sorry. I'm confused. Was my granddaddy supposed to have died there? I didn't know anything about that. All I know was he was a pilot in the RAF during the war, before he left to come here.'

'Mr Carter, is your father still alive?'

'He died last year, God rest his soul.'

'Is there anyone else alive who might know why Douglas Hunt left Britain?'

'Nobody here in the US.'

'What about Mrs Carew? Does she know about this?'

'As far as I know she has no idea. Bertrand's family never liked her. She was too low class for them. They never accepted her into the fold.'

'I'll try Mr Carew's family in that case.'

'I hate to be Debbie Downer, but I doubt you'll get anything out of them. They'd rather stick needles in their eyes than reveal anything that might spoil their reputation. I'm sure if you ask them they'll deny all knowledge of what I've said. Bertie's mom, Ernest Hunt's daughter, Marcia, was the worst of them all. I only met her once when I was a kid but, man, that woman had a stick up her ass.'

'I see. Thank you for being honest.'

'I just wish it would help Rupert.'

'It might. I'm not sure how yet, but it might.'

As she hung up, Shauna wondered if she'd given him false hope. She didn't know how the story of his grandfather could set Rupert Carew free. His involvement in the murder seemed undeniable, and the new information was one part of a very large puzzle, stretching back to the middle of the previous century.

'Lauren and Rupert Carew's school sent over their records,' Connor said from the other side of the incident room.

'Great. Let me know what you find.'

He pulled a face but set to work.

'DS Fiske, we're going to the British Legion.'

'To look for Bob Muncey? I thought you told Mrs Hendricks we weren't treating him as a missing person.'

'We're not. He got spooked when he heard we were asking about him. I want to know why.'

∽

ODOURS OF STALE cigarette smoke and beer leaked from the British Legion bar as soon as she opened the door. The place couldn't have been redecorated since the smoking ban fifteen years ago. The shiny, threadbare mock leather seating and carpet so worn the pattern had disappeared in places confirmed her impression.

The clientèle consisted entirely of old men, a handful of loners at the bar and a group of three huddled around a table. Mostly empty pints of beer seemed the tipple of the day.

She walked up to the bar with Will, ignoring the intense gazes.

'Are you a member, dear?' the bartender asked condescendingly.

Shauna took out her badge.

His sneer transformed to a puzzled frown. 'What do you want?'

'I'm looking for Bob Muncey. Has he been in recently?'

'Never heard of him.'

'I heard he's a regular here.'

The bartender looked out into the room. 'Anyone know a Bob Muncey?'

Like disturbed cattle, the men shook their heads and mumbled to each other.

'Sorry,' said the bartender, not sounding remotely sorry.

'Are you sure? He might have come in with his granddaughter.'

'Children aren't allowed in the bar area.'

'She isn't a child. She's in her twenties.'

'Look, I don't know any Munceys, Bob or otherwise, with or without grandchildren.'

Will took the photo he'd purloined from Muncey's house out of an inside pocket and slid it over the bar. It showed the old man with two younger men, their arms wrapped over each other's shoulders. 'This might help. He's the one in the middle.'

After giving the image a cursory glance, the bartender said, 'Well, it doesn't.'

Shauna asked, 'Do you have a list of members?'

'Yeah, but I don't see why I should—'

'I can come back tomorrow with a warrant if you want to do it that way.'

Huffing, the bartender lifted a section of bar and walked out into the main area. A minute later he returned with a ledger.

It took a while to go through all the names, which dated back to the sixties.

No variation of John Robert Muncey was among them.

P enelope had made a point of dressing down for her mission. She was wearing trousers, the pair she used for gardening, her oldest rain jacket, and flat shoes. It didn't help. She remained visibly, eminently, different from the locals, who wore track-suits and clothes from places like Primark. The women's hairstyles consisted mostly of greasy ponytails pulled tight over their scalps. Their eyelashes were false and claw-like nails in vivid colours over-hung the handles of their baby's pushchairs.

She knew the demographic too well. It was among people like this she'd grown up. Though her mother had tried her best to keep her apart from them, not allowing her to make friends with the children in her street, just classmates of known and approved families, that hadn't stopped her from developing familiarity.

She loathed them, their houses, their habits and smells, every-thing. This area was exactly the kind of place she hadn't wanted her own children to experience. How awful it was that Rupert was so well-acquainted with these types and had spent time here.

The address Rupert had given her was the worst of the houses on the street, and that was saying something. He hadn't given her the number, saying she would know it when she saw it. How right he was. The front door had long been absent. The windows that were not

boarded over were gaping holes, without glass. Graffiti covered the walls on the ground floor, the vandals apparently stymied in their efforts by lack of access to a ladder. Weeds grew tall between mattresses, supermarket trolleys and rusted bicycles in the front garden. Someone had lit a fire in the centre and the cold ashes remained.

Clutching her handbag tightly to her side and bolstering her resolve, she stepped through the gap where a gate should have stood and marched up the cracked concrete path to the dark doorway. Her closer vantage point revealed a figure lying in the hall, slumped against the wall, legs spread wide. She couldn't tell if it was a man or a woman.

'Excuse me.'

When the person didn't stir, she leaned in and repeated herself, louder.

'You won't get an answer out of her,' said a voice. 'Not for a couple of hours at least.'

Jean-clad legs descended halfway down the stairs. The man who had spoken squatted down to see her. His expression transformed from mild curiosity to suspicion. 'What do you want?'

'I'm here about my son.'

'You want something for him? There's motherly love. I wish my mum was like you.'

'No,' she replied stiffly, 'I don't *want something for him.* I want to know if he stayed here on the third of March.'

The man walked down the remaining steps, over the prone figure, and uncomfortably close to Penelope. He had piercings through his lip and eyebrows, and the same haggard, pale look as Rupert, though his skin was brown. She guessed his family was from India or Pakistan. His accent was British.

'Third of March?' he sneered. 'Let me check my calendar.'

Another person appeared at the end of the hall, a woman in a dirty duffle coat, the fur around the hood barely hanging by a thread. Her head was close shaven.

'Who's this, Sanjit?' She glared at Penelope. 'Who are you? Are you from the council? We have squatters' rights, you know.'

'I'm not from the council. I don't want any trouble. I'm just trying to help my son.'

'He isn't here,' said the woman. 'Now piss off. Sanjit, get her to piss off.'

'Keep your hair on,' said Sanjit. 'She's looking for her kid.'

'My son,' Penelope corrected. 'And I'm not looking for him. I know exactly where he is. I'm trying to find out if anyone remembers him staying here on the third of March.' She swallowed and her vision blurred. 'It's very important.'

'I might remember him,' said Skye. 'What's he look like?'

'Watch out, Skye,' said Sanjit. 'She's talking about an alibi.' He turned to Penelope. 'You want someone to give your kid an alibi, right? In court.'

'Talk to the Filth?!' Skye exclaimed. 'Forget it.' She returned to the back of the house.

'Excuse me!' Penelope called out. 'Please wait. If you did see him...'

But Skye had gone.

'Maybe I can help,' said Sanjit. 'What's your son called?'

'Rupert. Rupert Carew.'

'Carew? Wait.' His eyes widened. 'This is about that murder case. The brother killed the sister.'

'That's right, but it isn't true. Rupert's been accused and...' She was disgusted at herself for baring her soul to strangers, especially people of this type. 'I want to help him. He can't remember where he was when his sister was murdered. He thinks he might have been here.'

'We get people coming and going a lot. What date did you say? Third of March? Describe your kid.'

'He's tall, slim. He has dark brown hair and blue eyes. He's twenty-three, though he looks older.'

Sanjit shrugged. 'Not ringing any bells.'

She tried to think of something that would make Rupert memorable. 'His accent is similar to mine. And he has a tattoo on one of his arms.'

'That's more like it. I think I do remember him now.'

'You do? That's wonderful. And are you willing to help? You would have to give a statement to the police.'

'Yeah, no problem. I'll do it today if you like.'

'I could take you there now. I've parked about five minutes' walk away.' She didn't like the idea of this man sitting in her car but she could have it cleaned this afternoon.

'All right, but we haven't talked about how much.'

'How much?'

'I want five hundred now and if I'm called as a witness in the trial I'll want another monkey before I take the stand.'

'Oh, I can't pay you.'

'Course you can. A grand's nothing to someone like you. Don't you want your son to get off?'

'I came here to find someone who can genuinely vouch for him, not to commit a crime. I can't possibly buy him an alibi.'

'Sucks to be Rupert,' Sanjit sneered. 'His mum doesn't love him.'

'You don't remember him at all, do you.'

He turned to climb the stairs. 'If you change your mind, I'll be here.'

'Don't go,' she said. 'Is there anyone else who might have seen him?'

Sanjit ignored her.

Penelope hesitated, reluctant to go farther into the house. Doubtless, there were other people here. While she'd been talking to Sanjit and Skye, there had been footsteps and other sounds of movement overhead and the quiet murmur of voices. But she dreaded leaving the comparative safety of the doorway open into the street. If she went in among these addicts and tramps, who knew what might happen to her?

Her quest was hopeless. No one here was a reliable witness. It was time to leave. But as she retreated down the hall, something fastened around her ankle, making her fall to her knees. She let out a gasp of pain.

It was the supposedly comatose figure on the floor who had grabbed her.

She kicked her leg vigorously. 'Let go of me! Let go!' Looking out

of the door, she called, 'Help! Please help me!' She scrambled in her pocket for her phone.

'I r'member 'im,' said her captor. 'I r'member.' She released Penelope's leg.

'It doesn't matter,' she said, getting to her feet. Her skin crawled at the knowledge she'd been touched by this down-and-out. Did she have lice, or a skin disease?

'His tattoo,' said the woman. ''s a dragon, yeah? Y' don' have t' pay me.'

'It *is* a dragon, but what difference does it make? What jury would ever believe *you*?'

Revulsion coursed through her. She couldn't stay here another minute.

AS SHE WAS DRIVING HOME, her mobile rang. She pulled off the main road and into a side street to park and answer it.

'I thought you were ignoring me again,' said Rupert in his usual sardonic tone.

'I've never ignored you,' Penelope replied acidly. 'You might accuse me of many things, but not that.'

'Have you been to the house yet? Did anyone remember me?'

'I'm just on my way back from there, actually. What a horrible place. Rupert, how can you live as you do? What happened to all your trust fund money?'

'What do you think happened to it?'

'You can't have spent it all on drugs.'

'Numbing pain is expensive. I had a blissful year of escape, then it was all gone. Now I have to do other things to fund my habit. Would you like to hear about them?'

'You know I wouldn't. I don't want to know anything about your life. Visiting that house was as much of an education as I would like.'

'Did you find anyone who remembered me?' he reiterated.

'I...no, sorry. There was a man, Sanjit, who wanted money for saying he remembered you.'

'That might work.'

'No, it wouldn't. Any sane juror would see through him in a minute, and I'm certainly not incriminating myself by organising a fake alibi.'

'No one else?'

Penelope's stomach turned over as she recalled the awful drug den and the woman clutching at her ankle. 'No.'

'So that's it then.'

'You have a very good, very expensive lawyer. I'll have to sell Windleby to pay her and her team.' A twinge of guilt hit Penelope. She hadn't meant to let Rupert know about the loss of the family estate. She hadn't wanted him to think he was responsible.

'Good,' he spat. 'The old place was a chain around your neck anyway.'

'That isn't true! I love it and I loved my time there with...your father.'

There was a pause, then Rupert murmured, 'You loved him more than me. More than both of us.'

'That isn't true.' The words sounded hollow.

'And the life. You loved the life most of all.'

'We can talk about all this when you're released. I'm sure you'll be found innocent. You have the very best legal...' The sound quality on the line had changed. 'Rupert? Are you there?'

At some point as she'd been talking he'd hung up.

There it was. The motive. She didn't have the complete answer but it lurked at the edge of her mind like a shadow. All she needed was a few more facts, or, preferably a confession.

Shauna put together the copies of selected comments from two sets of school reports and slid them over the table to Will.

Catching her look, he reached out and read one, then the other. A crease formed between his eyebrows and he read them again.

She saw the exact moment the penny dropped.

The crease disappeared and his eyebrows lifted. '*Shit.*'

'Shit indeed.'

'Is that what Lauren Carew's death was about? Revenge? I still don't see how it's connected to the Spitfire crash and Douglas Hunt fleeing to the States, though.'

'I don't either, yet. But the connection has to be there, and Bob Muncey can tell us what it is.'

'If we find him.'

'When, not if. I'll tell Bryant what we've found and he can pull the trigger on a nationwide alert. An old man and his granddaughter can't hide forever.'

'Don't forget he's a Muncey. They might not be the OCG they once

were, but they'll have plenty of resources. Favours to call in and secrets they use as blackmail. I wouldn't underestimate them.'

'We'll see.' Shauna took the papers and left to speak to Bryant.

'ALL I CAN SAY IS,' he said when she'd finished explaining and shown him the evidence, 'I'm glad I allowed you to return to work. You are an excellent detective, Holt. If you get your emotions under control you should go far.'

She gritted her teeth. 'Thank you, sir. Do you agree we should—'

'Yes, yes. Leave it with me. I'll get on it right away. That pair won't get far.'

Reading between the lines and translating the euphemisms of Lauren Carew's reports, it was easy to see she'd been a vicious bully. Time and again she'd been placed in detention or given a suspension due to name-calling, shaming her victim on social media, or actual physical attacks. And they were only the documented cases, where there were witnesses and evidence. Who knew what other forms Lauren's bullying had taken? Ostracising, whispered insults, stealing and breaking personal items were just a few of the ways schoolchildren tortured their peers, and no one had made a proper effort to put a stop to Lauren Carew's exploits. She should have been expelled from school if not charged for assault and harassment. But it seemed her family's money had protected her.

It was ironic that money hadn't protected Gemma Hendricks from Carew's attacks. Rather, it had ensured she remained a victim throughout her educational career. By refusing to transfer her to a different school, her mother and stepfather had consigned her to years of abuse.

And her grandfather had found a way to engineer the ultimate revenge for it: murder.

Will had been ruminating on the revealing reports. 'How did Bob Muncey persuade Rupert Carew to murder his sister? I mean, I can see how Rupert would be the perfect person to lure her to a quiet, out-of-the-way place. She would never suspect her brother

might hurt her. But how could he bring himself to kill her? I haven't seen anything to suggest he hated her. He seemed upset over her death.'

Shauna replied, 'Just because he's upset, doesn't mean he didn't do it. Muncey might have bribed him with drug money and he would have got her trust fund too. Some addicts will do anything for their next fix.'

'Should we bring him in for another interview?'

'No point. I was too optimistic thinking we would get anything from him last time.'

Alfie hung up his phone and swung around in his chair to face them. 'The checkout operator's back from holiday.'

'On the other hand,' said Shauna, 'maybe it *is* time for a return visit from Rupert Carew.'

THE VIPER HAD TAKEN a couple of days to put together. Shauna preferred the video identification parade over the old style, which had often taken weeks to arrange. It was less intimidating for the witness and that probably meant more definite IDs. It had to be hard to point the finger at a suspect in real life, albeit behind a screen, knowing the implications.

The checkout operator was wearing her uniform. A small woman, she looked overwhelmed by the situation. Her neck and shoulders were rigid. Jas did a good job of settling her in, putting her at ease with her calm manner.

'Are you sure you wouldn't like something to drink?' she asked.

'No, I just want to get this over with. I won't have to go to court, will I?'

'Uh, we can talk about that later.' Jas threw an alarmed glance at Shauna.

She lifted a hand, gesturing *It's okay* behind the operator's back.

'You'll see a range of men,' said Jas. 'If you recognise the one who bought the parcel tape, let us know. You can watch the video as many times as you like. Take your time.'

Shauna folded her arms over her chest and waited as their potential witness viewed the images.

'I'm not sure I'll remember him,' said the operator. 'I serve hundreds of people a day, and this was a couple of weeks ago.'

'Just do your best,' Jas said.

Shauna was hoping Carew's distinctive tattoo would have set him apart from the other customers and make him more memorable. But she didn't want to prompt the witness. She had to recall Carew by herself for the evidence to be accepted by the court.

More faces appeared on the screen. Rupert Carew looked out. Seconds later he was gone.

The operator said nothing.

The video came to an end.

'Is that all of them?' asked the woman. 'None of them looked familiar. Sorry.'

'Would you like to see it again?' Jas asked.

'If you like, but I don't think there's a lot of point.'

Jas re-started the recording.

Disappointment settled on Shauna. She'd been hoping the checkout operator's testimony would be another nail in Carew's coffin. The case against him was better than before but it remained far from solid.

After a second showing of the video, the operator said, 'I'd like to help but I can't. If I did serve any of those men, I don't remember.'

42

The call came just as they were leaving. Connor, Jas and Alfie had already gone home. Outside the incident room windows, night had fallen and misty rain was softening the beams of street lights. Shauna flipped the switch on the wall, plunging the room into darkness matching the exterior, and her desk phone rang.

Her shoulders sagged. It had been a long day.

'Leave it,' Will said from the corridor. 'Whatever it is, it can wait until tomorrow.'

After a few rings, the phone was silent.

'See?' said Will. 'It wasn't important.'

Shauna closed the door.

At the same time, another door at the end of the corridor opened.

Bryant poked his head out. 'Ah, I thought you must have left. Just wanted you to know there's a hostage situation at Felixstowe. Gemma Hendricks.'

'Gemma Hendricks is holding someone hostage?!' Shauna spluttered.

'She's the hostage,' Bryant replied dryly.

'Yes, of course.' Shauna put a hand to her head. It really had been a long day.

'This whole thing could be over by the morning. Thought you'd want to know.'

'Should we go over there?' Will asked.

'The officer in charge isn't asking for you. I'm sure the Suffolk force has the situation in hand.'

Shauna stepped closer to the DCI. 'Did they say what's happening?'

'Information's a bit thin. It seems there was an attempt to smuggle the girl and her grandfather abroad in a shipping container. She didn't like that idea, apparently. Got hold of a phone, dialled 999 and tried to get away. Shots were fired and Armed Response called in. There's a stand off at the port. That's about as much as they could tell me.'

'We should go there,' said Shauna. 'We know the history of the case. We might be able to calm the situation down and get whoever's holding Hendricks hostage to give himself up.'

'You have my permission. Better put on your blues and twos if you want to arrive in time to make a difference.'

Will drove, pulling away as Shauna slapped the light to the roof of the unmarked vehicle.

TRAVELLING from Cambridge to Felixstowe took about an hour and a half in normal traffic. Will did it in forty minutes. By the end of the journey Shauna's hand ached from gripping the handle over the door and she was coated in sweat.

She had phoned the contact in Suffolk to let them know they were on their way, and the barrier lifted immediately as they drove into the port. Police cars formed a second barrier at the centre of the crisis, fifty metres or so from the shipping containers. Armed officers in bulletproof vests and helmets squatted behind the cars.

She couldn't see Gemma or any other subjects in the hostage situation among the rusty steel containers standing on the quayside.

A man in uniform and carrying a megaphone reached out to shake her hand. 'DI Holt? I'm Chief Superintendent Abbas.'

'Pleased to meet you, sir. I wish it was under better circumstances. This is DS Fiske. What's the situation?'

Abbas grimaced. 'Not much different from when I spoke to DCI Bryant. One of the port workers saw three figures arguing and tussling near a container. A woman and two men, one of the men was an older gentleman. The woman ran out into the yard, here, but the younger of the two men ran after her and dragged her back and into an open container. The fuss she kicked up, plus the phone call we received, led us to believe the woman is Gemma Hendricks. When our officers approached the container the man had taken her to, they were fired upon. That's when we called in the ARU. Naturally, we've been phoning the number Hendricks called from and I've tried to open a dialogue with a megaphone, to no avail.'

'What's the plan?'

'We continue to try to establish contact and we wait. They'll need water and food and eventually they'll need to sleep.'

'But if one of them is armed...'

'Storming the place will raise the stakes. Patience is key here, Detective Inspector. We'll wear them down eventually.'

Shauna said, 'Sir, far be it from me to question your reasoning...'

The Chief Superintendent's eyebrows lifted.

'...but when I was in the Met I saw a fair few hostage situations that went wrong. Waiting only gave the hostage takers free rein on their victims.'

He said, stiffly, 'We will follow standard protocol.'

'Yes, sir. But,' she blurted, 'I believe the younger man with Gemma Hendricks is the murderer we've been looking for. They're the two people who know what he's done. He might kill them both, thinking that if he manages to get away no one will be left alive to testify against him.'

In a softer tone, the Superintendent replied, 'This is news to me. Your DCI didn't mention this at all.'

'I put it together as Will drove us over. Fear of death apparently sharpens my mind. Neither Gemma nor her granddad are physically capable of killing someone or carrying a body out onto the fen. There had to be another person involved. We thought it was Rupert Carew,

but the idea never quite worked. He also isn't in great physical shape, and it's hard to imagine he would kill his own sister. This other man with Gemma and Bob Muncey has to be the murderer, and he has a great motive for seeing them dead.'

Abbas's jaw twitched.

'I've worked on this case since the beginning too,' said Will. 'I think DI Holt is right.'

'She may well be. That doesn't mean we should deviate from protocol.'

'Sir,' said Shauna, 'can I speak to them?'

With noticeable reluctance, the Superintendent handed the megaphone to her. 'You can try, but you must cease speaking immediately on my request.'

She took the device.

Floodlights cast harsh beams on the empty space between the circled police cars and shadowy steel containers. The rain that had been falling for hours was becoming heavier, and she was reminded of Lauren Carew's funeral, when they had chased down Rupert, cornering him and carting him away to jail. How much more torture had they inflicted on that already damaged individual?

It was time to put things right.

She lifted the megaphone to her lips and pressed the switch. 'Mr Muncey, this is Detective Inspector Shauna Holt. I came to your daughter's house the day she reported your granddaughter missing. You probably don't remember me, but I remember you and your family. You seemed like a nice, ordinary family. Maybe with a few problems, but whose doesn't?'

'Should you be talking to the murderer?' asked Abbas.

She ignored him. 'Bob, we know why you did what you did. We know what happened to Gemma and how you tried to protect her. You did your best but it wasn't enough. So you wanted to hurt the person who hurt her. We understand that. But what's happening now is hurting her more. She wants to give herself up. It's the right thing to do. You should let her go. Let her do what she wants to, to take control of her life. Let her grow up.'

She swung the megaphone down by her side and waited.

'I'm not sure what you're trying to achieve, DI Holt,' said Abbas. 'It isn't the grandfather who is keeping her there.'

'Maybe not, but he's important in the Muncey family. He might even be the head of it. We found out he'd spent long periods outside the family home, explaining his absences when he was too old to work by saying he was down the Legion. He wasn't even a member. What was he doing all that time?'

'Organising crime?' Abbas suggested.

Shauna shrugged. 'Whatever it was, he kept his daughter in the dark about it, so it was something shady. He must have a high status in the family. He'll hold some sway over the murderer.'

She lifted the megaphone again. 'Gemma, you did the right thing phoning us. The fact that you came forward voluntarily will count in your favour, and your background, everything you suffered at school, these are things the judge will take into consideration. Talk to your granddad. Make him see sense. This is going to end badly for all three of you if we don't resolve this situation soon.'

What else could she say? She couldn't think of anything. She just hoped it was enough.

Handing back the megaphone to Abbas, she peered in the direction of the containers.

Was there movement in the darkness?

A figure shot out.

A ripple of tension ran through the armed officers. Rifles were lifted and eyes moved to their sights.

At the same time, Abbas spoke into his radio. 'Deadly force not authorised. Suspect appears unarmed.'

It was Gemma. She was bolting across the space between the containers and the police cars.

Meanwhile, in the dark opening of a container, two other figures struggled. They were so deep in shadow it was almost impossible to make them out.

The armed officers shifted uneasily.

Shauna felt their quandary. At least one of the two men who were fighting was armed, but even with night vision it would be impossible to shoot the one with the gun without risking shooting the other. Yet

if they didn't take the armed man out, he might fire on Gemma before she reached safety.

The girl's eyes were wide and white as she sped through the night and rain, boots throwing up splashes on the wet concrete. As she drew nearer, her laboured, fear-filled breaths broke through the steady hiss of rain.

Two officers ran towards her, weapons aimed.

A shot shattered the night.

Shauna gasped.

She'd thought Gemma had been the target, but the young woman ran behind the cover of the armed officers and then to safety at the rear of a police car.

Over at the container, a man was down.

The survivor stumbled into the light. He was an old man, short and very dishevelled.

43

No one knew how to restrain Gemma Hendricks. How do you put handcuffs on someone with one arm? In the end, Shauna said she and Will would take her as she was, and that she doubted Gemma posed any threat.

Bob Muncey was to be transported in a separate vehicle, courtesy of Suffolk Police Service. The third suspect remained at Felixstowe Port, awaiting the arrival of the pathologist.

Shauna was tempted to insist on being the driver for the trip back to Cambridge, but she decided she would rather focus on Gemma. The young woman was in a bad way, almost incoherent with distress.

'I'm so sorry, so sorry,' she repeated over and over, crying as they drove away from the port.

Her face was a pale mask smeared and smudged with black make-up. Her black hair hung down in wet rats tails over her eyes and cheeks. She'd wrapped her arm over her middle and she rocked backward and forward, tugging on her seatbelt.

Shauna reached over the back of her seat and touched Gemma's knee. 'It's okay. It's all over now.'

The legging under her hand was cold and sodden. She turned up the car's heating to full.

'Take off your jacket, Gemma,' she said. 'It'll help you warm up.'

But the woman seemed not to hear her.

She waited as Will drove more sedately than before down the A14 while Gemma's sobs slowly petered to silence.

She tried again. 'Are you feeling better?'

A slow shake of the head.

'Are you warmer now?'

A nod.

'Good. We can stop for coffee and something hot to eat at the next services.'

'It wasn't me,' said Gemma. 'I didn't do it.'

'I didn't think you did, but you can give your statement later. Now isn't the right time.'

'But I lured her there!' she exclaimed, a catch in her voice. 'I lured her there, God help me.'

'Gemma, now you've heard your Right to Silence anything you say can be used against you. You do realise that, don't you? You can tell us what happened when we're back at the station and we can get you a solicitor if you want one.'

'She believed me. She believed I actually wanted to meet up with her. She-she...' Gemma swallowed '...she wanted to say sorry for everything she'd done. She started to apologise to me but then Craig took her. He-he took her away, and then...' The sobbing started up again.

Will threw Shauna a look.

So Lauren Carew had gone to meet Gemma the night she was murdered, the victim of her years of bullying. She'd been given the chance to make amends and she'd taken it, only to be killed.

'Craig Muncey?' Will asked.

Gemma murmured, 'Yeah, my cousin.'

'Not Rupert Carew?' asked Shauna, unable to resist the question.

'He didn't have anything to do with it. Pops set him up.'

'Pops is your granddad, right?' asked Will. 'How did he frame Rupert?'

'It was the tattoo. I knew Lauren and her brother had matching ones. You can see Lauren's on her Friendly Fans account. Pops got a tattoo artist to draw the other half of the dragon on Craig's arm, and

then he put on a hoodie and went and bought the parcel tape
to...to...'

As she wept again, Shauna said, 'It's okay. You can get it all off
your chest soon.'

'What did I do?!' Gemma cried. 'She was sorry. She said she was
sorry.'

BOB MUNCEY WAS FAR MORE stoic than his granddaughter. It was the
early hours of the morning when he was finally in the interview room
at Cambridge Central. He looked tired and he had a purple welt all
down one side of his face, but he exhibited none of Gemma's remorse.
His expression was defiant as Shauna started the recorder.

After stating the necessary information for the recording she
asked him to give his full name. Next, she asked him to confirm that
he'd refused the advice of a solicitor.

'No need,' he said. 'I admit to everything. How much longer do I
have left? Five or six years? I managed to stay out of jail all my life. It
won't be so bad to end my life in one. I arranged the murders of
Lauren Carew and Mike Battersby, and they were carried out by Craig
Muncey, my grandnephew.' He continued emphatically, 'But I want to
make one thing clear: Gemma had nothing to do with any of this.
Nothing at all. It was all my idea and she did not know anything that
went on, start to finish.'

'In that case,' said Shauna, 'why was she trying to flee the country
with you?'

Muncey's mouth opened and then snapped closed. After a
moment's consideration, he replied, 'That part was Craig's idea. You'll
have to ask him,' he added.

'It's a shame he's dead,' Shauna said.

'Unfortunate, but true.'

'Don't you mean fortunate—for you?'

'What can I say? It was an accident. The gun went off as we fought.
But if I hadn't tried to stop him he might have shot Gemma, and I
wasn't having that.'

'We already know how Gemma was involved. She's confessed everything. She'll serve time but not so much that she'll be old before she's released.'

The old man's face lost its hardened look. 'I'm glad. She deserves a good life. A better one than she's had.'

'What about Rupert Carew? Don't you think he deserves a good life too? You nearly sent an innocent man to jail.'

'He isn't so innocent. He wasn't as bad as his sister, but he made plenty of kids' lives miserable at that school.'

'So this was about punishing him too?'

'It was about punishing the whole family. If I could have got revenge on all of them I would have. But the twins were the worst. It was like all the bad blood in that family ended up in them, especially the girl. Boys will beat you up but girl bullies, they're more vicious. They'll screw with your head. Gemma was never the same after Lauren Carew had done her work. That family is all nastiness and snobbery. They were all holier-than-thou, thought they were better than everyone else. Well, I showed them, didn't I?'

'And Michael Battersby? Where does he come into it? Did he think he was better than every one else too?'

Muncey broke eye contact. 'Mike had figured it out. He knew what those twins were like. How their father thought the sun shone out their arses and turned a blind eye. He was a local lad too, from a family that's been here generations. He knew what had happened to Gemma and what us Munceys are like. He tried to blackmail me. In a way, I didn't blame him. His wages were a pittance and sure as hell he would have been turfed out of that cottage the second he couldn't work anymore. I had to shut him up. Felt a bit bad about that.'

'Mr Muncey, it's clear you hate the Carew family as a whole, or rather, the Hunts. What isn't clear is why. It isn't just because they're wealthy, is it?'

He looked up and smirked. 'Ha, you don't know all of it, do you?'

'Are you going to tell us?'

His gaze travelled from Shauna to Will and back again as the pregnant pause played out.

'Oh, all right. It was that dig that triggered it. You see, all my life I'd

been told my dad was a deserter. My poor mum never lived it down. And me? If you think what Gemma went through was bad, it was nothing compared to what the kid of a deserter suffered during and after the war. There wasn't a day passed that I didn't come home from school with a bruise, and that was the least of it. I had bones broken, shoes stolen, I was spat at and jabbed with pencils. The lot. And there wasn't anything Mum could do about it. You had to go to school in those days or the truant officer would be knocking at your door.'

'That must have been horrendous,' said Shauna.

'You don't know the half of it. When I heard about the dig, it raised a lot of memories. Bad ones. Douglas Hunt, war hero, who died test flying a Spitfire. I was only young at the time, but I remember all about Hunt. That wasn't what anyone called him before he died. They called him something else. Something that rhymed but started with a C.'

'I heard he wasn't liked.'

'You been speaking to the old Duxworth crowd? Yeah, they would remember him. Did they tell you what happened to my aunt?'

'No.' Was this the 'nasty business' Edith Brown had mentioned?

Muncey leaned forward. 'Got her pregnant. She was only sixteen. Just a child. The minute he heard about it he didn't want anything to do with her. Denied it was his. 'Course, in those days, the woman was blamed. I knew my aunt couldn't have been like that. He must have forced himself on her. But even if she was willing, it wasn't right for him to abandon her, was it? He should have done the right thing. But she wasn't up to scratch for those toffs.'

'Oh,' said Shauna, covering her mouth as she remembered Muncey's aunt had died and what she died from. 'She had a back-street abortion.'

'Christ,' Will murmured.

Muncey nodded, his rheumy eyes filling with tears. 'Even now, after all this time, it still cuts me up. The hospital said it was sepsis that killed her, and I suppose it was. But everyone knew, even years later. It was another insult the bullies threw at me, even years later.'

He paused to wipe his eyes before going on, 'The dig brought it all back. I started thinking about everything my family suffered at the

hands of the Hunts and Carews. And I wondered about my dad. He was a good man. Not like the rest of the Munceys, if I'm honest. He was from a humble background but he didn't go into petty crime and the black market, he trained to be a pilot and did one of the most dangerous jobs in the war. It had never made any sense to me that he'd deserted. And he would never have left Mum. She was a lovely woman. Never remarried, you know.

'I did a bit of digging of my own, and I found out that Douglas Hunt had been killed in an air crash the very same day my dad went missing.' He lifted a hand. 'An arsehole dies...' he lifted the other '...a good man runs off for no reason at all. What are the chances of that? Well, I'm a betting man and I can tell you, it's zero fucking chance.' He threw up both hands and returned them to his lap. 'I worked it out. What really happened was my dad had been killed and Douglas Hunt's brother, the camp commander, used Dad's death as a way to provide him a swift and easy exit from the scandal.'

'But surely there would have been records,' said Shauna.

'It was wartime, and if the Hunts didn't have any morals they had a bloody lot of money. Anyone who knew the truth, Ernest Hunt must have stuffed their gobs with cash. Dad probably didn't have many friends in that crowd, not with his background. They would have been happy to go along with the lie. I thought, why should they get away with it? One generation tarnishing my dad's memory, killing my aunt and making my life a misery, and another generation making Gemma's school life a living hell. Someone had to pay.'

Shauna said, 'You were right. Did you know?'

'Right about what?'

'About the whole thing. Jack Muncey's remains were found at the site of the crash. The RAF was planning to contact you. Douglas Hunt travelled to America and changed his surname. The families are still in touch.'

His mouth turned down at the corners, his lips pressed together and he nodded, seeming unable to speak. Eventually, he muttered, 'Poor Dad.'

'The record will be set straight,' said Shauna. 'Your father won't be remembered as a deserter anymore.'

'Fat lot of good that'll do. Mum's dead and who remembers the war now?' Despite his words, he seemed somewhat mollified.

Will asked, 'What was the point of going to all that trouble? You had Craig Muncey carry Lauren Carew's body all the way out to the dig, and only you knew the significance of it.'

'Not true. I knew it was risky but it was kind of the whole point. I wanted to shove it in the Hunt family's faces even if it took them a while to figure it out.'

Shauna recalled the aged men and women in tailored clothes at Lauren Carew's funeral.

'And I wanted to show Dad I'd got back at the bastards, finally. Maybe it was stupid and we would have got away with it if it wasn't for that. But it wasn't only me and Gemma I did it for. It was for the old Hunts. They knew. The ones who are left. They'll go to their graves knowing the Munceys got their revenge in the end.'

44

S hauna rubbed her aching neck and turned off her computer. She'd finished the paperwork on the Carew case.

'All done?' Will asked.

'Yes, finally. I swear they invent a new form to fill in every week.'

'Fancy a drink before you go home?'

It was Friday, drinks night at Cambridge Central. The DCs had already left for the pub.

'I think I'll give it a miss this week. I'm looking forward to a hot bath, a good book and an early night.'

'Careful with that racy living. It'll catch up with you sooner or later.'

She smiled. 'I'll watch out.' She felt a little bad about not going to the pub with him. He'd lost friends at the station due to the incident at Beth Parker's party. Connor was still angry though Beth had swiftly moved on to a new beau.

Will turned off his computer too. 'I heard through the grapevine that Rupert Carew was accepted into a residential addiction treatment programme.'

'That's great news. It always makes me feel like shit when we arrest the wrong person. And the state he was in, it was like kicking him when he was down.'

'Yeah, but you were just doing your job. You shouldn't feel bad. And it all turned out okay in the end.'

'Not for Lauren Carew or Mike Battersby.'

'No, but that's the world we live in.'

Shauna stood up, lifted her coat from the back of her chair and put it on.

'You sure about that drink?' Will asked.

'Maybe next time, when I've got this case out of my head.'

As they walked out to the car park, he asked, 'What's still bothering you?'

'I can't help thinking about Mrs Hendricks. Her father belonged to an OCG. Her daughter was utterly miserable all through school. How could she have been so blind as to not see what was going on?'

'Her dad seemed to have done a great job at shielding her from the seedier side of the family. I'd bet good money she was telling us what she thought was the truth when she said he spent his spare time at the British Legion. She wouldn't have made that up because she wanted us to find him. As for the bullying, I don't know. You were the one who spoke to her. Did she say anything about it?'

'She did. She said she'd wanted to transfer Gemma to another school, which means no one was doing anything about it. But her husband didn't agree. He wanted to keep her there regardless and he was the one paying so he got final say.'

'That's screwed up.'

'Honestly, it sounds like the stepfather liked the fact that Gemma was being bullied, or at least he didn't mind.'

'It's a shame her mother didn't stand up for her. Lauren Carew might still be alive.'

Shauna said quietly, 'I would never have allowed it with my kids.'

Will gave her a sideways hug.

They'd reached her car.

'Last chance for that drink,' he said.

'You know,' she said, narrowing her eyes at him, 'you're very persistent.'

'Some might call that a positive character trait.'

'The answer's still no.'

'Goodnight then.'

'See you Monday.'

As he was walking away, she said, 'But I am glad you're persistent sometimes.'

He replied without looking back, 'No problem, Shauna. Have a good weekend.'

It was after seven by the time she reached her street and most of the parking spaces were filled. With a great deal of manoeuvring, she managed to edge into a gap near the main road, leaving her car virtually bumper to bumper with the ones in front and behind. Their owners would probably be cursing her in the morning but that was just how things were. She took her bag from the passenger seat and locked the doors.

Lights in front room windows spilled into the dark street. The air was moist, as if rain was on its way again. It had been unremitting this spring but she didn't really mind. Bad weather kept people away from the countryside, making birds bolder and easier to see.

More than a year had passed since she'd come to Cambridge and, though the place had its downsides, she'd decided she would make it her home. She would begin her search for a home in earnest this summer. Buying a place would mean moving out to one of the new developments and a commute but she couldn't face living in a flat like Will and Beth Parker.

The street was empty save for a man walking towards her, the hood of his raincoat pulled over his head.

It took her a second or two to realise it wasn't raining yet.

She halted.

The man sped up.

She had to get away.

In her panic, she ran into the side of a parked car. Gasping at the impact, she altered direction and moved to run behind it.

The man had reached her.

He grabbed her neck and dragged her across the narrow pavement, pinning her against a wall. His face entirely in shadow, he leaned in close.

She tried to scream but his grip was so tight she couldn't take a

breath. Weakly, uselessly, she battered his head and chest. She'd been trained on how to respond to a physical assault. She knew what she should do but she couldn't do it. Fear had severed her conscious mind from her limbs.

'Long time no see, Shauna,' the man murmured. 'I should end you now for what you did.'

His hand squeezed tighter. Her head felt like it was going to burst.

'But I won't. Not because I have any more feelings for you except hate. Not because you don't deserve it. But because I want to see you suffer. All these years I've had to hide, never knowing when I might be found, when someone might recognise me. All these years I've spent always looking over my shoulder. Now you're going to know what that feels like. You're going to be the one wondering if you're being watched, wondering when it will all be over. And it *will* be over for you one day, Shauna. You'll just never know when.'

He released her and she dropped to the ground, choking. She rubbed her aching throat, struggling to breathe.

There was the sound of running feet on pavement, and he was gone.

HOLT & FISKE'S STORY CONTINUES IN...

MASK OF FEAR

For advanced notification of the latest Regan Barry releases, updates on works in progress and tastes of life in Cambridge, join the reader group here:
https://www.subscribepage.com/reganbarry